Politics As Usual

"According to your friend Castro," Harper said, "you know the Governor's chief of staff. Uh—what's his name?"

"John Armstrong," RaeLyn Hunter replied. "Yes, I know him—or I should say I *knew* him. We were in school together, but that was a long time ago."

"He seems to be the key to Heywood's future," Harper continued. "He knows more about running the Governor's office than the Governor does. As near as we can tell, the administration's been run as efficiently as hell. But I'd like to know more about this boy genius before we make a move."

"I'll tell you all I can," she said, a flood of memories washing over her mind. "But, like I say, it's been a few years."

"Well, our job is to save Heywood's skin. The people we're looking for don't care what happens to his hatchetmen." He looked at the woman straight on. "This is politics we're in now, sweetheart. Law has very little to do with it. The best we can do is find somebody else to blame. My guess is that this guy Armstrong is a likely candidate."

"It doesn't sound very honorable," RaeLyn said quietly.

We will send you a free catalog on request. Any titles not in your local book store can be purchased by mail. Send the price of the book plus 50¢ shipping charge to Tower Books, P.O. Box 270, Norwalk, Connecticut 06852.

Titles currently in print are available for industrial and sales promotion at reduced rates. Address inquiries to Tower Publications, Inc., Two Park Avenue, New York, New York 10016, Attention: Premium Sales Department.

THE BUDDY SYSTEM

Michael J. Stewart

TOWER BOOKS   NEW YORK CITY

A TOWER BOOK

Published by

Tower Publications, Inc.
Two Park Avenue
New York, N.Y. 10016

Copyright © 1980 Tower Publications, Inc.

All rights reserved
Printed in the United States

Prologue

The telephone rang, and reflexively I tensed and stopped pounding at the tired, battered machine I called a typewriter. Like a Pavlovian dog conditioned to respond, I reached for the phone and grasped air before I remembered that I had intentionally omitted having one of the contraptions installed in my cloistered hideaway. I had answered too many telephones for my years, and I hoped to create a tranquil atmosphere here, one more conducive to the brewing of my creative juices. Unfortunately, I could still hear the downstairs phone. It rang a second time, and I cursed silently, chiding myself for not having left the damn thing off the hook while I tried to hammer out a few pages of that elusive best-seller.

It did not ring again, so I knew my wife must have picked up the receiver downstairs. I leaned back in my chair to recapture the inspiration that had disappeared so suddenly. But, unavoidably, I found my attention drawn to the telephone conversation downstairs. That first ring had had an ominous sound to it. It is strange how you can almost sense when the telephone bears a message of bad news. I couldn't make out the words, but there was something about the soft, muffled voice drifting up the hallway that drew my attention and aroused my curiosity. My wife's side of the conversation seemed pointed and businesslike—no small talk. On the other hand, that was her nature—brief and to the point.

The sound of light steps on the carpeted stairway told me that the caller had borne tidings of some import, for my wife always respected the seclusion I required when I tried to bleed out some clever words that might attract the interest of some nameless editor. The door was ajar. She pushed it slowly open, as though she thought I might be asleep in the room and she did not want to wake me. Traces of moisture glinted in her sensitive brown eyes, and her full lips formed that little pout that always betrayed her unhappiness.

"What's the matter?" I asked.

"That was your mother on the phone," she said. "Doc Sedgewick died last night. She thought you'd want to know."

"Doc? I can't believe it; he looked great the last time I saw him."

"It's been over a year," she reminded. "Your mom said he was seventy-eight years old."

"Seventy-eight! He couldn't have been." Words have always been my stock in trade, but suddenly I couldn't think of a thing to say. It wasn't that I was overwhelmed with unquenchable sorrow. Doc was not a relative, or even a close family friend; he was just my old scoutmaster, the ex-head-honcho of Schonberg Troop 2. I had been one of Doc's Eagle Scouts, and there is a special kind of bond between a scoutmaster and his Eagle Scouts that you cannot even begin to explain to one who has not experienced it.

But looking back, I guess Doc Sedgewick was more than an old scoutmaster to me. He was more like a symbol of all the people who had been important to me in my youth; and you might say that Doc had created the Eager Beavers—although I doubt Doc would have claimed that notoriety. Over the years, he had been the one person from my past who remained unchanged. He was an anchor that held me fast to a time I did not want to forget. When I was growing up, there were two men I always thought of as being immortal—John Wayne and Doc Sedgewick. Now they were both gone.

I looked at my wife and knew she could see the invisible tears in my eyes, the ones that still, after all these years, would not come. Those tears that we both knew I needed so badly. But only sissies cry; big boys don't cry—that's what they tell us, anyway.

"I'm sorry, John," she said, "I really am. I know Doc meant a lot to you."

In spite of her enormous *enceinte* belly, she stepped gracefully around my desk and moved quickly behind my chair. She bent down and, pressing her cheek to mine, wrapped her arms around my neck and squeezed gently. She said nothing; we have rarely needed words between us.

I sat there silently for a few minutes, my spirits brightened by her nearness. "When's Doc's funeral?" I asked. "Did Mom say?"

"Day after tomorrow, two in the afternoon. Are you going to go?"

I knew it would be a wearing day's drive from our summer home near Ten Sleep, Wyoming, in the heart of the Big Horn Mountains, to Schonberg in south-central Nebraska. I also knew I would attend the funeral. "You can't go with me, you know," I said.

"I know."

"You're past seven months and, if you're carrying twins like Dr. Franklin said, they could come early. I hate like hell to leave right now."

"That's silly," she said. "The Thompsons are just across the road. Hank could drive me to the hospital, and Sarah's offered to take care of Karin whenever we need her." She nibbled on my ear. "Besides, I won't have the babies while you're gone . . . I promise. I'm going to go full-term and have a couple of elephants."

I smiled in spite of myself. "Well, if I leave for Schonberg early tomorrow morning and drive straight through, I can be there by late tomorrow night. I'll call Mom tonight and tell her I'm coming."

I swung the vinyl-covered swivel chair around and, locking my arms around the small of her back, held my wife close and placed my ear against her swollen abdomen. I could hear the strong duet of heartbeats pumping in her womb—or at least I convinced myself I could. "Sound like pretty tough kids in there," I said. "You're going to have your hands full."

She tossled my hair like a mother with her small boy. "*We* will have our hands full," she replied. "And they *should* be tough . . . they're ours."

I liked the sound of that word: Ours.

"Are you going to write some more this afternoon?" she asked.

"I doubt it. Don't feel much like it now."

"Karin's taking her nap," she said meaningfully.

My precious, golden-haired daughter—no, *our* daughter—wise beyond her five years. She loved this woman no less than I did.

"What do you mean, Karin's asleep?" I asked, knowing very well what she meant.

"And you graduated magna cum laude? I don't believe it."

I rose, kissed her lightly on the lips and put my arms around her shoulders as we deserted my study and walked like young lovers to our bedroom down the hall. It was not a quickie. We did not make raging, passionate love. She preferred tenderness and, instinctively, because of her condition, I was especially gentle. Our union might have been more aptly called a coupling. Our bodies moved slowly and harmoniously like the familiar, practiced lovers that we were. When finally I could hold back no longer, I came in a way I never had before, emptying my loins with a series of gentle spasms. When she followed a moment later, I could sense that it must have been much the same for her.

After our disjoining, we lay naked and silent on the bed, she with her head cradled against my shoulder, her warm, damp body pressed close to mine. Suddenly, my eyes burned and I felt tears welling up inside. They seeped out of the corners of my eyes, and I moved my hand to brush them away.

She looked at me, her brow wrinkling with concern. "John? What's wrong?" she whispered.

I sniffled and wiped my eyes again. "Christ, I think I'm going to cry." At that moment the tears erupted and began to gush down my cheeks in torrents. She scooted up and gently pulled my head to her breast, burying my face in her fullness as though I were a suckling baby, caressing my back and shoulders with her hands. First I sobbed softly, slowly, getting a grasp on my emotions momentarily, nearly regaining my composure. But finally I surrendered and let the flood come, weeping freely and uncontrollably, only vaguely aware of the wetness of my wife's skin as I permitted my tears to soak and slicken her breasts and belly.

Was I a boy again? Did the reality of Doc's death trigger something in my subconscious that had vaulted me back to my childhood? Or had I finally become a man and, with my tears, washed away time and events that were best laid to rest and forgotten?

The simple, bronze-colored casket remained closed during the funeral. I was glad. I wanted to remember Doc the way I had always known him—sharp-witted, animated, vigorous even in old age.

The small Methodist church was drab and grim, devoid of the modernistic symbols and the colorful, inspiring decor of the new churches in our larger cities. On the other hand, I had little basis for comparison, since my visits to God's house in recent years had been confined to obligatory attendance at weddings and funerals.

I did not hear the funeral sermon. Even in my churchgoing days, I had often done my best thinking during the preacher's message. It was as though I had a built-in radar device that tripped the signal and launched my thoughts to another place as soon as the minister's words began.

From my pew off to one side near the rear of the church, I

discreetly scanned the tiny congregation. The church was less than half full, the large majority of mourners tired, elderly people of Doc's generation. Where were the generations of young and middle-aged who had been scouts in Doc's Troop 2? I had expected to see them swarming to the church, filling it to overflowing to pay tribute to the one who had given so much of himself to his boys. Oh, I recognized a few of the old scouts, all right, but there could not have been more than a dozen. And Doc had touched the lives of literally hundreds. Cynically, I thought of how quickly one's good works were forgotten, and how much easier we recollected and tallied the wrongs of a man's life.

Then my eyes came to rest on a familiar face. Yes, it was Sambo, but he had changed dramatically in the past two years. He was a burly man and heavy-jowled, but he had been that way when I last saw him. The difference was in his coloring. His face had a yellow cast to it, and his skin appeared slick and oily. He was my age, no more than thirty. He looked a sickly fifty.

Sherm did not attend the funeral, of course. He would have been too busy. He also would have guessed that I would be there, and I doubted that Sherm had any desire to ever meet me face-to-face again. Not that there was any malice on my part: Sherm was Sherm.

I almost jumped to my feet when the organ roared and the buxom, middle-aged woman started to howl strains of "The Old Rugged Cross." Reared in the tradition of small-town funerals, I knew this would be followed by the family pastor's droning of Doc's eulogy. The soloist would doubtless complete the ritual with her interpretation of "Beyond the Sunset." I was right.

When the funeral services were over, we filed silently out of the church, past the closed casket and out into the scorching, July heat. Even Schonberg Methodist had air conditioning.

As I stepped onto the walk that led from the church to the narrower public sidewalks that ran past it, I could feel the heat rising from the burning concrete as though it would sear through the soles of my shoes. It made me think of a boyhood day when I had watched a local restaurant owner fry an egg on the sidewalk in front of his business establishment as part of a publicity stunt one hot, July date. This was a day like that.

I approached the black hearse waiting at the end of the church walk, then turned and walked up the street a ways before I paused to await the emergence from the church of the pallbearers with their macabre burden. They would be followed, of course, by Doc's still-attractive, white-haired widow and the rest of the family members.

I caught sight of Sambo as he neared the hearse, and I waved acknowledgement, motioning him toward me. He hesitated and smiled uncertainly, then lumbered in my direction.

He approached, puffing laboriously from the heat, beads of perspiration breaking out on his broad forehead. He had a beer gut now that lapped over the waist of the too-tight pants that clung to his hips. He was a far cry from Schonberg's premier athlete.

I moved toward him. "Sambo," I said, "good to see you. It's been a while." I extended my hand and pressed it firmly to his; it was like taking hold of a dead fish—the grip of a man defeated by life.

"Yeah, Prof, long time, no see."

"Too bad about Doc. Schonberg won't be the same without him."

"No, I'll never forget him," Sambo said. "We had some great times. He's the one that gave us the name . . . remember? The Eager Beavers."

"Yeah, and it stuck for a long time. Clear through high school."

I didn't feel like reminiscing about the Beavers, so I changed the subject quickly. "How's Connie and the kids? Mom said you've got quite a family. Five kids?"

"Six. We had another last winter."

"You're still working at the packing plant?" I asked.

"Technically, but I've been on sick leave the last month

. . . liver trouble. The doctor says I can get back to work in a few weeks, but I'll just have to watch myself. Too goddamn much booze, Prof, and now I'm paying for it. You always were the smart one . . . in more ways than one."

"Not so damn smart," I said. "Look at what happened a few years back."

"It was Sherm that should have been in hot water, Prof," Sambo said, "not you. Hell, even when we were kids, somebody took the rap for Sherm. Usually you . . . but if not, it was Red or me." He shook his head sadly. "Good old Red. Nothing was ever the same after that, was it?"

"No, I guess not, but it wasn't just that, Sambo. You grow up . . . go on to other things."

Simultaneously, we saw the casket rocking its way snail-like down the church walk as the solemn pallbearers carried it toward the hearse. Silently, we watched them load the ominous vehicle with its sad cargo. As I studied the grief-stricken faces of Doc's family, I found myself increasingly depressed and anxious to break up my awkward conversation with Sambo. The cortege pulled away from the church to escort Doc to his last resting place. I turned back to Sambo and asked, "You going to the cemetery?"

Sambo replied, "I don't think I'm up to it, Prof. I've got to get home and get some rest. Damn heat's too much for me."

"Well, maybe we can talk next time I'm back. And, Sambo . . . if there's anything I can do, let me know. I owe you for when I was with the Governor."

"You don't owe me nothing, Prof. I wouldn't have been much of a man, knowing what I did and letting Sherm screw you like he planned to."

"Just the same, Sambo, thanks." I extended my hand, "Tell Connie hi."

"Sure, you bet."

Again, he shook my hand limply, then, seemingly embarrassed, he turned and walked away. We would not get together when I was in town; we both knew that. Once we had been friends. Now we were no more than acquaintances. I was not nostalgic about the Eager Beavers, and I found the prospect of any journey into my past unsettling.

Prof was a real professor now, an aspiring writer who sought refuge every summer in a small, comfortable lodge in the Wyoming Rockies. Everything I truly held dear in life was waiting for me in the mountain hideaway right now— the woman I loved, my child and children-to-be, my writing. I had already decided I would pass up the trip to the cemetery. I would pay a call on the Sedgewick family early in the evening, then I would spend the night with Mom. She would be disappointed that I was not staying longer, but Mom would understand.

Schonberg would always be an important part of my life, but it was no longer home. Home was where I would be going the next morning.

PART 1

1965–1966

1

Sherm brushed the curly, black locks off his forehead, then stood with arms folded across his bare, hairless chest, blinking his wide, dark eyes like a wise old owl in a Disney cartoon. Turning his head slowly, he studied his comrades appraisingly, like a cattle judge at the county fair, pondering, carefully weighing each animal's strong points and deficiencies before selecting the prize bull.

John was stretched out on the narrow, shaded patch of sand next to Red's '59 Dodge. He was absorbed in one of the paperback novels that always protruded from the hip pocket of his jeans. Sherm was reminded of a cowboy in a western movie who claimed he was naked without a gun on his hip; Prof must feel the same way when he doesn't have a damn book next to his butt. Anyway, he would be lost in another world until they were ready to leave, unless he came across something sexy enough to show the other guys.

Could Prof handle the responsibility Sherm had in mind? Mentally, he stripped Prof of the black, heavy-rimmed glasses. Without them, Prof was better looking than the other prospects by a damn sight. The girls liked him well enough, many of them apparently attracted by his quiet, reserved manner. But Prof would never do it. He would struggle with his conscience, research it, read on it for a few months, then decide the time was not right. If it were not for his damn scruples, he would be perfect.

Sherm swung around, turning his eyes toward the river. Red's milk-white buttocks popped out of the water as he swooped like a porpoise deep into the lazy current, disappearing from sight for some moments before his orange-cropped head shot out fifty feet downstream. Red would be willing to do it. Happy, fun-loving Red. He would be crazy to do it, but he could not handle the job. The girls considered him a screwball, a weirdo. Besides, he had terminal halitosis and insisted deodorant was for sissies. No, Red did not measure up.

Sambo lay spread-eagle and stark naked on the warm, sandy beach near the river's edge, staring at the pale, blue sky like some ancient sunworshiper. He reveled in the baking rays that bathed his bronzed, muscular body and savored the cooling breezes that gusted off the river this muggy June afternoon. His hand moved suddenly to his genitals, where he dug at some microscopic creature that was attacking his testicles, and his giant "prong," as he called it, began to swell.

Yes, Sambo would be the best bet. Put together like some Greek god, he had the physique for it—and the desire. Besides, he was the only one of the Beavers with a steady girl. That would save a hell of a lot of time. They could get this done before the month was out. Like Prof, Sambo was occasionally inhibited by his conscience, but with a little pep talk, that could be handled. Unlike Prof, Sambo was short on brains and could be manipulated.

It had not occurred to Sherman Reinwald to consider his own qualifications for the job. He was the idea man, the technician planning a new jet's first flight. He pulled a comb from his pocket and fussed with his thick hair. He was the son of one of Schonberg's elite, German families, but his smooth, unblemished skin had an olive tint to it, and his features were more characteristic of the Latins. He was slickly handsome but sensitive about his small stature.

He turned again toward the Dodge and marched deliberately to Prof, stopping at the latter's feet, waiting in vain for some acknowledgement of his presence. After a moment, he turned toward the river and cupped his hands around his mouth. "Everybody up here!" he bellowed like a drill sergeant.

Perturbed at the interruption, John Armstrong put down his book and sat up, cocking his head to one side and peering quizzically at Sherm. He caught that maniacal look in Sherm's eyes and knew that his comrade had just given birth to a new crusade. He maintained his silence and absently brushed the moist sand off his jeans and flicked some of the tiny grains out of the fine, rusty fuzz that cloaked his chest and belly. Then he took off his glasses and put them in the leather case at his side.

"Okay, Sherm," he said, "what is it?"

Sherm was glad Prof had taken off his glasses. He did not seem nearly so sinister and disapproving without them. "I've got a new project for the Beavers. I'll tell you about it in a minute; we've got to have all the guys up here."

Red and Sambo had evidently chosen not to hear the thunderous summons. Red floated like a cork on the water near the far bank of the river; Sambo still lay unmoving, statuelike, on the beach. Only now, his hands were interlaced behind his head, and his eyes were fastened hypnotically on the stiff pole between his legs.

Sherm yelled again. "God damn it, Sambo! Get your ass up here."

This time, Sambo turned his head. His face reddened slightly, and he grinned sheepishly before he got up and joined the others.

"Christ," Sherm said, "you'd think that pecker of his was some kind of trained cobra or something."

"Python," John corrected.

Red stood up in the shallow water, dived into the river's channel and swam toward his friends.

When they were assembled by the Dodge, Sherm said,

"Get dressed; sit down. We've got business to tend to."

"Jesus, Sherm," Red protested, "I just got in. I ain't ready to quit yet."

Sherm looked at him with a withering glare, and Red opened the car door and pulled out his pants. He started to pull them over his skinny, freckled legs.

"Jesus Christ!" Sherman snapped. "Don't you have any underwear?"

Red grinned, showing white, even teeth that seemed out of place on his scrunched-up face. "Shit, I ain't ever worn underwear in the summer."

"Jesus, Red, you're an animal. You're crude and uncouth, and that's why you don't get the job."

Red Murphy's face turned scarlet. He jerked up his breeches and snapped them before he lowered his head and charged at Sherm with arms swinging. "Lousy motherfucker," he yelled. "You sawed-off shrimp. I'll pound your face in."

Red's Irish temper had boiled over again, but Sambo's powerful arms as usual crossed Red's chest and pulled him back before he could vent his frustrations on Sherm.

Sherm knew he was no match physically for Red, although Red was only a few inches taller. Red was a born street fighter, and there was no one meaner in a fight when his ire was aroused. In all of the years of their fragile friendship, however, he had never executed a threat against Sherm. Sherman was too shrewd to let that happen. He never baited Red unless Prof or Sambo, preferably both, were around to restrain Red. This little episode had gone according to script.

"You son-of-a-bitch," Red spat as he strained against the arms that held him like steel bands.

"Sorry about that," Sherm said, "nothing personal. Now, let's all cool down. . . I've got a proposal."

I don't think I want to hear this," John said.

"No lip, Prof," Sherm said. "Wait till you hear what I've got to say."

"Okay," John said, "what is it?"

Sherm looked steadily at Sambo, who nervously averted his gaze. "Sambo," Sherm said, "have you ever been laid?" Sambo's face turned crimson. "Well? Have you? Come on, now, just between us guys."

Red grinned broadly. John shook his head disgustedly. "No, not really," Sambo said, "but Connie lets me feel her boobs sometimes, and then. . ." He paused. There was silence.

Sherm asked, "Then what?"

Well, sometimes. . . we get in the back seat and I rub against her until I shoot my wad."

Red's eyes opened wide in amazement, and he swallowed hard. "Jesus Christ, he's a fucking pervert!"

Incredulous, Sherm asked, "You mean you had your clothes off? Bare-assed naked?"

"Well, no. We keep our clothes on, just get to necking, and. . . and. . . I can't hold it back, that's all. Connie doesn't even know it." He laughed nervously. "My shorts are gummy as hell the rest of the night."

"I knew you were my man," Sherm said. "Sambo, how old are you?"

"Seventeen."

"And still a virgin. We're all virgins. Not a piece of ass between the bunch of us." His eyes moved challengingly from one to the other. "That is, unless somebody here can say otherwise."

Red shrugged, "I finger-fucked Suzie Swartz when I was a freshman."

"You perverted bastard," Sherman said, "that doesn't count." He turned to John, "Does it, Prof?"

"No, I guess not."

"Okay," Sherm said, "Sambo's going to change all that. We're going to have what they call a learning experience. We're going to help Sambo lay Connie."

John stood up, brushing the sand off his pants. "Sherm, you're crazy. I'm leaving. They call it rape, you know."

"Oh, shit, Prof, don't get your balls tight. We're not going to rape anybody. We're just going to initiate Sambo into the rites of manhood, and we'll all learn along with him. It's education, Prof. Think of it that way."

Mollified, John sat down again. "Sambo," Sherm said, "things are even better than I thought. Hell, you've almost gone all the way without us. With our help you'll have that cock of yours nestled in Connie's soft pussy in less than a week. You'll be a man, Sambo. . . just think of that."

Sambo looked uncertain, but he shifted position and tugged at the rising bulge in his trousers. "I don't see how you guys are going to help me."

"We're going to give you information and encouragement. Moral support. Confidence. That's all you need."

"How do you know Connie's gonna buy this?"

"No problem. Everybody knows she's crazy about you. You said she let you feel her boobs. Hell, you've been almost home and didn't even know it. We'll coach you a little bit. . . tell you the right things to do. . . give you the proper words. We'll have old Prof here do a little research on this. You're going to go first-class, Sambo."

Always first to see the practical implications, John asked, "What if she gets pregnant?"

Sambo's face turned glum, and he looked worriedly at Sherm. "Yeah, Sherm, what about that? God, I wouldn't want to get Connie knocked up. She's a great kid, and I'm nuts about her, but I don't want that kind of trouble. I'm not ready for that."

Sherm paced back and forth next to the Dodge, his hands knotted behind his back, a sign that he was preoccupied with the problem and did not want to be interrupted. Red and Sambo watched him attentively; John started to pull the paperback out of his back pocket.

Suddenly, Sherm came to a halt, stiffened his back and lifted his eyebrows slightly, looking at the others with contempt. "Simple," he said, "you use a condom."

"That's a bird, ain't it?" Red chimed in. "What the hell's a bird go to do with screwin'?"

"Jesus Christ, you nitwit!" Sambo looked thoroughly perplexed, but he was not about to risk invoking Sherm's wrath.

Finally John explained, "It's a rubber, guys. You put it on, so a girl won't get pregnant."

Red's freckled nose crinkled as he grinned knowingly. "Oh, why didn't you say so? I know about rubbers."

Sambo asked, "You got any, Sherm?"

"No, but you'll get some. All the drug stores have them."

"God, Sherm, I couldn't go to Doc Sedgewick for something like that. . . He'd know what it was for. He'd tell my old man. Worse yet, Connie's."

"Dummy," Sherm said, "we won't buy it in Schonberg. "We'll drive into Hastings and buy them. They've got millions of rubbers in Hastings. All shapes and sizes."

Sambo paled and scratched his head, "I don't know, Sherm."

"We'll run up there, day after tomorrow," Sherm said. "Prof, you study this. We want Sambo to have the best scientific information." He strutted over to Sambo and looked up at the huge young man who, nearly six feet four inches tall, towered over him. He patted him gently on his sinewy biceps. "Just think of it, Sambo. Samuel Hanson, Jr. The first of the Eager Beavers to score. You can do it, Sambo. I know you can."

John knew there was no stopping Sherm now. Besides, it did sound like an interesting project. He would have to get to the library the first thing tomorrow. George Bauer used to work at Doc Sedgewick's; he might have some insight into this condom business.

2

The Beavers sat in Red's battered green Dodge which was parked across the street from the Hastings Rexall Drugstore. Red slumped down in the seat, the top of his head barely sticking above window level. His eyes rolled warily, and his hands clutched the steering wheel tightly, like those of a tense get-away driver for a gang of bank robbers. Sambo fidgeted on the other side of the front seat, perspiration streaming down his flushed cheeks. John sat in the backseat directly behind Red, his hands clasped behind his neck. On the other side Sherm leaned forward, rattling off last-minute instructions to a badly-shaken Sambo.

"Now, you just go to the back of the store," Sherm said, "where it says 'Prescriptions.' They'll have a guy in a white coat back there, and you just tell him you want some condoms. Condoms. Can you remember that?"

"Condoms," Sambo answered obediently.

"Right. Tell them you want the biggest size they got. Christ, I hope they make them big enough for that cock of yours. Geez, what do you think, Prof?"

"No problem," John answered. "Don't worry about the size, Sambo. They're all the same; they're just a thin rubber sheath. They'll stretch over anything from a Vienna sausage to a roll of minced ham. Don't waste time trying to pick out the best brand. Tell the man you want Peacocks with a reservoir tip."

"Peacocks?" Sambo asked.

"I thought this didn't have anything to do with birds," Red interjected.

"It's a brand name, Red," John said. "They sold more of those at Doc Sedgewick's than anything."

"All right," Sambo said. "Peacocks with a . . . what?"

"Reservoir tip."

"Yeah, Peacocks with a reservoir tip . . . What's that?"

"What's what?"

"A reservoir tip."

"Oh," John answered. "It's a condom with an extra pocket to catch your sperm. It won't bust as easy."

"Bust! What do you mean bust?" Sambo said, fright showing in his voice.

John answered, "What do you mean 'what do I mean, bust?'"

Sambo's face had gone from red to ashen, and he turned back to Sherm. "Oh, Christ, Sherm, let's forget about this."

"Sambo, you chicken shit. Get your ass out there and go buy your rubbers . . . now."

As Sambo climbed out of the car and proceeded slowly across the street, his stomach tightened, and he felt on the verge of nausea. He was certain the other Beavers could hear the sound of his heart thumping. He paused in front of the store and looked up and down the sidewalk. No one in sight. He wiped his clammy palms on his jeans and started for the door.

Suddenly panic seized him, and he stopped and backed away. He turned around, stepped off the curb and moved toward the car when he saw Sherm waving frantically and pointing toward the drugstore. Sherm would raise hell if he did not go through with it. He gave Sherm the finger before he turned back toward the store; he would go in when he was damn well good and ready.

He paced back and forth in front of the store for a few minutes, intentionally not looking in the direction of his friends. Fortunately, there was little activity and the coast was clear. Abruptly, he darted for the store entrance.

It was just as Sherm said—the prescription sign was at the rear of the store. Sambo was positive that all eyes in the building were boring in on him, everyone wondering, he supposed, what a kid like himself wanted with rubbers. He shoved his hands in his back pockets and ambled nonchalantly down the nearest aisle, pretending interest in the rows of hair oil and aftershave that filled the men's department, while casing the layout of the prescription center from the corners of his eyes.

"May I help you, young man?" a woman's voice said.

He bolted upright and almost tripped over his feet before he turned to face the plump, matronly clerk who had sneaked up behind him. "Uh, no, just looking right now. Thank you, ma'am."

"Let me know if I can be of some help," she said, and smiled amicably before she walked away.

He took a deep breath and commenced the walk down death row toward the prescription counter. Yes, there was a guy in a white coat. Oh, Christ. It wasn't a guy—it was a woman. A woman rubber salesman! What was the world coming to?

He did an about-face and made a beeline toward the door without so much as a glance sideways. Outside, he bent over to catch his wind and to hold back the vomit that was beginning to well up in his throat.

After a pep-talk from Sherm and some calming reassurances from Prof, Sambo reluctantly agreed to try again at another store. He was relieved upon entering the Cornhusker Pharmacy to find that the firm had the good sense to employ a male pharmacist. He was boosted by a surge of confidence and, swaggering to the prescription counter, he nodded a greeting to the diminutive, bald man at the cash register.

"May I help you, young fellow?" the white-coated pharmacist asked.

"Yes," Sambo squeaked. What was wrong with his voice? Christ, the words wouldn't come out. "I'd like some con . . ." He coughed and cleared his throat. "Peacocks," he said.

"Peacocks?" the old man asked, eyeing him curiously.

The stupid old fart. He worked in a drugstore and didn't know what Peacocks were? What next? He found his hands starting to tremble, and he was tempted to make a run for the door.

"Oh . . . oh-h-h-h," the pharmacist said, a smirk crossing his lips, "you need some condoms. I see."

Smart-ass, Sambo thought.

"You probably want the Peacocks . . . the reservoir tips, I presume."

"Yeah . . . yeah . . . that's right," Sambo choked. Why did his voice keep cracking like that?

"How many?"

"Oh, God, he had not even thought about that. Maybe he should just go out and ask Prof. No, if he did that, he would probably never come back.

"How many will you need?" the man asked.

He only had five bucks. "Uh, make it three," Sambo said.

The pharmacist raised his eyebrows and, with an incredulous look, said, "Three boxes? There's a dozen in the box, you know, My, my."

"Oh, that's right . . . I forgot. How much is a box?"

"They're on special right now—$2.39 a box."

"I'll take a box."

"These are lubricated, you know. Can I find you anything else?"

"No, that should be all for now." His voice was stronger.

A few moments later, he strutted out the front door like a big rooster, flourishing the little paper sack so that the other Beavers across the street could see that he had accomplished his mission.

No sooner was Sambo seated in the Dodge, than Sherm

pounced upon the prize, yanking the sack from Sambo's hand and tearing away the white paper to expose the gold and green cardboard box decorated with the Peacock logo.

Even John was caught up in the excitement now. "Open them," he said.

Sherm did, and out slipped a dozen, individually wrapped, tinfoil packets of condoms. "God damn," Sherm said. "They're even gold-lined."

"Open one," Sambo urged.

"You do it," Sherm said, handing one of the packets ceremoniously to John.

"All right," John said, "put the others back in the box. We don't want to waste them."

Carefully and tenderly, he peeled away the foil wrapper. A slimy fluid dripped on to his blue jeans as the packet broke open and he grabbed the slippery white object encased within. He pulled it out and held up the condom for his comrades to view.

"Sambo, you big ox," Red said, "you got the midget size! That won't even go over the tip of your dick."

"No, wait a minute," John said and began to unroll the balloon-like receptacle from its base. "See, I think you just roll it over your penis."

"Your what?" Red asked.

"Your pecker," John corrected himself.

Sherm pinched the round, firm rim at the condom's base, shaking his head sadly. "He'll never get it on that big cock."

John took command. "He'll get it on. I told you, it fits anything . . . even Sambo's. Now, this is a Beaver project; let's chip in and split up the cost. Red, you and I and Sherm each get two of these things. Counting the one we wasted, that leaves five for Sambo. He'll need practice putting it on a few times, but that should still leave a couple for Connie." John had no idea what he was going to do with his own trophies, but somehow his new acquisitions gave him a sense of security and masculinity.

3

Sambo felt the slightest twinge of guilt for what he planned to do that evening. Connie had been more than willing to pass up the movie and take on the view at Cedar Ridge. They had engaged in heavy petting before, and he was certain Connie did not anticipate it would go beyond that tonight. But she would like it—Sherman had promised she would. If he could just remember everything Prof had told him about technique, the sensuous places and all that stuff. Prof had made him horny as hell just telling him about it. But Prof seemed to know what he was talking about. The rubbers fit just as he had promised. He had wasted two of them in his private practice sessions, and he was sure he had the knack now. If tonight worked out, he would use them up in no time. But he could always buy more.

As he nosed his father's new, red Buick up the twisting, gravel road to the top of the ridge, Connie moved closer and leaned her head on his shoulder, resting her hand lightly on Sambo's knee. God, she must be hot to trot—it was going to be too easy.

Connie looked up at him with her limpid blue eyes and brushed her long, blond tresses back over her shoulders. The guys all envied him. She was a tall girl with a cute, button nose and a pretty, natural smile. She was built like a brick craphouse. He had seen bigger boobs, but hers fit her body perfectly. She was reasonably bright, and a sweet kid besides.

Guilt began to set in again. He felt like a creep. But the Beavers would be waiting at midnight for a report. There was no way out. He was a lousy liar, and he knew it, so they would not buy any fairy tale he brought back.

His Buick crept over the crest of the hill, and Sambo pulled out onto the lush, grassy meadows that overlooked Schonberg's myriad of twinkling lights. Occupants of a few other cars had already staked out places at the far end of the meadow. It was an unwritten law among Schonberg teenagers that parkers not be disturbed. Spotlighters or other pests faced the wrath and contempt of the vast majority of Schonberg High students.

Sambo drove the car to a spot on the meadow's edge and pulled to a stop not far from a grove of towering cottonwoods, finding solace in the screen they formed on one side of the vehicle. Leaning back in the seat, he put his arm around Connie's shoulder. They sat there quietly until he was startled by the rustling of fragile cottonwood leaves, as a mild breeze drifted over the ridge. He sat up suddenly and tossed a nervous glance over his shoulder.

"What's the matter, Sambo?" Connie asked.

"Nothing . . . just edgy tonight, I guess."

"Why?"

"Beautiful girls always make me nervous."

"You're sweet," she said, turning and wrapping her arms around his neck, planting her full, moist lips on his.

He felt pressure in his pants and banged his knee sharply against the steering wheel as he moved to make the necessary adjustments. "Ouch!" he said, "it's too crowded up here. Want to get in back?"

"Okay, sounds like a good idea."

They had done this before, so he anticipated that the move from the front to the back seat would be a simple matter. From here on, he would have to remember his lessons, though.

As they climbed in back, he appraised the obstacles. He was too damned big for the car seat, and he would need to leave one door partially open for some stretching room. Connie was wearing a lightweight, pleated skirt; that would be less formidable than slacks or jeans. It was too hot for a sweater, so only the sleeveless, cotton blouse and whatever lay underneath covered her breasts. It could be a lot worse.

He felt the outside of his pants pocket—the condoms were there. He had brought two. John had told him to take two, in case he lost one. Sherm had added he might want to do it twice.

Settled in the back seat, he took her in his arms again, pressing his lips tight against hers, then, as they spread, probing into her mouth with his tongue—French kissing the kids called it. She was breathing heavier now, and he felt the firmness of her breasts as they pressed tighter against his chest. He pulled his head away and whispered, "Oh, Connie, I love you." Prof had provided the script, but right now, he believed it—he honestly did.

A fire smoldered in his loins. They slid down the seat in a semi-prone position, and as they did, he inched his hand to her breast, squeezing it gently before he fumbled at the top button of her blouse. The button seemed twice as big as the hole. He tugged at the blouse sharply. The button snapped off and feel on the floor. "Sorry," he said.

"It's all right," she answered. "Here, let me."

He pulled back momentarily while she unbuttoned the blouse and slipped it off. Then she unhooked the bra. As the straps slid down her arms, emancipating the grapefruitlike bulges of flesh beneath, the throbbing in his loins became unbearable. There could be no turning back.

He brushed his fingers lightly over her breasts, kissing her long and deeply. Tease her nipples, Prof had said. He did, delighted as they rose and hardened at his touch.

Now, to get at her pussy. Her vagina, Prof had called it. He pressed his body on top of hers, kissing her neck and ears ardently as he moved one hand to her thigh. He was relieved when he felt warm, bare flesh there. Her skirt had hiked up in the course of their wrestling. Another good omen. Unbelieable. Everything was going just the way the Beavers had planned it.

He placed his hand on the inside of her thigh and moved it up slowly, inch by inch, toward her crotch, stopping only when he felt the soft silkiness of her panties. Geez, it was hot and damp there. Had she peed in her pants? No, Prof had said it got that way when it was ripe and ready for his prong.

"Connie," he said, "I love you . . . I want you. Oh, God, I want to make love to you." Again, he meant it—especially the last part.

"Oh, Sambo," she said, "I love you, too, but we can't. You can feel me, touch me, anything . . . but we can't do that."

"But I want to, sweetheart. This is . . . is . . ." What had Prof said? Yes. ". . . the ultimate expression of our love. Oh, please, honey, please."

"I would Sambo, really I would, but I'm scared I might get pregnant."

Again he opened his mouth and placed it over hers, darting his tongue in and out, lightly touching her own, rubbing the inside of her thighs, holding her tightly. Her breathing was nearly as labored as his. She wanted to also—he was sure of it. Now was the touchy part. He could mess things up, if this looked too well-planned.

"Connie," he said, "we can do it. I have something with me . . . something that prevents babies." The moonlight streamed through the car window, casting its light upon her Nordic face. He caught the sudden glint of suspicion in her eyes. "I've always had them." he said quickly, "but I've never used them with anybody . . . I swear. You're the only one I ever wanted." He pressed his fingers under her panties, feeling the upraised, bushy mound of her pubes. She writhed and moaned, closing her eyes and breathing heavier, as though something were torturing her from within. "Are you all right?" he asked.

"Okay," she said, "let's do it . . . but hurry."

They sat up, and he fumbled with his own clothes, as Connie kicked off her sandals and wriggled out of her skirt and finally her panties. When they both sat stark-naked, he glanced at her embarrassedly as he rummaged through his pants pockets, hunting frantically for the tinfoil packets. He had never seen a girl completely nude before, and the sight of her milky skin around her forbidden parts excited him, maddened him to an insane frenzy. From Sherm's description, he had expected to discover a giant, black bush to match his own between her thighs. But it was only a light-brown, silky triangle exposed there in the pale light. That should make it easier to find whatever it was he was looking for.

Finally, his fingers closed on the packet. Just finding it made his prong ache and started the unrelenting throb again. As he tore away the foil, he looked again at Connie, who sat on the other side of the seat, her head tilted quizzically as she watched him. He could see that this ritual was taking away the spontaneity, somehow making the act less right. And her passion was obviously cooling. He had better speed it up.

He pulled out the soggy condom, and her eyes widened in astonishment. "What is that?"

He held it up front of him. "It's a con . . . rubber," he said.

"I've heard of them, but I've never seen one. What in God's name are you going to do with that thing?"

"It keeps you from having babies."

"I know that, you idiot. How does it work?"

Suddenly she was being very clinical about the whole thing, and he found himself on the defensive, and his damn prong was beginning to lose some of its hardness. "Well, I put it on my . . . you know."

"You put that thing on your penis?"

He gulped, taken aback; he had never heard a girl use that word. But he was determined. "Yes, it keeps the babies from going in."

"It looks like a balloon," she noted. "I understand it catches the semen."

"Yeah, that's right."

"All right, let's go ahead."

She slipped down in the seat, and with her knees raised and legs spread slightly, she waited. Her signal heightened his ardor. He started to slip on the condom when he bumped his elbow on the car door and the rubber dropped out of his hands onto the floor. "Oh, Christ," he muttered, feeling around on the floor, trying to find the rubber sheath that eluded him.

"What's the matter?" Connie said impatiently.

"I dropped it. I can't find it."

"Well, then, we'd better not," she said. "I just don't want to take any chances."

She was more curious now than passionate, and he was not going to score without his rubber. "Wait," he said, "I've got another one in my pants pocket."

She lifted herself up on her elbow and seemed to be studying him. What in the hell was she looking at? His hand trembled palsylike, when he finally found his trousers and his fingers closed around that all-important packet. "I found it," he said like a prospector who had just discovered gold. "I found it! I'll be just a minute."

This time he concentrated only on the task of the moment and artfully opened the packet, deftly pulling the condom over his tumescence. He turned to Connie and found she was still staring at him. "I'm ready," he said.

She pointed at his penis. "It's so big," she said. "Are they all that big?"

He was not certain whether to be proud or embarrassed— he opted for the former. "No, as a matter of fact, they're not. The guys say I've got the biggest cock in the whole school. When I went to scout camp, they used to call me Python."

"You're kidding," she giggled. Then her eyes narrowed, and she took on a worried look. "Sambo, I don't know if I can get that in me. I've never done this before."

"No problem," he said, "you'll stretch." That's what Prof had told him, anyway—but you have to go careful with a virgin he had warned.

"Okay, but would you just kiss me and feel me a little bit . . . like you did before? Before we do it?"

"Sure," he said, as he moved to her, gouging his heel on the handle of the open car door. The damn backseat was made for midgets. He moved his hand again to the soft fur of her crotch and kissed her ears, nose, mouth, neck. Then each again in turn. Shortly, Connie began to moan and squirm again. Christ, he did not know how long he could hold out. Then he became aware of the pinching and tightening of the condom on his prong. Suddenly, he remembered Prof had told him not to let it get dry. It would be harder to get in and might hurt Connie.

"Connie," he said, "we've got to do it . . . quick."

"Do it. Do it now!"

She spread her legs, one foot slipping off the car seat and thumping on the floor. He mounted her and braced one foot against the back of the front seat, cursing silently about the logistical problems confronting him. Her arms went around his back and pulled him down. "Hurry," she said, "hurry."

He reared his buttocks and drove with all the force he could muster, then winced as his prong hit a dead end.

"Sambo, you idiot! Not my belly button . . . between my legs . . . lower."

"I know," he said, "I know. I just couldn't tell where I was at."

"Here, let me help you," she said.

He could feel her hand closing over his encased prong, pressing it lower so that it was aimed at some hidden place between her thighs. He had known there was an extra hole there—Prof had promised him there would be. It was not that he did not have some vague knowledge of the female anatomy, but he had found the precise arrangement of the receptacle a bit confusing. Anyhow, she evidently was ready now.

"Okay," she said, "that's it."

He thrust again and thought he had sprained his prong when it crashed against a solid wall in his vain attempt to enter. "Oh, no," she cried, "it hurts. Don't." But he rammed again. This time he felt it give a little. He began to bore like a human posthole digger, and he thought he was going to wedge his way in, when her blood-curdling scream pierced the still, night air. Her legs closed, and he jumped away, fearful that his genitals had been mutilated beyond reapir. Instinctively, he clutched his testicles and doubled in pain, struggling to catch his breath.

"Jesus," he said, "what's the matter with you? You about killed me!"

"You about killed me, Sambo. You're an animal!" She scooted up on the seat, suddenly demure and modest, trying to cover her breasts with one arm while guarding her assaulted pubes with her other.

His penis deflated like a popped balloon and went hopelessly flaccid. The crusty, dry condom dropped off. He picked it up and flicked it out the car door. Suddenly, he was conscious of an automobile engine roaring from the meadow. Momentarily, he was blinded by two beacons of light headed straight for his Buick.

"Christ," he said, "get your things on. Somebody's coming down here." They both began to rummage frantically through the jumbled heaps of clothing on the car floor. He came up with one of his socks and Connie's panties before the car came up beside them. He pulled his door closed.

"Everything okay in there?" came a gruff voice.

"Uh, we're fine," answered Sambo.

"What about the lady?" the voice queried.

Connie stared coldly at Sambo. "For Christ's sake, Connie," Sambo whispered, "tell them you're all right. You want to climb out of the car stark-naked?"

In a squeaky voice she answered, "I'm fine, thanks. I thought I heard something in the woods; I was just scared."

"Okay," the man said, "but try not to make so much noise down here, okay?"

The engine roared, and the car peeled away, heading back to its own place on the meadow. "I want to go home," Connie said.

He moved toward her, "Hell, Connie, I'm sorry. I didn't mean anything; I've never done this before."

She backed away from him, clenching her fists menacingly. "Get away from me you. . .you. . . rapist! I want to go home, and if you don't get me out of here right now, I'm going to scream bloody murder."

"Yeah, sure, Connie, I'll take you home." he sighed. "But first we've got to sort out our things and get dressed." He bent over again, groping for his clothes on the floor. The first thing he touched was the lost condom. It swiftly joined the other in the meadow.

It was still early, not much past 10:30, when Sambo pulled the Buick up in front of John Armstrong's house. The other Beavers were sprawled out on the front porch, congregated dutifully to receive Sambo's report. He should have gone home, but he would still have to face them later. Goddamn Sherm and his screwy ideas. You could bet Connie would never go out with him again.

As he got out of the car, Sherm came down to meet him.

"Sambo, baby. Geez, you're a fast worker. You look weak; you must have given her the works."

"You and your bright ideas. I ought to set you flat on your ass."

"It didn't work?"

"You're goddamn right it didn't work. And I lost me the best girl a guy could have. She called me an animal."

"Ah, don't worry," Sherm said. "She'll get over it. We'll get Prof to talk to her."

Sambo brightened. Connie would listen to Prof; the girls liked him and respected him, and he was a peacemaker. "Yeah," he said, "maybe Prof can straighten this out with

Connie."

As they approached the porch, Sherm called out to John and Red, "It didn't work, guys—we're still virgins. Back to the drawing board."

4

John squirmed in his sleeping bag, trying to work his hip and shoulder into some niches in the hard earth, where they might find some small comfort. Their campsite at Twin Lakes was carpeted with springy grass, but it felt like granite beneath his aching bones, and the Beavers were crammed in Sherm's two-man wall tent like sardines in a can. He had the downhill spot next to the tent's front opening and fully expected to be crowded out from under the canvas shelter before morning. He would have opted for sleeping under the stars anyway, if he had not sighted the silent, electrifying bolts that were intermittently lighting up the pitch-black sky to the west. Rain was likely before the morning, and he preferred sleeping dry.

It was after 1:00 a.m., and he still had little prospect of sleep. Sherm lay beside him, sleeping soundly, snorting like a hog on occasion—usually about the time sleep promised to come to himself. This campout fiasco had been Sherm's idea—a visit into their nostalgic past, he had called it. Troop Number 2 had camped and fished at Twin Lakes many times over the years, and Sherm suggested they would have a ball camping near the secluded lakes in the rolling hills south of Schonberg.

Sambo and Red had been enthusiastic and, with reservations, John had agreed to come along. He did not care much for fishing, but he did appreciate the quiet beauty of the hills and had anticipated the pleasure of catching up on some reading amidst the solitude.

Since their arrival yesterday afternoon, however, he had spent most of his time refereeing squabbles between his companions. Even normally docile Sambo seemed short-tempered on this trip. The bullheads and channel catfish were not biting either, and John guessed that probably did not help his friends' dispositions any.

Anyway, he was glad he had brought his own car. The others planned to make the camping trip a two-night adventure. He hoped they had a good time, but he was going home in the morning.

For some reason, he had found his outings with the Beavers increasingly less enjoyable in recent weeks. He was becoming a reluctant participant in their escapades and was beginning to treasure the time he spent away from the others. Still, they were his friends and he was not going to desert them.

Sambo and Red were at the other end of the tent on the other side of Sherm. John rolled over when he heard them giggling like two kindergarten children. He sat up and winced as the brightness of the flashlight beam caught him in the eyes. "Damn it! Get that light out of my eyes," he said. The beam moved off to the side of the tent, and he saw Red's grinning face in the dim light. Then he realized that spindly Red and massive Sambo were both sitting on top of their sleeping bags, naked and cross-legged like a couple of savages. "What are you guys doing?" John asked irritably.

"Sambo's showing me his scar," Red said. "Want to see it?"

"What scar?"

"The one on his prick . . . where he got it caught in the zipper that time."

"No thanks, I've seen it."

Undaunted and cheerful, Red said, "Want to jack off

with us? Sambo's got three days stored up."

"Yeah," Sambo added, "come on over."

"Go to hell," John said. "I just want to get some sleep. Don't you guys know you'll get pimples from that?"

"You serious?" Red asked. "Jesus, my mom thought I should go to some kind of a skin doctor.

"He's filling you full of shit," Sambo said. "God, Red, you're a gullible bastard."

Well, even if it did," Red said, "I'd rather have pimples than quit."

"It'll make you go blind, too," John added for good measure, but this time the others did not respond.

He rolled back over and struggled to find a comfortable spot again, assuming that Red and Sambo were now absorbed in their nocturnal games. It seemed like everywhere Sambo went, he was set on making his big prong the center of attention. Of course, John could not blame him entirely. Sambo's instrument was enormous and was something of a legend among the guys at Schonberg High. Some claimed it reached his knees, and there was frequent speculation that the huge thing, if coaxed, would peek out of his pant leg and wink. The guys who had seen it in the locker room after football practice knew better. It was not quite that long, but there was considerable banter on just how long the thing might be at full erection. What would happen if he turned that snake loose on some unsuspecting girl—certainly there would be no Schonberg virgin with a pussy big enough to swallow the whole thing? She'd have to have stitches when he was finished. Was it lethal? Would he kill somebody with that weapon?

Sambo carried his appendage with pride, and he always had a preference for skin-tight jeans that presented a suggestive outline for any fair damsel to study. John knew that Sambo worshipped his penis as a god before all gods and chuckled to himself when he thought of the tragic time when Sambo was certain he was going to lose it.

The scar was Sambo's souvenir of that occasion. It happened one night in the locker room after football practice.

Sambo had showered and was getting dressed. He often went without underwear, and that night he pulled his tight jeans over his still-damp hips. He started to zip his pants, when the end of his pecker got caught in the zipper. Sambo was circumcized, and the zipper teeth latched onto the thing's bare head, holding it like a vice grip on a bolt. John stood by helplessly as panic gripped Sambo and he began to moan. Tears dripped from his eyes as he tried to rip the thing loose, but when he could not get the job done, he commenced screaming bloody murder. The coach came in, worked at it a little bit as Sambo sobbed, but he could not get it free either. The audience that had gathered around the disaster was not supportive. Sherm suggested flippantly that they might have to cut the damn thing off. Sambo immediately fainted dead away and had to be carried to the coach's car for delivery to the Schonberg Hospital's emergency room. There his dilemma was remedied quickly. A physician administered a local anesthetic and relieved him quickly of his pain. In a matter of moments, he removed the zipper by cutting a chunk of skin off the marble-smooth end of the organ.

Sambo still displayed the nasty little red scar left by the surgeon's scalpel. He wore it as a badge of honor.

John had started to drift off to sleep when a roar of thunder crashed and a bolt of lightning erupted from the sky, sparkling and sizzling just outside the tent—or so it seemed. Then the rain came, but it seemed to be a gentle, cooling rain, without the devastating winds that usually accompanied Nebraska thunderstorms. The soft pitter-patter of the drops against the tight canvas roof soothed him and made him drowsy again, and soon he was in a deep sleep.

When he poked his head out of the sleeping bag the next morning, he was nearly blinded by the glaring rays of the June sun as the fiery glow crept over the ridge east of the campsite. He crawled out sleepily, orienting himself before he realized that his sleeping bag was soaked like a sponge and that the underwear he had worn to bed had been drenched with it. As he feared, his tentmates had, unintentionally, forced him out of the tent during the night and he had spent a good part of the early morning hours sleeping unsheltered in the rain. Well, it was not the first time, but somehow he did not find it as adventuresome as he might have a few years back.

A change into some dry underwear and clothes would make things better. Still wrapped in his sleeping bag, he scooted toward the tent to find his knapsack. He did not have to go far because it was directly outside the tent opening, evidently having joined him on the expedition into the elements. So much for dry clothes.

He stood up and pulled back the tent flap, sticking his head under the canvas to check on the others. Sleeping like babies. Then the stench struck his nostrils and he backed away quickly, gagging as he fought the urge to vomit. He recognized the odor—human defecation. One of them had crapped in his sleeping bag. Christ, did he have to diaper these guys, too?

Carefully keeping his distance, he yelled through the tent opening, "Hey, you guys, wake up!"

"Go to hell," came Sambo's sleepy voice.

"Wake up," he yelled again, "and take a whiff . . . a deep one."

"Oh, shit," Sherm groaned.

"You're right, Sherm, that's what it is," John said dryly.

Sherm came out of the tent like a shot; Sambo, like a mad bull, charged out behind him. John moved away.

"Sherm, I hate to tell you this," he said, "but you've got some on your face."

Sherm's hand went instinctively to his cheek. His fingers touched the creamy blotch. He pulled his hand back and studied the rich, brown stain on his finger tips. "Oh, shit," he said, "oh, shit," then took off on a dead run for the nearby lake.

Sambo did not bother with self-examination. He followed Sherm's example and soon passed him by on the way to the cleansing waters. Shortly, Red emerged, yawning and stretching like a sleepy coon hound as he stepped naked onto the wet, ankle-high grass outside the tent.

"What's going on, Prof? Where's Sherm and Sambo?"

"Down at the lake, taking their morning bath."

"What for?"

"Somebody crapped in the tent last night."

"They did?" He ran his fingers through the curly locks that were fiery-orange under the glow of the morning sun. Then he grinned sheepishly. "Yeah, that's right—they did. I remember now . . . I had to take a shit and it was raining, so I just squatted in the corner." He leaned back into the tent to identify the spot. "Well, it *was* in the corner anyhow."

"Yeah, it probably was once," John agreed, "but I guess it's spread all over the tent by now." John knelt on the ground and commenced rolling up his sleeping bag. "And Red," John said, "if I were you, I wouldn't tell Sherm to eat shit for a few days."

"Huh? What do you mean?"

"Just what I said."

"Hey, John," Red said, "remember that time at scout camp when I crapped in the tent just before inspection?"

"Yeah, I remember."

"This is just about as funny as that, ain't it?"

"Yeah, real funny, Red."

"What's the matter, Prof? You mad or something?"

"No, I'm just losing my sense of humor." John picked up his sleeping bag and reached down for the straps of his knapsack.

"What are you doing, John?"

"I'm going home. You guys have a nice camping trip."

"You can't go. I was going to run in and get some beer tonight."

"Good. Disinfect the tent with it. I'll see you around."

5

"Hey, there's Sally Hooper," Red whispered excitedly, sticking his head out of the car window as he swung the Dodge around the corner of the courthouse square. "Let's take her for a ride . . . have a gang-bang, maybe, huh?"

"That's the only way you'll ever get a piece of ass," needled Sherm from the other side of the front seat. "You've been jacking off so long you wouldn't know what to do with it anyhow."

Indignant, Red countered, "Oh, yeah? I haven't seen you getting so much of it yourself. You're all talk, Sherm, that's what you are . . . all talk."

"Hey, Red," Sambo interrupted from the back seat, "when are we going to bring out the beer?"

"When I say so, that's when," snapped Red. "Nobody else has paid for their share yet, so I guess I say when we drink the beer."

John folded his arms and sighed, leaning back against the seat, and glanced sideways out the back window as the car rolled slowly by Sally Hooper, then sped away as it went past. The Beavers were in a nasty mood tonight, and Sherm, Red and Sambo had been at each others' throats ever since Red picked them up after supper.

Red bragged that he had purchased a couple of cases of beer across the state line in Kansas, using the fake ID John had fabricated for him a few months back. The Nebraska drinking age was twenty-one; Kansas was eighteen. Red did not quite qualify on either count, but certainly was more believably eighteen.

John had had second thoughts about tonight, especially when he heard about the booze. He had access to some crude printing equipment in the high school journalism room and had faked a few documents for his buddies from time to time, but he was never really comfortable around the guys when they started drinking. He could never quite see the logic to the view that one had to dull one's sensibilities in order to have a good time. He had never been drunk, and only occasionally had he joined the Beavers and their pals in a beer. Besides, he had plans for college and a future, and criminal charges filed against him as a minor in possession of alcoholic beverages would not quite jibe with those plans.

But Sherm had insisted on calling it a back-to-school party. They would begin their senior year at Schonberg High next week, and they hadn't been together much since the ill-fated camping trip.

John had taken a highway construction job, and the long, hot hours had given him an excuse not to join his friends in the evenings. He actually had been too tired for such nightlife that summer; he welcomed the excuse to stay home. Outings with the Beavers would have left little time for reading, and he found himself wondering more and more what he had in common with the others.

After John convinced Connie to give Sambo another chance, the two had become inseperable companions. John suspected that Sambo had, by this time, accomplished his sexual mission without any assistance from the Beavers.

Sherm had pursued exploits of his own with a vengeance in recent weeks, and had suddenly emerged as Schonberg High's leading man-on-the-make. On the few occasions the Beavers had gotten together, Sherm rattled on endlessly about his conquests, and his explicit descriptions of his sexual relations with Sarah Remington convinced John that there was some substance to Sherm's bragging.

Red had a part-time job as a carry-out boy at the Steinmetz Supermarket. At nights, he just drove around in the Dodge. John felt sorry for him and had joined him a few times, but he found he and Red had little to talk about when the others were not around.

Red headed the Dodge around the square again, and John caught sight of Sally down the street, walking nonchalantly, hips swinging, along the sidewalk that edged the courthouse lawn. Sally was a girl with a reputation for being easy, and she could frequently be found strolling along the courthouse square early on a summer evening. She was available for pickup and did not seem to mind climbing into the car with a gang of boys. Being the only girl never seemed to bother her. In fact, she appeared to prefer being the center of attention.

John liked to dance with Sally and, even now, the thought of it stirred life in his loins. She could just about drive you wild on the slow ones. She had that way of grinding her hips against you that made you sure she was ready for action. It was impossible to dance with Sally without getting a healthy erection, and she was always more than willing to step outside to take a little breather between dances. The guys always claimed she was good for a quick lay out in the bushes, but John had never had guts enough to advance that far. Rumor was she was a nympho, which made the thought of an evening with Sally all the more exciting.

As though he had read John's mind, Sambo said, "Doesn't she give you a hard-on just watching her walk? What an ass!"

John could not ignore the rising turbulence in his own genitals and, as they neared Sally, the gang-bang idea did not sound bad. "Why don't we offer Sally a ride?" he suggested.

Red pulled the car close to the curb. When it reached

Sally, she turned and smiled. Red slammed on the brakes, and the old jalopy jerked to a halt. "Want to go for a ride?"

Sally smiled eagerly and brushed back her long, sable-black hair. "Sure," he said.

For once, Sambo beat Sherm to the starting gate and hopped out to open the car door, letting Sally in to the backseat between him and John. When she sat down, her short-shorts pulled up even further on her thighs, and John gawked like a country bumpkin at the smooth, shapely legs. When he looked up, he saw her eyeing him mischievously, but she only smiled and made no effort to cover the willowy limbs.

"Haven't seen you much this summer, Prof," she said.

"No. No, I had a job—highway construction."

"You look like it," she said, patting his biceps gently. "Muscles."

"Yeah," he said, "I guess it hasn't hurt me." It was unbelievable what a compliment from a girl could do for a guy. It buoyed him up, made him feel masculine. He knew that the manual labor had filled out his six foot frame, and, while he was not grotesquely muscular like Sambo, he was in good shape now. But there was nothing like having a girl notice.

Red drove around the square a few times, then Sambo said, "Want a beer, Sally? Red's got a whole trunkload."

"Well," she said, suddenly hesitant, "I don't know. I can't be out too late."

"Aw, come on, Sally," Sherm interjected, "it won't take long. We'll go out to the beach."

She looked at John with questioning eyes, as though seeking reassurance. "What about it, Prof? Are you going, too? I didn't think you'd want to."

Suddenly, he was discomforted. He did not like being Sally's conscience; he had enough trouble being his own. "Well, I . . . uh . . . don't mind a beer once in a while; I'm just not a guzzler like these squirrels."

"Well, okay, I'll go along."

At the narrow beach that edged the river, Red, Sambo

and Sherm tore into the beer and downed several cans each as Sally and John looked on. Sherm walked up with a can of beer and ripped off the tab. "Come on, Sally, have a beer."

Again, she looked uncertainly to John. "Are you going to have one, Prof?"

Damn it. Why did she keep asking him? He wasn't her goddamn guardian. "Uh, yeah, I'll have one, I guess."

He was going to quit after the first one, but the others needled him to take another. Finally, Sherm came over and said, "You bastard, you'd better not blow this. She's not going to drink unless you do; why spoil all of our fun?" So John had another—and another. Soon, he felt light-headed and he could see that the others, including Sally, were well on their way to getting soused.

Sambo called out, "Hey, let's take a swim," and promptly kicked off his shoes and started pulling down his jeans. Momentarily, the thickly muscled young man stood naked on the beach, his giant phallus sticking straight out like a huge spear protruding from his groin. Sally followed suit, then the others, including John, followed without further encouragement.

Sally stood on the beach in the middle of the excited males, oblivious to their nudity. The Beavers were not unaware of her presence, however, and John eyed her enviable figure with delight. She was a truly pretty girl. A good, firm pairs of boobs. Her rounded butt might have stuck out too much, but overall, her hips complemented the rest of her well-formed body. But his eyes were drawn to the thick, black mound of curly hair between her thighs. He remembered the times when the guys at the swimming pool had speculated about that hair of Sally's. She had never been especially discreet about keeping it within the confines of her bathing suit, and her admirers were always sneaking looks at the long, crinkly pubic hairs that stuck out. John found the pubic coif stimulating, and it renewed his enthusiasm for what might transpire that evening.

Soon they were all splashing in the shallow river, and it cooled John's ardor for a spell. As he swam out into the current, his stomach began to churn and ache, so he turned around and swam back to the beach. Sobered up now, he realized he was paying for his over-indulgence. He had a low tolerance of alcohol. It would serve him right if he puked up his guts now. He got dressed and stretched out on the soft sand, hoping that would pacify his queasiness.

Shortly, everyone was back on the beach, and it was not long before the others were hitting the booze again. John watched while Sambo and Sally ran races along the sandy beach, with Red and Sherm shouting encouragement. John was acutely aware of the throbbing in his semi-erect organ as he watched Sally run back and forth, giggling and squealing, as her tits sprang up and down like two perfectly-coordinated basketballs bouncing on a gym floor.

Every so often, Sherm would run after her, pinching and grabbing at her butt. The she would whirl, slap at him playfully and chase him down the beach, with Sambo following. In the meantime, Red had lost interest. As usual, he had outdrunk everyone else and, as usual, he was devastatingly sick, doubled up in agony as he vomited up the contents of his stomach.

Finally, Sambo staggered over to John and pointed to Sally who, by this time, had collapsed and lay spread-eagle on the soft, moist sand. "Gang-bang time."

Sherm came up and said, "Me first."

"No, me first," Sambo said.

"You big son-of-a-bitch," Sherm said, "You do everything first. You're a pig, that's what you are."

"Don't call me a pig, you little piss-ant, or I'll bash your teeth in." Sambo straightened up and clenched his fists; his eyes widened and took on an insane look. "Me first," he said.

Sherm's erection shriveled. "Aw, go ahead. Who gives a shit?"

Sambo generally got mean when he was drunk, and John could see he meant business. Fortunately for Sherm, he was still sober enough to see it.

Sambo whirled and stalked toward Sally. He was confident, like a giant stud horse, and John could see that Sambo knew exactly what he wanted to do and how he was going to go about it. This was a different Sambo from the one he had known earlier in the summer. Sherm just shrugged, his lower lip sliding out in a firm pout. He took a can of beer and followed Sambo over to where Sally lay.

She was stretched out, dead drunk, sound asleep. A snoring, rasping sound came from her throat. She sounded, John thought, like an emphysemic old man he had once known.

"Well, what are you waiting for, Sambo?" Sherm asked. "We don't have all night."

Sambo had sobered up considerably now, and John wondered if he had ever been as drunk as he had seemed. Suddenly, he pounced on Sally like an old tomcat after a female in heat, driving his prong into the tangled nest between her thighs. Astonished, John got up, discovering he had an excellent view of the mating as the moonlight cast its soft rays with a spotlight like effect on the naked bodies.

When Sambo's engorged organ struck her with full force, Sally's eyes popped open in shock. She looked frightened, scared to death. She tried to squirm away, but Sambo's powerful arms held her tight, and he coaxed, "Come on, Sally; come on, Sally baby." There was going to be no stopping him. Sambo was like a man possessed, and John could see that as far as Sambo was concerned, there was no one else on the beach—only him and Sally.

But John was puzzled. Sambo kept raising his muscular buttocks and thrusting, but his prong did not seem to be making any progress. Sally was sobbing and crying, "No, don't . . . don't! Please, don't!"

Sambo yelled, "Spread your cunt . . . help me get it in." He grabbed her hand and tried to get her to take hold of his phallus and guide it. She pulled her hand away and started pounding him on the back, struggling, trying to wriggle away.

John took a hesitant step toward them, dazed and confused. He could not understand this. Sally was supposed to be easy. God, a nympho like her ought to be hungry for a cock like Sambo's.

Sherm doubled up in laughter, cheering Sambo on, chiding him for his apparent ineptness. "What's the matter, don't you know how? Too big for her?"

Unhearing, Sambo suddenly placed his own hand between his legs and guided his burning tumescence home. The muscles in Sambo's buttock tightened as he pressed his weight against her with full force. Then she screamed like a knife had been rammed into her belly and started crying again, louder now, miserably, as Sambo's prong slid in to the hilt. In a moment, Sambo was huffing and puffing, pumping away with an animallike fervor.

In a few minutes, he grunted like a hog and came. He collapsed on top of her and lay quietly for a bit. Suddenly, she pulled free, rolling out from under him and got up and started racing down the beach, whimpering pathetically as her fear-glazed eyes darted from place to place, seeking refuge from her attackers. Sherm started after her, his own organ rising to the occasion.

The scene suddenly sickened John. It was the terror he saw in her eyes. This was no longer a game. Sally was not a nymphomaniac offering her insatiable body freely to anyone who would take it. She was a frightened little girl, violated and debased. He was ashamed.

Sambo stumbled toward him, sweat-soaked and pale. "God, Sambo," John said, "what were you doing to her? She acted like you were killing her. She was scared to death."

Sambo had calmed down considerably now and was humble, perhaps embarrassed. "I didn't mean to hurt her. Geez, I think I must have busted her cherry; it wouldn't go in. I don't think she'd ever done it before."

An icy chill danced down John's spine, and he was seized by a moment of near panic. Looking down the beach, he saw that Sherm had caught up with Sally and was wrestling her to the sand. This was not gang-bang anymore—what had taken place was rape, or pretty damn close to it. And he was right in the middle of it.

He began to run—faster than he ever dreamed he could—toward Sherm and Sally. Sherm was on top of her, but she was fighting, kicking, scratching now. Evidently, the shock of the assault had jolted her back to sobriety. John closed in on them, grabbing Sherm's arm and yanking him sharply off the girl. She scrambled away.

Sherm turned to John like a snarling bear, and John could see the anger and frustration burning in his dark eyes. When Sherm charged and swung wildly, John ducked under his attacker's flailing arms and let loose with several quick, hammerlike punches to Sherm's belly. Sherm gasped frantically for air, then doubled up and collapsed face-down in the sand.

John moved to Sally, who was huddled near a pile of driftwood, sobbing and shaking spasmodically. "Sally . . . are you all right?" he said lamely.

She looked at him with red, swollen eyes, raising her knees and crossing her arms over her bare breasts in an attempt to cover herself. "I . . . I'll be okay," she choked. "Would you get my things?"

"Yeah . . . sure." He hurried away to retrieve her clothing.

After she had dressed, John approached her again. She stood, hunched over slightly, her arms folded tightly across her stomach, still trembling. Her eyes were still glazed and trancelike. "Sally," he said softly, "I'm sorry. Nobody meant for anything to happen; things just got out of hand. It was the booze."

"I know," she said. "I just want to go home."

John drove Red's car back to town, with Sally in front and the other three sick, repentant Beavers in back. The short journey was completed in silence. When John pulled the automobile up outside Sally's house, the door flew open and she jumped out before he had come to a complete stop. She ran into the house, sobbing.

Red looked after her, his head bobbing stupidly. "Christ, Prof, I can't remember anything. Did we have a good fuck?"

John turned in his seat and glared disgustedly at the sad, slovenly creatures in back. "Shut up, Red."

6

The combo cut loose with "Hang On, Sloopy" for what must have been the third or fourth time. John got up and headed for the punch bowl. He was not that crazy about the fast ones, and he did not have a date, so he did not feel obligated to dance this one. John and Red had come to the mixer stag. Sambo, of course, had brought Connie, and they had already departed for what John presumed was more lively action.

Sherm was wearing out the gym floor with Shelly Whiteside, who had the biggest boobs in the junior class. During intermission, Sherm had confided to John that Shelly had all but promised Sherm a screw when he took her home. John guessed that would be nothing new for Sherm—or Shelly, for that matter—but he wondered how Sherm was going to deal with Sarah Remington, whom he had escorted to the dance. Sarah considered herself Sherm's steady, and she was insanely possessive and could be witchy as hell when crossed. Sherm had always protested to the guys that he had no steady—Sarah was steady ass, but that was all she was to him.

Red did not dance and, as usual, devoted the evening to clowning. Increasingly, John found himself bored with

Red's juvenile humor, and tonight he kept his distance from his friend, preferring not to be identified with Red's unimaginative practical jokes.

He had not found it the least bit funny when Red poured a cup of crimson punch down the front of Cathy Morton's white blouse a short time ago. Red had been dancing a slow one, with a push broom in one hand and a cup of punch in the other. Working his way along the edge of the dance floor, he had pretended to stumble and fell against Cathy, who was seated at a table with her date. She became furious and, after letting loose a few choice expletives unbecoming to a young lady, whacked Red sharply on the side of the head with the broom. Poor Cathy, she did not know that Red was hopelessly in love with her and that was just his way of attracting her attention.

With his persistent B.O. and his repulsive personality, Red was the best girl-repellent around. Still, despite their gradual estrangement over the past weeks, John felt imprisoned by bonds of loyalty to the Beavers, and there had always been something of an unwritten law among the comrades that someone keep perpetually dateless Red company. More often than not, good old Prof got stuck with the job. Not that he had to, but there was this sense of responsibility he had never been able to shake.

John helped himself to a cup of the red juice at the table, moved off to the edge of the gym floor and leaned back against the concrete-block wall to survey the scene. With only casual interest, his eyes scanned the bleachers that lined both sides of the basketball court. The dateless boys sat on one side, the unescorted girls on the other. He suddenly regretted that he had not invited a girl to the mixer. There were several he knew who would have been available and would have made good dates.

He never had difficulty getting dates, but he always felt a little awkward around girls and recognized he was probably inhibited by a natural shyness.

His eyes moved along the gray rows of bleachers on the girls' side of the gymnasium, stopping from time to time to study one who seemed especially interesting. Then his eyes were drawn to a girl sitting alone well up in the bleachers, signaling, it seemed, that she was there as an observer of the scene and not as a part of it. Who was she? Some shy, unattractive wallflower? He could not make out her face, but she appeared slender and sharply dressed in a burnt-orange matching sweater and skirt that suited the cool October weather. But it was her hair that held his attention. He would not say it was golden; it was more the color of fresh, light honey, and it curled and swirled down her neck and over her shoulders like windswept ocean waves.

He found himself moving slowly out onto the gymnasium floor, inching his way through the melee to the girls' bleachers, his eyes fastened on the mysterious blonde. The closer he drew, the more intriguing she became. He thought he caught her glance, but then she shifted and turned her head away. He noted now that her pullover sweater fit snugly, but not indecently, over well-defined breasts.

Then he recognized her. It was RaeLyn Hunter. She was a junior. He had seen her in the halls at school, exchanged an occasional "hi" with her once in a while. He had thought her attractive, but she always seemed reserved and something of a loner. He remembered now that some of the guys who had dated her said she was a cold fish—definitely a hands-off type. She was something of an intellectual, he recalled, and many of the guys were in awe of the brainy ones. They did not want to go out with a girl who made them feel inferior. He might be shy, but he was not insecure about his own mental prowess.

Drawing close to the bleachers, he paused. She was less than a hundred feet away. He could make out her features quite clearly. She was pretty, slender, willowy. She was fair-skinned, with slightly chiseled facial features. Her nose was perhaps a bit too straight, but it fit her face. Why was she sitting up there alone? Maybe she didn't dance. Would she dance with him if he asked her?

Suddenly, her head turned again and he realized she was looking at him, studying him as though she were returning the scrutiny she had received. Her face was impassive but not unfriendly.

He moved toward the bleachers, then hesitated before starting to climb to where she sat. She certainly did not seem shy; he could see her eyes following him curiously as he climbed the steps. When he approached, her lips parted to form a mischievous smile, revealing white, remarkably even teeth. Her doelike brown eyes sparkled with a zest he had not expected to see in one who had apparently divorced herself from the evening's social activities.

"Hi," he said. "You're RaeLyn Hunter, aren't you? I'm John Armstrong."

"Hi," she answered. "Yes, I know who you are . . . everybody knows John Armstrong."

She had a sure, pleasant voice. "I doubt that," he answered.

"Oh yes. President of the senior class, editor of the school rag, valedictorian-to-be. . .you're famous."

She was teasing him, and they had only just met. Still, there was something about her that made him feel bold. "Would you like to dance?" he asked.

She hesitated just a moment, "Okay."

When they reached the edge of the dance floor, he stopped. The combo was in the middle of "Hang on, Sloopy" again. "Do you mind if we wait a minute? I'm not very good at the fast ones."

"That's fine with me," she said agreeably. "It would be nice if the band could learn another."

"You noticed that, too, huh?"

They stood there silently. The din generated by the band made conversation difficult. John was grateful for the loud music that gave him a chance to collect his thoughts. His trek from the gym floor to the bleachers and back again had transpired all too quickly. He stole a sideways glance at his soon-to-be dancing partner. Her eyes seemed to be fixed on the rocking, swaying dancers, but there was an intensity about them that suggested her mind was not totally absorbed with the dance-floor activity.

She was taller than he remembered, perhaps five foot eight or nine. She carried herself well, and there was a natural poise in her bearing not always present in teenage girls of her height. She was not a classic beauty, not the kind who won Miss America contests, but she was pretty enough and she exuded class. He had a hunch there was nothing phony about this girl.

When the band wrapped up its most recent "Sloopy" rendition, it turned to a slow one, "Unchained Melody." John took RaeLyn's hand and they glided onto the dance floor. Unbelievable. She was graceful as a gazelle, moving easily in his arms, not struggling to lead, like most of the Schonberg High girls he had danced with. He thought of himself as an adequate dancer, but with her he felt accomplished, although he admitted to himself that it was probably more her doing than his.

Still, as they danced and exchanged pleasantries, he understood why some of the guys shied away from her. She spoke with confidence and at times seemed a little distant and unattentive. She had a maturity in her manner that would threaten an inferiority complex. But this made her more interesting, he thought, and he found himself strangely curious about this girl.

Another dancing couple bumped against them and pushed him closer to RaeLyn, momentarily pressing her firm breasts gently against his chest. He caught the intoxicating aroma of her perfume, and her soft hair brushed against his cheeks. His thoughts turned to the woman in her, and he found himself captivated by her femininity.

"I never see you around much," he commented.

She was tall enough to look slightly upward and reach his eyes quite directly. He saw an impish twinkle there.

"Maybe you haven't been looking," she said.

"Oh, I've seen you in the hall at school. I mean, I don't see you at many of the school activites. . .football games, dances, things like that."

"I don't go to many of them," she said matter-of-factly.

"Why not?"

She answered his question with a question. "Why?"

"Well, for fun. . .to be with other kids. Uh, just to. . .uh. . ."

"You haven't given me many good reasons," she said, smiling. Then she must have sensed his frustration, for her face turned serious now. "John, I'm not trying to be flip. I do study a lot. I love to read. I enjoy dancing, and I don't mind going out with the kids once in a while, but I don't feel the need some people do to always be with a gang. I can take it or leave it, I guess."

"Such as?" The music stopped. He did not want to escort her back to the bleachers, but he did not want to dance. "Would you like to sit at a table with me?" he asked. "I'll get some punch."

"I'd like that," she said.

He found a table as far away from the dance band as he could. When they were seated, he asked, "Where were we?"

"Such as," she said.

"What do you mean 'such as?'"

"I said I've always been interested on other things, and you said 'such as.'"

"Oh. All right. Such as?"

"Well, I'm going to be a lawyer. That means a lot of other things have to take second place."

She did not *want* to be a lawyer. She did not *plan* to be a lawyer. She was *going* to be a lawyer.

"You seem awfully sure of yourself," he said. "Why do you want to be one?"

"You'll be disappointed if you're looking for something noble," she said. "I'm not going to be a lawyer because I want to help the downtrodden poor or anything like that. I've thought about it a lot, and I don't think there's any other field that gives you as many options—especially for a woman. There's so much versatility in a law degree. So many fields you can use the knowledge in—private practice, business, government—you name it. And there's a flexibility with that kind of background that doesn't rule out being a mother and homemaker, too."

"You seem to have it all figured out."

"I think so. What about you, John, what are you going to do?"

"I don't know. I'm not as certain as you are about things. Journalism, maybe. The guys call me Prof—maybe I'll be an English professor. I like words, working with language. There's something exciting about taking a collection of words and putting them together, making them say something, then taking the same words and putting them together in another way and making them say something else. Or taking some different words and saying the same thing another way. I've always been fascinated by words; I could read my life away. I understand what you mean by not always needing the company of other people. I have some friends I've run around with a long time. Still, I've known them all these years, and I've never been close to them in the sense of being able to confide or share my serious thoughts about something. They'd just laugh. I'm happier when I'm alone." He smiled. "I sorry, I'm lecturing. . . that's why they call me Prof. . .I don't know when to shut up."

She was across the table from him, leaning forward, her chin resting on interlaced fingers. He had the feeling she was studying him, sizing him up.

"I think you give wonderful lectures," she said, "and you *will* do something with words, John. I can hardly wait to see what it will be."

"You can call me Prof, if you want."

"No, that name was made up in fun. I'd rather call you John."

"It sounds strange to have someone call me John. Only my mother does that anymore. Even my dad and older sisters call me Prof."

"I'm afraid you'll have to be John to me."

"That's fine. I've never been too crazy about my nickname."

"Well, what have we here?" came a smooth-as-satin

voice from behind.

It was Sherm. John could not think of anyone he would rather not see right now, unless it was Red.

John turned. "Hi, Sherm."

Sherm ignored his greeting, his eyes fixed on RaeLyn, and John seethed silently as he observed the brazen appraisal she was receiving.

"Hello, RaeLyn. You're gorgeous this evening."

"Thank you."

"You and Prof didn't come together, did you?"

"No, John and I just met here."

"Would you like to dance?"

The little son-of-a-bitch, John thought, he'll look like a dwarf beside her.

"No, not right now. Thank you, but I'd rather not."

Sherm flushed perceptibly. "Maybe later," he said coldly.

"I think he's mad," John said as Sherm whirled and walked away.

"Yes, I think so."

"I take it you know him."

"Yes, my father works for Reinwald Electronics. He's executive vice president there."

"You're not worried about your dad's job?"

"No, my father is an electrical engineer, and he's a shrewd businessman too. Reinwald needs him more than he needs them. Besides, I'm an only child, and I'm spoiled rotten. I'm used to doing what I want."

"I believe that," he said. "Are you sure you don't want to dance?"

"Not with Sherm."

"Would you like to dance with me?"

"Do you want to dance?"

He grinned sheepishly. "Not really. . .just being polite."

"I don't want to either. I'd rather talk."

"Okay, let's talk."

They did not dance any more that evening. They talked. And they were still talking through the last strains of the combo's grand finale. John told her things he had never shared with any other person, and he had a feeling she was reciprocating his confidence. Never in his wildest dreams had he imagined he would find intellectual companionship with someone of the opposite sex—especially one who make him feel so aware of his own maleness with her every unconscious gesture.

John was struck by near panic when the students started to file out of the gym. He wanted to hold her there, somehow freeze these moments in time. She rose to leave, and he stood up with her.

"I have to go now," she said.

"I have my car," John said. "May I take you home?"

"Thanks, but my father's supposed to pick me up."

"Oh." Downcast, he joined her on the walk across the gym floor toward the exit. Near the door, he touched her elbow softly and stopped. They faced each other, their eyes locked as the other departing students poured past them. "RaeLyn," he said. "I had a good time this evening. . .being with you, I mean."

"So did I, John. I can't remember a nicer evening. Thanks for everything."

Her warm eyes melted his heart and, as she started away, he did not think he was going to choke out the words to stall her departure. "RaeLyn, wait a minute." She turned toward him, appearing less sure of herself. "Do you like movies?"

"Yes. I guess there aren't many I don't like. I'm kind of a movie freak."

"Would you like to go to one with me next Saturday? I don't even know what's showing."

"Sure," she said, "sounds like fun."

"I'll see you at school and let you know what time, okay?"

"Great. Good night, John."

As he watched her walk away, Red came up behind him and jabbed him sharply in the ribs. "Hey Prof," Red said, "what are you doing with that stuck-up broad? She's got a padlock on her pussy; you'll never get any place with her."

Crimson spread over John's face, and his fists clenched

involuntarily. "Don't say another word, Red. if you want a ride home."

7

John squinted and shielded his eyes with his gloved hand, trying to ward off the sun's glare magnified by the white blanket of snow that shrouded the surrounding hills. RaeLyn had promised him she would be back in a few minutes; it had been a half hour, and he was getting restless—also a little irritable.

The steep, rocky slopes of the Bobcat Hills Recreation Area swept up and down like an endless, natural roller coaster. They were covered with sleds, snowmobiles and skiers this day before New Years. The Schonberg High students had invaded the state-maintained park some ten miles south of Schonberg at the commencement of Christmas vacation. The weatherman cooperated above and beyond the call of duty, and nearly twenty inches of snow had been dumped on south-central Nebraska since mid-December. With the mass usage of recent days, the best slopes were packed hard. They were not comparable to the Rocky Mountain ski trails, of course, but no one was complaining.

This was their second trip to the hills. John had rented a snowmobile from the local dealer who ran a snowmobile concession at Bobcat Hills when there was enough snow on the ground. A brisk wind had come up in the last hour, and John was ready to call it quits—or at least move to one of the fires that burned in one of the cavelike recesses that dotted the steeper hillsides. He shivered as a sudden gust of icy air slapped his cheeks, and he hunched over and pulled his head deeper into the hooded, fur-lined parka, like a turtle retreating into its shell.

The he saw her, scampering toward him like a child. He could not miss her in her insulated snowsuit, its deep, royal purple contrasting sharply with the blinding whiteness of the snow. Her red nose almost glowed. Rudolph, he had called her teasingly, but otherwise she seemed immune to the cold and had stubbornly refused to call it a day. She needled him unmercifully about his own aversion to the cold.

She was smiling as she approached him and breathing heavily from the climb. For one who professed to be a bookworm, she had surprising stamina.

"It's about time," he said as she came up and wrapped her arm around his own. "Where have you been, anyway?"

"I told you I had to go potty."

The crude restroom facilities were few and far between at Bobcat Hills.

"It shouldn't have taken that long."

"Oh? How do you happen to be so knowledgeable about a lady's requirements in that regard?"

"That isn't what I meant, and you know it."

"Do you really want the truth?"

"It would be nice for a change," he said, feigning indignation.

"Well," she said, "it's like this. I really have two boyfriends. I spend part of the day with you and part of it with the other one. You've got the next half hour, then I'll have to leave and go see the other one again. You don't mind do you?"

"Funny. I'll bet you were just watching someone ski and forgot I was up here."

"That's close enough," she said.

"Hey, I'm about to freeze my tail off. Do you suppose we could call it quits for the day?" He pulled up his coat sleeve and looked at his watch, hoping his emphasis would have some effect on her. "It's almost 4:00."

"Pansy," she said.

"I like warm-weather sports. I'm a heck of a good swimmer."

"I'm probably better."

"I doubt it."

"Well, we aren't going to find out today. It's winter, in case you haven't noticed."

"I have noticed...that's what I've been trying to tell you. Let's find us a fire."

"Not yet. Don't be a spoil sport."

"We have to get back to town before too long. You'll want to go home and change before the New Year's Eve party at Sherm's house."

"I don't want to go to a New Year's Eve party."

"Why not? Everybody wants to go to a New Year's Eve party."

"I don't. You don't either."

"I didn't say that."

"You didn't have to. I know you don't like parties."

"Sometimes I do," said John. "Why don't you want to go?"

"I'm not that crazy about parties...and I don't like Sherm."

"You don't? Why not?"

"He's devious, and he's selfish. He uses people, and you can't trust him."

"That's a pretty harsh judgment."

"You don't like him either."

"I've never said that. What makes you say that? Sherm and I have been buddies for years."

"He's used you for years, and you've always known it . . . and you've always put up with it, for some reason. That's what I'd like to know . . . why?"

"Look, RaeLyn, I don't know how we ever got into this

conversation, but I know what Sherm's like . . . probably better than you. I know he uses people, that he's used me sometimes. But the Beavers had some good times together. Maybe we all used each other in a way. God, I don't know what held us together, and if I don't understand it myself, I can't explain it to you."

She kissed him on the cheek, repentent now. "Hey, I didn't mean to upset you, John. I was just being a smart-ass."

He was shocked at her terminology; he had never heard her use a word that even bordered on the profane. She was no prude, but somehow her choice of words now made her seem more human to him.

"Now, about the party," she said, "your wish is my command. If you would like to go to the party, I would be pleased and honored to accompany you."

"I don't want to go to the party," he said.

"I already told you that. Why don't you come over to my house? My folks will let us have the rec room. We'll build a fire in the fireplace, pop some popcorn. We can play the stereo, and we'll think of something to do." Impulsively, she hugged and kissed him again. "Now, what about the snowmobile? You've got it rented till 5:00. We don't want the rent money to go to waste. You've been driving this thing around all afternoon, and I've had to hang on for dear life, going where you decided to take us. You even got to take it down the big run by yourself. Now it's my turn."

"But you've never driven one."

"I drive a car, don't I?"

"It's not the same thing."

"Oh, I see," she said, her lips forming into a pout. "Okay, Mr. Snowmobile Expert, tell me about your experience. How long have you been driving one of these things?"

"Long enough."

"How long?"

"All right, all right. Last week was the first time. But you're a . . ." He stopped, realizing he was about to say the

65

wrong thing.

"I'm a what?"

"Nothing."

"A girl, right?"

He shrugged. "I didn't mean it that way. You know I think you're the smartest girl I've ever known."

"Oh-h . . . the smartest *girl* you've ever known, huh? Meaning of course, that girls are naturally dumber than boys, and a smart girl, obviously, can't fit in the same league as a smart boy. Right?" Her eyes shot sparks.

He had put his foot in his mouth, that was for certain. If he had expected to dissuade her from the snowmobile cruise, he had said all the wrong things. And damn it, she knew better. He had not meant things that way at all. He admired her intelligence and, as far as he was concerned, there was no one, male or female, who could compete with her keen mind.

"You know better, Rae . . . " His response was cut off by the chunk of icy snow that was suddenly mashed brutally against his face. As he wiped away the cold, white residue, RaeLyn moved to the snowmobile. "Rae, I'm sorry," he said, hurrying after her. "Go ahead, but try it first on the west slope over there. It's not as steep. Just so you get the feel of it."

She was already snapping on the silver-painted protective headgear and was crouched like an Indianapolis Speedway driver when he reached her. He bent over to give her additional instructions, just as she turned the ignition and the engine roared.

She rammed the compact machine into gear and shot free of the snow with rocketlike force, heading for the east slope. He shoved his hands into the pockets of his bulky coat and, shaking his head in disgust, trudged after the speeding vehicle.

Suddenly, he went numb with panic. She was going too far east. The slopes were not especially treacherous where John stood, but a half mile away in the direction RaeLyn was going, they became steep and rocky, scarred intermittently with clusters of hidden boulders buried like hunters' traps beneath the snow to catch the unwary driver. In spots, sizable chunks of the hills had been sheared away by erosion and resulting cave-ins to form clifflike dropoffs of ten to twenty feet in many cases. These, too, could not be observed by a speeding driver until he was already upon them. Even experienced amateurs steered clear of the eastern slopes.

Damn it. Couldn't she see that no one had been sledding down there? He started to run, calling after her. "Rae, Rae! Not there!" Even as he yelled, he knew there was no chance she could hear him over the engine's ear-splitting noise, but he had to try. He followed her along the white-capped ridge that overlooked the narrow valley below. As he moved in the unpacked, virgin snow, he found that it sucked at his feet and legs, holding him like an insect on fly paper. He could do no more than plod, pulling his feet free one at a time as he struggled through.

He stopped and bent over, hands on his knees, breathing heavily, frantically trying to catch his breath, wincing at the knifelike pains that tore through his abdomen. When he straightened up and looked to the east again, he saw that she was turning south, down the slope, still moving at breakneck speed. He had a clear view of her zigzag journey. And all he could do was watch.

She weaved down the slope, first angling left, then sharply right and then swinging back again. She was handling it beautifully, like a pro. He would gladly eat his words if she made it to the bottom unscathed.

She slowed the vehicle, though only slightly, so perhaps she recognized her danger. His optimism was short-lived. The bright orange machine, vivid against the white background, accelerated noticeably again and veered further east. "Jesus Christ! She doesn't see it," he said under his breath.

The snowmobile nosed to the higher ground that swept up like an ocean wave to RaeLyn's left. The crest of snow concealed a sheer cliff that dropped off abruptly on the other side.

She wasn't slowing. *Jesus, she still doesn't see it! She'll break her neck! She's going to kill herself!*

The snowmobile swerved suddenly, then catapulted over the cliff. At the same moment, a purple-clad rag doll somersaulted in midair and crashed to earth on the top side of the cliff, precariously close to the edge.

Stunned, he stood momentarily watching the orange blur that had been the snowmobile flipping, then rolling like a giant ball driven by its own inertia, until it crashed against a massive outcropping of sandstone that blocked its course not far from the bottom of the slope.

His eyes darted back to the crumpled form that lay half-buried in the snow at the top of the cliff. It was totally unmoving. Unaware now of the deep, sticky snow that tried to slow him, driven by the fear of what he might find there, he angled southeasterly down the slope, leaving a snakelike trail in the snow, as he dodged first one way, then another, like a football halfback trying to elude the obstacles in his path. He stumbled, torpedoing through a drift, then rolling downhill some ten feet before he struggled up and continued his frenzied charge.

When finally he fought his way up to the rise where RaeLyn lay, fear gnawed at his gut and he was overcome by a sense of foreboding. He moved to her, brushing the snow away from her face as he knelt beside her on the knoll. She was unconscious, her face deathly pale. Her head was tilted to one side, and scarlet splattered the snow near her forehead. He pulled off his gloves and gently touched her forehead, knowing instinctively he should make no attempt to move her. He could see that she was breathing and he noted that her chest rose and dropped evenly, like a person lost in peaceful slumber.

But she was so still, lying there on her back like a department store mannequin stretched out on a bed of snow. Had she broken her neck? Visions of a paralyzed, paraplegic RaeLyn raced through his mind and intensified his anxiety.

He glanced back up the slope, observing that others were

swarming down the hillside now, like an army of ants moving to a picnic gathering. He felt both relieved and angered at the sight of the persons who would be there soon—relieved for RaeLyn's sake that help was coming; angered at the certain knowledge that many would be curiosity seekers. There were always those who eagerly, if not maliciously, anticipated the opportunity to be first-hand observers and messengers of someone else's misfortune.

He looked back at RaeLyn, studying her bleeding face, trying to ferret out some positive sign that she would be all right. "RaeLyn," he said, his voice cracking. "RaeLyn!" Tears welled up in his eyes, and he rubbed her cheeks softly, hoping that his touch might awaken her. "Goddamn it," he whispered, "why didn't you listen to me? I tried to tell you. Stubborn, spoiled brat."

"I told you I was spoiled," came a slow, uncertain voice, and her eyelids fluttered and came open. Faint traces of a smile showed on her quivering lips.

"Thank God," he said softly. But instantly he saw the pain in her glazed eyes as she started to turn her head. "RaeLyn, don't move . . . don't try to move anything."

"Why . . . why not?" she asked, her voice shaky.

"Because I said so," he snapped. Then, imploringly, "Please, ReaLyn, do what I say."

"I will, John. I'll do whatever you say."

Okay, where do you hurt?"

"All over. My neck, the back of it, feels like somebody's stabbing a burning knife in it. It goes clear down to my shoulders."

"Okay, where else?"

"My right side hurts . . . and my right leg below the knee. It hurts and feels sort of numb at the same time."

"But you can feel it?"

"Yes, I can feel it . . . but I wish I couldn't."

Tears were streaming down her cheeks now, but he could see she was trying to tough it out. "Be glad it hurts, RaeLyn. It means you'll be all right." He was no doctor, but he was confident that the fact she had feeling in her lower extremities was a good sign—at least nothing had severed her spinal cord. But he was worried about the neck injury. He knew that if there was damage, she was in a precarious situation; the wrong move could be life-threatening or result in a crippling injury.

At the sound of labored breathing and soft thumping in the snow behind him, he turned to see several young men approaching well ahead of the others who were streaming down the slopes. He recognized Hal Kassebaum, halfback for the Schonberg High football team, and his younger brother, Wes.

"Prof," Hal said as he approached, huffing deeply, "what happened?"

With his thumb, John gestured over his shoulder in the direction of the twisted snowmobile. "Tried to ride that damn thing over here."

"How is she?"

"Hurt bad, but she's conscious now."

John folded his glove and pressed it firmly against the wicked, ragged gash on RaeLyn's forehead. After a few moments, he removed it to assure himself that the bleeding had ebbed. It had.

"Hal," John said, "do you know . . . has anyone called an ambulance?"

"Yeah, Dan Shambaugh was up there; he saw it happen. He sent me and Wes down here. He went back to his car to radio to town."

Shambaugh was a young deputy sheriff who was a snowmobile freak in his off hours. John knew him as a cool and confident officer, one highly respectd by Schonberg's young people. It reassured him to know that Dan was around and would be there soon.

Other onlookers started to crowd in now. "Is she dying?" he heard someone ask. "Help her up," yelled another. "Let's carry her up the hill," came a third voice.

John stood up, his angry eyes sweeping the gathering throng, almost daring them to step closer. "Everybody get the hell away from her! Get back! Get out of the way." He turned. "Hal, would you and Wes just keep people back? She can't be moved; we've got to let the ambulance people handle this."

He let himself back down, sitting next to RaeLyn's head, reapplying his crude compress when he saw that blood was beginning to ooze from the nasty laceration. "You'll be all right," he said. "The ambulance should be on its way. I can see Dan Shambaugh coming down the hill; he'll help get things organized. We'll have you to the hospital in no time."

"John," she said, "my leg's starting to hurt worse. I'm getting dizzy."

"Just don't move, Rae. You'll be all right . . . I promise."

"John, promise me something."

"Sure, what."

"Don't leave me when they take me to the hospital. Promise?"

"Promise."

"John . . . John, do you know what I need right now?"

"Yes, you need to be in a nice, warm hospital."

"No, I need to pee. John, if I go in my pants, don't let anybody see, okay?"

Her speech was slurred, and she sounded like a drunk. Her eyelids closed, then opened. She looked at him blankly, then blinked her eyelids a few times before they closed and she lost consciousness again.

8

The pendulum on the wall clock struck twelve times. John looked up at it from his chair in the Schonberg Memorial waiting area. January 1, 1966. Happy New Year.

He was alone in the waiting room now. RaeLyn's parents, Jack and Louise Hunter, had sat with him most of the early evening hours, while they waited nervously for a report on RaeLyn's condition. The Hunters were nice people. Mrs. Hunter was a slender, striking woman in her early forties, shorter than RaeLyn, but otherwise an older version of her daughter. John and Mr. Hunter had hit it off well at their first meeting. Mr. Hunter, tall with hair that was dark, but prematurely streaked with gray, was a confident man who still had a way about him that made him easy to be with. That was doubtless his contribution to RaeLyn.

John got up from the vinyl-covered chair and began to pace the floor, periodically looking down the hall for some bearer of news. Perhaps the Hunters had forgotten he was there. At least they did not seem to be blaming him. Mr. Hunter had thanked him for staying with RaeLyn through the ordeal at Bobcat Hills and on the ambulance trip to the hospital. John had not provided any details of the accident, but somehow Jack Hunter seemed to have things pretty well figured out.

"As you know, John," he had said, "RaeLyn's ordinarily a very gentle person . . . uses good common sense . . . but every once in a while she has a stubborn streak that shows. When it does, she's more than headstrong. You just can't reason with her, and she's too damned old to spank . . . just like her mother." He smiled weakly and winked.

A prim, middle-aged nurse had come to the waiting area over an hour ago and, after eyeing John disapprovingly, had asked the Hunters to come with her, presumably for a status report on RaeLyn. John keenly felt their absence and, without company to keep his mind preoccupied, found his imagination working overtime.

He fantasized that RaeLyn was critically injured and her parents had been called to be with her in her final moments. Or she had already died and, in despair, the Hunters had forgotten about John waiting there alone for some news of RaeLyn. Or she was paralyzed and did not want to see him, so devastated was she by the bleakness of her future.

Why didn't they come? Why didn't someone come?

He glanced up at the clock again—fifteen minutes into the new year. It seemed like fifteen hours. He sat down again and picked up a magazine, absently leafing through the pages. He could not even have said what publication he was looking at, but it gave him something to do.

"John," came the familiar voice. He looked up to see Jack Hunter. "RaeLyn would like to see you. Louise and I are going for a cup of coffee."

"Is she all . . ."

"She'll be fine, John. It'll take some time, but she'll be fine."

Jack Hunter had that presence that inspires confidence, and the tenseness suddenly escaped from John like air out of a busted balloon. She would be fine. Thank God. He had never kept a vigil for a stricken loved one before.

Loved one. Yes, the caring he had for RaeLyn was love, at least in every way he'd ever thought about it.

"John?" Mr. Hunter asked. "Did you want to see

RaeLyn?"

John smiled and stood up. "I'm sorry, I'm just so glad. I guess I was almost numb."

Hunter smiled back. "I understand, John. Believe me, I do. And, John?"

"Yes, sir."

"Thanks for everything."

"What do you mean, sir?"

"Just thanks. I'll let RaeLyn tell you about it."

Hospitals always made him feel a little queasy. Subconsciously, although he knew better, he guessed he thought of hospitals as a place to die. Since his birth, he had not spent a night in one and he intended to keep it that way. Whenever he visited a friend or relative confined to a hospital, his mind always leaped back to a time when he was seven or eight years old when, with his parents, he made a pilgrimage to see his ailing grandmother, Grandma Armstrong, a sensitive, vibrant woman, always full of energy and enthusiasm. She had been John's favorite; they had understood each other.

But Grandma Armstrong was not in the hospital room when they got there. Oh, there was a lady whom he dutifully called Grandma, whose cheek he kissed lightly and quickly when instructed by his father. But the feeble, cancer-ravished lady was white and drawn, barely able to work out the raspy words from her throat. Her eyes were dull and filmy, her body emaciated to a point that it seemed that loose hide was draped over her thin skeleton.

She died two days later. He never saw the real Grandma Armstrong again. He assumed that a psychiatrist would tell him that his childhood experience was the root of his irrational fears, but even now he wondered if he would see RaeLyn again.

Opening the door to RaeLyn's hospital room, he was greeted by a white, shrouded form that gave him no assurance. As he approached her bed, he could see that she was immobile. An assortment of wires and pullies stretched from steel frames above her bed to her right leg and to bracelike contraptions about her neck and skull. A huge, canvas belt was strung across her hips, anchoring her fast to the bed's steel frame.

"RaeLyn?" he called softly and uncertainly.

"John?" Is that you?"

Realizing she could not turn her head to see him, he moved to her bedside and, resting his hands on the bedrail, leaned over. Her brown eyes rolled to meet his, and it elated him to see some sparkle there again, however faint.

"Hi," he said.

"Hi," she answered, forcing a slight smile.

"How do you feel?" Then he shrugged. "I guess that's a dumb question."

"Better than I deserve. That was a pretty stupid thing I did, wasn't it?"

"Yeah," he agreed, "that was pretty stupid, all right."

"I don't know what got into me. Sometimes, I'm just so . . . so . . . unpredictable."

Most of us are," he said, "so I guess you're entitled to be once in a while."

Her eyes were moist. "You don't hate me then? You don't think I'm a stubborn, spoiled brat?"

"You couldn't do anything to make me hate you, Rae."

"I'm glad," she said, "that helps a lot. Did they tell you everything?"

"No. Your dad said you'd be fine, but that you'd give me the details."

"Well, I'm a mess," she said, "but Dr. Anderson said I'll be good as new in time. You want the gory details, or not?"

"If you feel like talking about them."

"My mouth is fine," she said, "and don't you say a word. Now, my forehead. It took eight stitches to close the gash. The doctor says there may be a little scar, but I can have it fixed with plastic surgery, if I want to someday. I may just keep it as a souvenir."

"Some souvenir," he said.

"I have two broken vertebrae in my neck, but no spinal damage. If you had let them move me, I might be dead. Or paralyzed for life—that might have been worse. Dr. Anderson told dad I was lucky you were there. How did you know I shouldn't be moved?"

"I really didn't, but I'm an old boy scout, remember? Every once in a while I remember something Doc Sedgewick told me. This was one of them. If there's a neck or back injury and you don't know how bad it is, don't do anything. Let somebody who knows what they're doing take care of it."

"Well, anyway, they're taking me to Lincoln sometime this morning to have a neurologist check me out. I may be there a while. Will you come see me?"

"You know I will."

Oh, I've got some cracked ribs, too," she said, "so you can't squeeze me too hard for a while. And a broken leg, too. Simple fracture of the fibula, the doctor said. He said it will be okay. I'll still have neat-looking legs."

"You nut. Whoever said you had neat-looking legs?"

"Nobody, really, but you think so. I can tell by the way you're always noticing them."

"You noticed?"

"Sure."

"I'm sorry, Rae, but I can't help myself."

"I'm flattered." She yawned. "And I'm sleepy. I think they gave me something."

He could see she was fighting to keep her eyes open. "I'd better go, Rae, and let you get some sleep. I'll keep in touch with your folks. If you're going to be in Lincoln, I'll drive in to see you at least a couple of times a week. Maybe we can talk on the phone."

"John?"

"Yes."

"I'm still scared. I don't like this hospital business."

"I don't blame you, Rae, but you'll be all right."

"John?"

"Yes."

"Would you kiss me before you leave?"

"I was just waiting to be invited." He bent down and

touched his lips gently to hers.

"M-m-m," she said drowsily, "you don't ever have to wait to be invited."

"I know," he said. "Now you'd better get to sleep. Be good, Rae."

"Whatever you say, John. I love you. Good night."

Her eyes closed, and she was asleep before he could respond. Had he heard her right? She said "love," but she was sleepy, drunk with whatever they had given her. She probably had no idea what she was saying. Still, it was nice to hear.

He watched her quietly a few moments, then turned and stepped softly out of the room.

9

"Let's go down to Doc's," John said as he met RaeLyn outside the ancient, two-story Schonberg High building. He was leaning against his father's custom Ford, savoring the balmy March breezes that reminded him spring was officially just a week away.

RaeLyn walked slowly, a little tentatively, but there were no traces of the limp that had faded quickly since her return to school a month earlier. She was following a rigid exercise program developed by the physical therapist at Schonberg Memorial, and it was working. It felt good to see a vibrant, healthy RaeLyn again.

The wound on her forehead was only a white sliver of slightly indented scar tissue now, and she still maintained she was going to leave it there. "Self-punishment," she said.

"It does give you a certain character," John had replied. "Sort of a beauty mark." And he meant it.

"I could go for a Coke," RaeLyn said as she came up to him and took his hand. "Did Sambo talk to you?"

"No."

"I saw him in the hall this afternoon; he seemed upset about something. He asked me if I'd have you wait after school, if he didn't see you in the meantime."

"He didn't say what he wanted?"

"No. Very mysterious."

"I don't know what he would want to see me about, but I guess I can wait . . . if you don't mind."

"No, it's nice out."

John had seen even less of the Beavers since RaeLyn's accident. After her few weeks at the Lincoln Medical Center, she had been hospitalized at Schonberg Memorial for nearly three weeks. He had been a daily visitor there and had become a part of the Hunter household after she went home.

But the other Beavers had interests of their own, too. Sambo was absorbed with Connie; Sherm was absorbed in whatever girl he was with at the moment. Red had his job at Steinmetz's Supermarket.

Red, alone, probably missed the comradeship of the Beavers. Often John saw his old cohort driving his Dodge aimlessly through the streets of Schonberg, a lost, forlorn look on his face. John felt sorry for him.

He saw Sambo coming down the sidewalk that led from the gray-brick school building. Sambo usually sauntered leisurely; today he walked like a young man with something on his mind.

"Over here, Sambo," John called, waving a greeting.

"Hi, Prof," Sambo answered, tucking his white T-shirt, that barely contained his muscular arms and shoulders, into his jeans.

John noticed that Sambo pushed his hand a bit too far down the front of his trousers, probably making an adjustment for some tightness there. Same old Sambo. He glanced sideways to see if RaeLyn noticed. She looked at him with raised eyebrows and smiled. She had.

"Rae said you were looking for me."

Sambo jammed his hands in his front pockets and stood, glancing uneasily at RaeLyn. "Yeah, I'd like to talk to you, Prof."

"Well, here I am," John said. "What's up?"

"Well . . .uh. . . could we talk alone? If you don't mind . . . I mean, it's private."

"RaeLyn and I don't have any secrets," John said.

"It's okay, John," RaeLyn interrupted, "I don't mind."

"I'm sorry, RaeLyn," Sambo said, "I mean . . ."

"It's all right, Sambo. I see Connie's waiting for you on the corner; I'll go talk to her."

"Yeah, that would be great. Thanks a lot, RaeLyn." When RaeLyn was a safe distance away, Sambo said, "I've got trouble, Prof. Big trouble."

John leaned back against his car and raised himself up on the front fender. "What kind of trouble, Sambo?"

"Enough to keep me from graduating in May if I don't get it straightened out."

"You flunking something? Need some tutoring?"

"No. Hell, no, Prof, nothing like that. I'm getting the best grades I've ever had this year. All C's except for two D's. Goddamn Advanced Algebra and English."

"Well, they usually give seniors the benefit of the doubt. It looks like you've about got it made."

"That's what I thought. But I got called into old man Steen's office this afternoon. He's going to kick my ass out for a week. Suspend me. Cancel my English credits. Shit, the English hours are required. No credits no diploma."

"Why?" John asked. "What happened?"

"They made a locker search and found copies of the English midterms in my locker."

"Jesus, Sambo, how did you get hold of them? What did you do that for? You said you were squeaking through anyway."

"I didn't take them, Prof. I ain't much on books, but I don't cheat. You know that. I never have."

John had to admit that. Sambo was like a big, playful Saint Bernard—not a scholastic bone in his body—but physically powerful enough to be a devastating force. Honesty was an unconscious part of his nature, and deviousness was alien to his character. Cornered to help a friend, he might tell a white lie on the spur of the moment. But deceit by design? Not likely.

"If you didn't take them, how'd they get there?"

"Sherm. He put them there."

"Sherm? Why? He doesn't need to steal exams to get through English."

"He doesn't do it for himself. He gets the exams, photocopies them and sells them."

"I never heard that before. When did this start?"

"Oh, last fall. A lot of the guys buy them; I never have though."

"How did he get hold of them?"

"I don't know."

"Why did he put them in your locker?"

"He heard about the locker search. He said he thought they were going to start on first floor where his locker is, so he put them in mine on second floor. He said he would switch them as soon as they checked his locker. They went through the second floor first."

"What did you tell Steen when he called you in?"

"I told him they weren't mine, that I didn't take them."

"He didn't believe you, I assume."

"No, he asked me who did take them then. I lied and said I didn't know. He didn't believe that either. I'll be suspended starting tomorrow after school, if I don't satisfy him some way. And my English credits will go down the tube."

"Did you talk to Sherm?"

"Yeah, hell of a lot of good it did."

"What did he say?" asked John.

"Cool as a cucumber. He said he wasn't going to turn himself in; that I'd have to rat on him if I want him to take the blame. He said he'd deny it anyway, and that if I was any kind of a friend, I wouldn't squeal. Jesus, Prof, I don't know what to do. I can't tell on him . . . it just don't seem right. I mean, he's one of the Beavers and everything. Know what I mean?"

"Yeah, I know what you mean, Sambo. Still, he's not much of a friend, if he'll let you take the blame for this."

"I still can't do it, Prof. But I've got to graduate."

Sambo looked down at his feet and kicked aimlessly at the front tire of John's car. "There's something else."

"What's that?"

"Well . . . I don't know for sure . . . but Connie might be pregnant."

"Pregnant?"

"Yeah, she missed her period last week and . . . well . . . we . . ."

"You don't need to explain to me, Sambo."

"I know, Prof, but if Connie's knocked up, I won't just run out on her. We'll get married. You know how important that high school diploma would be then."

"Geez, Sambo, you do have problems." John sighed and rubbed the back of his neck thoughtfully. "Let me talk to Sherm and think this over a little bit. I'll see what I can do. Be here about 8:00 tomorrow morning; we'll talk about it again. I'll think of something."

"Jesus, thanks, Prof. I knew I could count on you. You'll come up with something . . . I know you will. See you." Sambo turned and ambled down the street toward Connie.

It was that simple. The black cloud that had hung over Sambo's head evaporated. He had faith that old Prof would take care of it. It was quite a burden, one that John could have done without.

RaeLyn returned after Sambo joined Connie. "What are you doing to do?" she asked.

"You know?"

"I think so. Sambo might not graduate. Connie could be pregnant. Prof's supposed to solve it all."

"That's about it," John said. "Connie told you all this?"

"Yes. I think she needed somebody to talk to, and I guess she figured if Sambo could trust you, she could trust me. I think you can take that as a compliment. They look up to you."

"Hell of a lot of good that does me. It just makes a lot of trouble, as near as I can see."

"I don't think you'll have time for that Coke," she said. "You'll want to find Sherm, won't you?"

"How did you know?"

"I can read your mind."

"I believe it."

"Listen, I've got some studying to do, John. Why don't you take me home, then you can try to run down Sherm. Come over later tonight if you have time."

"I'll have time."

10

John sat parked on the street in front of the Reinwalds' sprawling mansion. He had not been able to locate Sherm after school, but it was nearly 6:30 now, and it was a good bet Sherm would be showing up for supper. John had stopped by his own home to let his mother know he would be late.

Coming from his own modest home in a quiet, middle-class neighborhood to the Reinwald manor on what Schonberg residents enviously called Snob Avenue, made John aware of the sharp contrasts in life-styles between the two families. Not that he resented the Reinwald wealth. He had heard the rags-to-riches story of Sherm's father, Max, a boy orphaned in his teens. Lacking in formal education, but driven by ambition and unafraid of hard work, he had founded a small electronics firm that was now one of the Midwest's largest. John believed in the American dream and admired Max Reinwald for what he had done with his life—even if the man had neglected, on his upward climb, to instill in his son any solid values beyond the desire to make a buck.

At least the Reinwalds seemed to enjoy their wealth, John thought. They were the pillars of the country club, guardians of the social elite. They traveled widely—Europe, Mexico, the big cities of the east and west coasts. They had a second home in Phoenix, a condominium in Vale.

From what John had gleaned from his newfound interest in the Hunter family, RaeLyn's father directed the fortunes of Reinwald Electronics now. Max Reinwald simply played the role of president, put in an appearance often enough to justify his corporate salary and to be certain that dividends would be paid each quarter

Although the white, southern-style home at the end of the long, paved driveway dwarfed his own dwelling place, John had no complaints. He had never known hunger or insecurity of any kind, as far as his physical comforts were concerned. His father, Benjamin, was a small building contractor, one of the old school, who took pride in his craftmanship and stubbornly refused to take on new jobs that he could not personally oversee himself. Their home was a simple, brick bungalow that Ben Armstrong had fashioned with his own hands some thirty years before. He had provided a comfortable living for his wife, Ruth, and their family. As his father approached 65, John had heard Ben assure Ruth, some fifteen years his junior, that they would have enough to provide for his old age and Ruth's, too, if "the damn government didn't let the inflation thing get out of hand." But Ben had made it clear that the kids were on their own, that he did not have the resources to carry them beyond high school. John suspected that Ben's statement and insistence on his children making their own way in the world, was more a lesson in self-reliance than a necessity, but he accepted it.

His two older sisters, Laura, now 28 years old, and Linda, 23, had both worked their way through college, Laura through some eight years of the grind and several years of residency before she recently became associated as a pediatrician with an Omaha practice. Linda had married midway through college, but had received her degree last spring and was teaching English at a high school in the western part of the state, despite the pregnancy that would bring John his first niece or nephew in July.

No, he would not trade the stability and sense of family he had grown up with for all of the Reinwald wealth.

The roar of Sherm's yellow Corvette racing up the street behind him jolted John back from his dreaming, and he turned in the driver's seat of his own vehicle to meet Sherm's friendly wave. John notice that Sherm was flashing that cocky, good-to-see-you smile of his, as he pulled the sportscar up beside John's automobile.

"Proffie, baby, how are you doing?"

"I need to talk to you, Sherm," John replied.

"Jesus, don't look so sober about it, kid. Nothing could be that bad. Wait a minute, be right with you." Sherm gunned the accelerator, causing the Corvette to let loose an unnecessary racket and whipped the car in front of John's. When he got out, he came back and climbed in the front seat of the Ford, the confident smile still frozen on his face. "What's up, Prof?" he asked as he slammed the door shut.

"Sambo's in trouble," John said.

"He is?" Sherm said, feigning surprise. "What do you mean?"

"I think you know what I mean. The English Midterms...the copies that were found in Sambo's locker."

"Oh, those."

"Yeah. I assume you know Sambo's about to get suspended, and he's apt to lose his English credits. That means he won't graduate."

"Yeah, poor Sambo. That's tough as shit. The big, dumb bastard needs that diploma."

"That's not the point, Sherm. He said he didn't take those exams; he claims you did . . . but he won't tell. Is that right, Sherm? Did you take them?"

Sherm's smile dissoved; his eyes narrowed and turned ice-cold. "Maybe I did."

"I want more than maybe."

"Okay, what if you get it . . . what are you going to do? Tell old man Steen?"

John was silent for a moment; he did not want to make a

commitment he could not keep. He could not desert Sambo right now, but on the other hand, whatever it was that held the Beavers together would keep him from laying the blame where it belonged. "No, I won't use your name. I promise you that. But, I'm going to try to think of some way to help Sambo. I just want to be completely satisfied that Sambo's innocent."

"All right," Sherm said, "I did it. I swiped the key from the principal's office one day, had another one made, then took the old one back. I left it on the floor, so they figured it was just misplaced or got knocked off the desk or something. No sweat. All I've got to do before exam time is hide out in the restroom or furnace room until everybody leaves the building, then open the principal's office and help myself. The photocopying machine down at the plant takes care of the rest. Made myself a small fortune—English, algebra, history, the whole works. Of course, you've got to be careful who you sell them to. The wrong kid gets hold of one and you've got trouble."

"But why, Sherm? You don't need the money."

"Hell, Prof, I've got pride. I want to do something on my own."

"Sherm, you're just a cheap thief, that's all it makes you. And you let Sambo take the rap for this thing. With a friend like you, who needs enemies?" He could see Sherm was unfazed. He was amoral. He had no sense of right or wrong.

"Sherm," John said, "you're an asshole."

Sherm smiled again, "Gee, thanks, Prof. That's the nicest thing you ever said to me."

John sighed. "I take it you're not going to turn yourself in."

"You take it right, Prof, and I don't think you or Sambo will do it either."

"How can you be so damn sure of yourself?"

"It would go against Sambo's grain to rat on a buddy. And you, Prof? You're too fucking honorable. You already said you wouldn't tell Steen. You're supposed to be so goddamned smart, but you're a dumb shit when it comes to something like that. You'd go to hell before you'd turn me in."

He glowered at Sherm, despising him but still knowing that what Sherm said was true. "I've got to go, Sherm," John said. "Thanks for nothing."

Sherm opened the door. "You bet, Prof, anytime . . . anytime."

11

John glanced nervously at Sambo, whose fingers tightened around the hard plastic of his chair's arms. Sambo's tension always manifested itself in perspiration. His pale, blue sweatshirt was dark and wet around the neck and underarms and he had the appearance of a condemnèd prisoner strapped to an electric chair. John did not feel too comfortable himself.

They were seated in Principal Steen's office. The secretary had informed him that the principal would be with them shortly. John had decided to bank on what he believed to be Steen's essential sense of fairness. The kids called him old man Steen. In fact, he was less than forty, had teenagers of his own and, although he could be tough as nails in meting out his sometimes arbitrary concept of justice, he was approachable. Sambo had nearly fainted when John met him outside the school building and informed him that they were going directly to the principal's office.

"What are you going to do, Prof?" Sambo had asked.

John had answered, "Play it by ear."

"Did you talk to Sherm?"

Yeah, you won't get any help there."

"We...we can't rat on Sherm, can we?"

"No, I suppose not. We should, but we won't."

"Then what the hell are you going to do?"

"Talk to Mr. Steen."

"I figured that much," Sambo had said, "But what are you going to tell him?"

"The truth as far as I can go with it."

"I don't understand."

"I don't either, Sambo...I don't understand how I got involved in this whole mess."

Sambo had not pursued his inquiries, apparently satisfied that everything was in John's capable hands and content to let his friend resolve the problem.

Principal Steen opened the door to his office and Sambo and John stood up like the accused rising for a judge entering a courtroom. Only this judge with black, curly hair tumbling casually over his forehead and short, stocky build, resembled a dock worker more than an administrator of justice. He looked like he could handle the inch-thick plywood paddle that hung symbolically behind his desk. Corporal punishment was outmoded, a throwback to a barbarian past, but evidently no one had bothered to tell that to Principal Steen.

"Sit down, guys," he growled as he took the seat behind his desk. Steen glared at Sambo, rubbing his jaw as he studied the school's prize athlete. "Well, Mr. Hanson," he said, "I take it you have something further to say for your cause this morning."

Sambo looked at the floor, then nodded at John. "Uh...I think Prof here has something to say."

Steen's dark eyes bore down on John, and, as much as he was grabbed by the urge to turn away, John met them unflinchingly. It was as though they were locked in a test of wills, each daring the other to turn away first.

"What about it, John?" Steen asked. "You Hanson's lawyer?"

"No, sir, I wouldn't call it that, but I'm his friend, and I know some things that I have to tell you."

"About the senior English exams?

"Yes, sir. Sambo didn't have anything to do with it," he blurted out.

Steen leaned back in his chair and cocked his head to one side, at the same time lifting his shaggy eyebrows in disbelief. "Is that all, John? You're asking me to take that at face value? That's not evidence. We found the papers in Hanson's locker. Now I've got to have more than your say so."

"Okay, sir. First of all, I suggest you change locks on your doors, then hang on to your keys. Somebody has a key to your office. That person's been getting hold of exams for senior classes all year long and selling them to some of the students."

Steen's eyes narrowed and John could see that he was getting a thorough appraisal from the Principal. "Well, go on."

"This person got word through the grapevine there was going to be a locker search; he put the papers in Sambo's locker and planned to move them back to his own after it had been searched."

"That sounds a little far out," said the principal.

"Sambo told me he didn't do it, Mr. Steen. I've known Sambo for a long time; he's not a liar and he's not a cheat."

"Well, I have to admit, if Hanson here is a cheater, he's a damn poor one," said Steen. "His grades sure haven't improved because of it."

"He's not involved in this, Mr. Steen. I can promise you that."

"How else can you assure me?" Steen asked.

"I've talked to the guy who did it. He admits it. He told me everything I've told you."

Steen leaned forward, his hands clasping the edge of his desk. "We've got a simple solution to our problem then," he said.

"What's that?" John asked.

"Tell me who the guilty person is, and your friend here is off the hook. I'll take it from there."

"I can't."

"What do you mean, you can't? You just told me you know who the person is."

"I mean, I won't."

Steen's face flushed scarlet with anger. He vaulted out of his chair, cracking his knee on the desk. "God damn it," he whispered, rubbing tenderly, distracted from his inquiry momentarily. He turned again toward John.

John felt more menaced by the man now that the principal was standing crouched over the desk like a provoked grizzly bear on the verge of attack.

"What do you mean, you won't?" Steen roared. "Listen, Armstrong, you don't have this valedictorian thing all sewed up. I can suspend you as an accessory to this. Hell, what am I saying? I can cut off your credits in required courses. You not only wouldn't make valedictorian, you wouldn't graduate. Think about that."

John still held the man's gaze. "I have, sir. I gave it a lot of thought before I came here. I know you can do all that, but I don't think it would be right, I don't think you would do it."

As though he had been hit sharply in his soft paunch, Steen dropped down in his chair. "Jesus, kid," he said grudgingly, "you're slippery as hell."

Suddenly John felt better. The principal's eyes softened, and John thought he detected a twinkle there, like the man saw some ironic humor in the situation, though was not about to acknowledge it.

"All right," Steen said, "let's back up. Why in the hell can't you tell me about this?"

"Because there's trust involved," John said. "I found out what I did because somebody trusted me not to tell. I won't . . . I want to . . but I won't."

"How do I know you didn't concoct this whole story?" Steen asked. "How do I know you're not the guilty one?" He shook his head negatively, as though answering his own questions. "No, I know better than that; you could write the damned exams if you wanted to. But you're asking me to trust you, to drop this thing against Hanson, just because you say so."

"Yes, sir," John replied, "I guess I am. I'm not lying. Sambo's not either, but we can't give you any more proof. You'll just have to make up you own mind whether you want to believe us or not.

The principal looked dourly at Sambo, who was white-faced and awed by the entire dialogue. "Hanson," Steen snapped, "do you know how far your friend here has gone for you? You know I could kick his ass out of school? Torpedo his class standing?"

Sambo shook his head, tears glistening in his eyes, but this time he did not avert Steen's withering stare. "Yes, sir, I know that, Mr. Steen."

"Why don't you two get the hell out of here? We'll forget this damn thing ever happened."

Sambo grinned and stood up. John joined him, breathing a sigh of relief as the tension disappeared. "Thank you, Mr. Steen," John said as he moved to the door.

"Yeah,...thanks a lot," Sambo said.

"Just a minute, guys," Steen replied, stopping the two young men in their tracks. "I don't want you to go out of here thinking I'm a fool. I know about the Eager Beavers. I've got a damn good hunch who you're covering up for, but I won't lean on you guys to get him." He looked up at John. "I appreciate loyalty in a person, John, but I think your loyalty is misplaced here. I hope it doesn't get you into trouble someday."

12

The old-fashioned, steel yard swing squeaked rhythmically as RaeLyn swung lazily back and forth on the green carpeted lawn in back of her family's ranch-style home. Her long ponytail bobbed up and down with the motion of the swing, and she shivered as the silky ends of hair brushed and tickled her bare shoulders.

It was a warm evening, unseasonably so for late April, although a little breezy. The red-orange glow of the sun was fading in the west, threatening to pull over the horizon with it the welcome warmth it had provided during the day. She wore a mint-green sundress, suspended from her tan shoulders with little spaghetti straps, tastefully exposing just a beginning of the cleavage between her full, firm breasts and showing just a trace of the whiteness where her early spring tan ran out.

She looked at her watch. John was a few minutes late. She knew he would have a good reason; sometimes he was so punctual it was disgusting. He always said he didn't like to wait on people, so he didn't want to make someone else wait for him. She understood that; she was not very good at waiting either.

The evening promised to be an interesting one. For as

long as they had been going together, John had talked about the Beavers and the wild, crazy things they had done together. She knew all of the guys as individuals, of course—Red, Sambo, and Sherm—especially Sherm. Red and Sambo sometimes seemed a little cool and distant when she was around, but Sherm always went out of his way to be friendly. Of course, they were acquainted because of their fathers' mutual business interests, and Sherm always managed to remind her of that. She had never liked Sherm and thought she detected a certain mocking insincerity in his manner. He was, perhaps, a bit too nice, too smooth and confident. He was the best-looking of the guys, she admitted, even better looking than John, and he had a certain charm and poise she found intriguing. She had read about tall girls often being attracted to short men. Sherm was significantly shorter than she was, but in spite of her instinctive hostility toward the young man, she conceded he had a definite magnetism.

But he could not hold a candle to John. There was only one John Armstrong. He was tall, handsome enough, with sandy hair and gray eyes that spoke even when his lips did not. He was a bit serious-looking maybe—no, scholarly, that was the word. She could see why the guys had nicknamed him Prof; it fit. But she still did not like the name. She was drawn to his intelligence, and there was a gentleness, a vulnerability about him she had never seen in other young men she had encountered. He was strong and confident, yet still burdened by an insecurity, a sense of loneliness that she knew instinctively she complemented. He needed her as much as she needed him.

There had never really been anyone but John, and she did not think there ever could be. He would graduate from Schonberg High next month. They would have the summer together, but then John would be heading for the University of Missouri to what he maintained was the best journalism school in the country. He would get home during the few holiday breaks, maybe a weekend or two, but she would not see much of him. Who could say what their future would be? The thought of John's leaving dampened her spirits momentarily, turned her melancholy. On several occasions John had professed his love for her, actually said, "I love you, RaeLyn." She was certain she loved him, although as articulate as she was supposed to be, she had always only affirmed it with, "Me, too, you," or like words. She had never said "I love you, John."

She sensed his disappointment that she had not, and she wanted to, but subconsciously, she supposed, she saw it as something of a surrender, an acknowledgement that her own life was subservient to someone else's. If she was going to be a lawyer, she had to hold fast to her plans for the future, and she feared that any commitment to John might interfere with those plans. Not that John would ever expect her to put aside her own ambitions, but she might abandon them all too easily herself if the circumstances were right.

These days John seemed to be a part of everything she wanted. Sometimes, caught up in the heat of passion, he was all she wanted. She had never had sex with a boy, but more than once she had wanted to with John, had sensed the quickening of her pulse as he held her tight, felt the gentle, unrelenting throbbing between her thighs.

She suspected that John had never done it with a girl either. He would have been too shy, too much the gentleman, unless he truly knew the girl, convinced himself he loved her and had been caught up in the fever of the moment.

Would they be able to make it through the summer? Their petting had become increasingly uninhibited and familiar, their hands moving precariously close to forbidden places in recent days. Just last night, as she lay back on the car seat, John had pressed tight against her, and she had been acutely aware of the fustrated hardness in his trousers. In the course of their playful wrestling, her skirt had hiked up almost to her waist and John's hands had moved tentatively up her thighs, creeping under the elastic of her panties. She could not say now how she might have reacted if he had yanked them off and moved to finish what they had started. But at the last minute he had made a strategic retreat, moving away from her and apologizing profusely. He had been contrite, coolly polite, the remainder of the evening. She had sensed his embarrassment and reassured him that she understood, even admitted she was having difficulty keeping a hold on her own emotions.

His conscience, his perhaps out-dated notions about morality, made him all the more special, and she loved him for it. If they ever did it, she knew it would not be a cheap thing, something casually undertaken. It would mean something to both of them, no matter how much they might regret it later.

Tonight, the Beavers were going to be together again, sort of a pre-graduation reunion, she supposed. Sherm had invited all of the Beavers and their dates to his home. It would be perfectly respectable, Sherm had assured John. Sherm would play some of his new records, they would dance, drink Coke and eat themselves sick. She credited Sherm with having a sentimental side she had not recognized before. Maybe she was wrong about him. Perhaps the other guys in the group had been something more to Sherm, after all, than so many tools to get his way.

She had always felt a little guilty because of her own contribution to the Beavers' dissolution, although of course, it had not been an intentional thing. She would not have begrudged John some companionship with his old pals, or at least she did not think so, but she had never been put to a test in that regard. She had been John's best friend from the moment of their meeting, and he had never expressed any interest in being with his old gang after that. In fact, he had seemed strangely ambivalent in his feelings when he talked about the Beavers and, of course, the cheating episode had driven another wedge between John and his old comrades.

She heard the familiar groan of John's old Ford pull up in front of the house. She jumped up and scampered out to meet him. As he came toward her, he reached for her hand and said, "Sorry Rae, flat tire right in the driveway. I was going to call, but I figured I could change it as fast as I could make the call."

"It's okay," she said. "Are you ready to go to Sherm's now?"

His expression was dour, definitely unenthusiastic. "Uh, why don't we sit on the swing for a while," he said. "Sherm won't be ready; he never is. He didn't even set a time; things won't get going until nine. It's not even eight yet."

"All right," she said, "it's nice on the swing tonight. A few more weeks and the bugs will start to come out. The mosquitoes will drive us back in the house."

They sat down in the swing. John gave it a shove with his foot to start it rocking, and they sat there silently, swinging slowly, surrendering to the calming, soothing effect of the gentle spring breeze.

RaeLyn finally broke the silence, "You don't seem very excited about Sherm's party. Don't you want to go?"

"Not very badly."

"Why not?"

"You know how I feel about Sherm. . .especially since that trouble with Sambo. He's no good, RaeLyn. He hurts anyone who has anything to do with him."

"But you didn't always feel that way. You were friends once. . .you, Sherm, Sambo and Red. . .you're always talking about the good times you had."

"I suppose, in a way, but you have to use the word friends in a loose sense. I think of a friend as somebody you can trust, depend upon. . .somebody you can talk to, share your secrets with. . .count on them to stand by you when things get tough. We were always just a bunch of guys who hung around together. I look back now and I realize, in a lot of ways. . .in the ways that really count. . .we hardly even knew each other." He took her hand in his and bent his head toward her so that their foreheads touched, "You're a friend, Rae. You're more than that, but you're a friend."

She placed her hand behind his head and pressed her lips gently against his, shivering slightly when he held her kiss a bit longer than she had expected. "I like being your friend,

John," she said. Then she smiled mischievously. "I like the 'more' part, too. But what about Sherm's party? Are we going?"

"I don't want to," he said, "but what about you?"

"It doesn't really matter," she said, "but I don't mind going. I think I'd enjoy seeing the house from the inside. My folks have been there a lot when the Reinwalds have given dinner parties for business associates, but I've never been there. You know, without fail, I get a Christmas gift and birthday present from the Reinwalds every year. . .I guess because of daddy's position with the company. I always send a thank you note, but that's about as close as we ever get. I've never even met them."

"Well," John said, "their place is the closest thing we've got to a mansion in Schonberg. I guess they're loaded; I suppose you know more about that than I do. You'll probably meet his folks tonight; you'll like them. Sherm's dad is an ordinary kind of guy. His mother is real pretty and young-looking."

"You sound like we're going."

"Yeah, I guess so. I thought maybe I could get you to talk me out of it, but you didn't help much. I'd feel pretty crumby, I guess, if I didn't show up."

"Who all's going to be there?" she asked. "Girls, I mean."

"Well, Sambo will be there with Connie, I suppose, but I'm not sure. They've been acting funny lately; they seem kind of quiet when they're together. Not as lovy-dovy as they used to be. And Sambo, he's nervous and jumpy. He had an athletic scholarship at Kearney State, but the other day he said he's not going on to school. I'm not sure his grades would meet the scholarship level anyway. Maybe it all has to do with Connie being pregnant."

"I can understand that," RaeLyn said. "They're sure, then?"

"Yeah, Sambo told me yesterday they were going to wait until school's out before they get married. She'll be almost four months along then, but they thought it would be better to finish out the school year."

"They're going to have the baby and get married then?"

"Sure, what else would they do?"

"A girl can get abortions in some places now."

He frowned and looked at her incredulously. "Abortion! Would you go through with something like that?"

She hesitated. "No, but I wouldn't get pregnant in the first place."

"You can't say that."

"I can too. I wouldn't let it happen." The conversation was suddenly making her uneasy. "Getting back to the original subject," she said, "who's Sherm bringing?"

"Probably Sarah Remington. He's been taking her out a lot again lately."

"If what the girls say about her is true, he's not taking her to any movies," she said.

"Your claws are showing."

"You're right. I'll shut up. What about Red?"

"I imagine he'll be alone." John paused for a moment. "Rae, would you dance with Red if he asked you?"

"Of course, I don't have anything against Red. I'm not that much of a snot."

"I didn't mean it that way. I know most of the girls don't care much for Red, but he's lonely as the devil. I feel sorry for him. The Beavers were all he ever had, and I guess I still feel kind of responsible for him. We'll all be going our separate ways as soon as school's out, and I don't know what will became of Red. I doubt if his grades are good enough to get him into college. Besides, his dad died when he was just a little kid, and his mom's health has never been real good. They've always been pretty hard up. I don't think he'd want to go to college anyway. He'll probably get a construction job or something. He's not afraid to work. I wish he'd make some new friends. . .or find a girl, like I did."

"I'll give Red special attention tonight," she promised.

He put his arm around her and squeezed her gently. "I knew you would. Thanks."

What was it John always said?—When a friend is involved, loyalty is more important than truth. She had countered, "I always thought newspapermen were supposed to be seekers of the truth."

"They're supposed to be objective, too," he had said, "I try to be, and I'm not trying to defend lying as an art. I think we should look for the truth. But I think friends are entitled to loyalty, too. The problem most of the time is to decide who your friends are, who deserves your loyalty. Sometimes I'm not very good at that. Once that's decided, the rest is simple, as far as I'm concerned."

Loyalty. Yes, that was one of the reasons she cared about him so much. She knew she commanded that kind of loyalty from him, but she had a gnawing feeling that someday that loyalty to a friend would be John's undoing.

13

The Reinwald home was a palace. RaeLyn had only seen homes like it in the movies—crystal chandeliers, a high-domed entryway, winding staircase, beautifully carpeted halls. And, fittingly, Sherm, as host, was prince charming. Attentive and polite, he was suave and debonair in the elegant setting. He belonged here, and tonight seemed mature beyond his years.

John had the guest list pegged perfectly. Sambo and Connie, Sarah Remington was there. You couldn't miss her. Her boobs were about to pop out of her dress. Poor Red was alone.

John had been wrong about one thing, though. RaeLyn would not meet the prominent Reinwalds. Sherm informed them that his parents were gone for a few days; they would have the house to themselves tonight. RaeLyn suspected that his parents were unaware of the party plans, but the guests were not junior high students, and the absence of chaperones did not especially alarm her.

After he had met John and RaeLyn at the massive double doors of the front entryway, Sherm led them to what he called the recreation room. RaeLyn had seen high school gymnasiums that were smaller. She chided herself for standing there awestruck like a country bumpkin, as she surveyed the magnificent setting.

There was even a shiny, hardwood dance floor, an island in the middle of rich green carpet. She could not identify the ivory-colored paneling that covered the walls, but it reeked of money. Appropriately, the room was a paradise for an electronics nut. An enormous stereo system lined nearly the full width of one wall, and speakers were located strategically about the room. There were several television sets surrounded by clusters of plush furnishings, apparently to permit guests a choice of television viewing.

At the end of the room opposite the stereo was a bar with an area behind it that was a well-equipped kitchen area.

Her own family was comfortable financially and enjoyed a relatively affluent lifestyle, but she felt like a little beggar girl here, awkward and out of place. She was utterly captivated, enraptured by the atmosphere.

Red was already stationed at the stereo, and Elvis was taking off with "All Shook Up." Any freeze between Sambo and Connie was obviously thawing quickly tonight. They were swaying slowly on the dancing area, pressing their bodies almost obscenely close, RaeLyn thought, apparently unaware that their movements were not even remotely in time with the fast music.

"Over here," Sherm said, leading them to the kitchenette. He opened the large refrigerator, revealing well-stocked shelves. There was plenty of Coca Cola, all right, and any other soft drink one might desire. There was also an ample supply of beer. The shelves behind the nearby bar suggested that a connoisseur of fine liquor would be very happy here. RaeLyn glanced nervously at John and shrugged.

"Anybody for a beer?" Sherm called.

"Bring me one," Red yelled from across the room.

"Come get your own, fat-ass," Sherm responded. "I'm not a goddamn waiter." He turned to RaeLyn and smiled disarmingly, "Excuse my French," he said. "Red doesn't understand English." He reached into the refrigerator and started to remove the frosty cans of beer, lining them up like tin soldiers on the bar.

"Coke for RaeLyn and me," John said.

Coke was fine with her. She did not especially like the taste of beer, but she was mildly irritated that John presumed to speak for her. He was not that way about most things, but she had noticed before that he was strangely uncomfortable whenever they were around alcohol.

"Aw, come on, Prof," Sherm said, "for old times' sake." He winked at RaeLyn. "He wasn't always such a prude; he was never a major league guzzler, but he could handle his share. Come on, Prof. RaeLyn will have one." He turned to RaeLyn, "Won't you, Rae?"

John's eyes shot daggers at Sherm. "I said we'll have Coke."

"Coke's fine with me," she said, trying to ease the tension.

"Yeah, sure, whatever you want. Maybe you'll feel like a beer later."

Once over the initial volley between Sherm and John, RaeLyn found herself enjoying the evening, relaxing more as she became accustomed to the dazzling surroundings. In spite of John's urgings, shy Red had declined to ask her to dance, so she had asked him. He could not politely refuse and she had found him amazingly graceful on the dance floor. He had asked her to dance twice after that, and she was flattered by the sudden infatuation that had overtaken him. After their last, she said, "You're a good dancer, Red."

His face turned almost the color of his hair. "Thanks," he said, "thanks a lot."

She saw him as a boy who had more promise than any of his friends suspected. He was lonely, lacking in confidence; his unorthodox behavior was likely a cry for attention. Underneath the facade, there was a beautiful person who only wanted acceptance. She hoped he found it soon.

Sambo rendered her a duty dance while John danced with Connie. Sherm was apparently enraptured with his partner for the evening. RaeLyn had cast him furtive glances throughout the evening, but since their initial encounter, he was oblivious to her presence.

Sherm carefully orchestrated the lights throughout the evening. Now the room was dimly lit. Over Red's protests, Sherm had insisted they play the slow records now, and the music suited her mood. She liked the feel of John's body pressed next to hers as they stepped slowly and softly around the floor. The smell of his aftershave was intoxicating, and there was a certain sensuality about the way her breasts brushed against his chest as they moved in each other's arms. She slid her hand down his back and imagined herself naked against his own nakedness.

Perhaps it was the house, a latent eroticism there, but it seemed like it almost had the smell of sex. Then she had that tingling, that wanting, between her thighs again.

Sherm tapped John on the shoulder. "May I cut in?" he asked. "I haven't danced with this charming lady all evening."

John looked questioningly at RaeLyn and, apparently reading assent in her eyes, released her from his embrace. Sherm eased between her and John, took her in his arms and swept her away. He was every bit as graceful as he looked and, unlike John, a natural dancer with an inborn sense of rhythm. Maybe it was something genetic with people of his class. In any case, she could understand his success with girls. There was a presence about him that made him taller than his height, more powerful than his slight frame would suggest. Perhaps it was what politicians called charisma.

She had attended political meetings with her father from time to time, and she had been surprised on more than one occasion to find that the six foot four inch senator who overpowered her on the television screen was five foot three when he looked at her and shook her hand. Still, once over her initial surprise, she had found that the man's small stature had not diminished his standing with her.

They made a little swirl on the floor, and RaeLyn caught sight of John. Damn him. He was dancing with that Sarah

Remington, and, God, the way she was throwing her hips at him, she looked like she was going to rape him right on the dance floor. And he had that secret smile. He was enjoying it! She would be damned if he wasn't. It occurred to her that John wasn't any different than the rest of them. He'd probably screw Sarah on the dance floor, if he got the chance.

What was she thinking? She wore John's class ring, and they had always been loyal to each other. Jealousy was a new emotion in their relationship, and she was disappointed with herself. Nonetheless, she pressed her body closer to Sherm's and his response was instant. His arms tightened around her, and she could feel his rising hardness pushing against her. And her own throbbing was there again. Why was she feeling this way? Her palms were slippery with perspiration, and she worried that her face was flushed. Her distress had not gone unnoticed.

"You're warm," Sherm said, "how about something cold to drink?"

Snatching at the opportunity to regain her composure, she responded, "Sounds good," and followed him to the refrigerator. Tossing a quick look over her shoulder, she saw that John and Sarah were sitting on one of the couches, engaged in animated conversation. Sarah suddenly cut loose with a burst of laughter at something John said, and RaeLyn saw her squeeze John's knee playfully. She fumed.

Sherm opened the refrigerator again. "How about a beer this time, RaeLyn?"

"Well, I don't think so."

"Now you're too smart a lady to let Prof tell you what to drink. Have just one with me, will you?"

She shot a quick glance at John and Sarah again. She still had her hand on John's knee. "Okay," RaeLyn said, accepting the beer. Then she moved with Sherm to a studio couch, where they sat down and leisurely sipped their beers.

Sherm was a total gentleman tonight—gracious, well-mannered. Not like Miss Hotpants over there with John. She locked her eyes on her boyfriend and the cheap flirt across the room, and, as though he had received her message, John looked her way. Then, excusing himself, he rose and walked toward RaeLyn. As he approached, he looked disapprovingly at the beer can in her hand, but said nothing.

"Shall we dance?"

"Okay," she said agreeably. Then, turning to Sherm, "Thank you, Sherm, you dance beautifully."

"Thank you," Sherm said, "so do you. Maybe we can try it again later."

I'd like that," she said. Then for emphasis, added, "Very much."

She could sense John's tenseness as they danced. He was distant and detached now, but she knew he would not say anything unless she goaded him into it. She was in a mood to do just that. She had felt unexplainably bitchy ever since they had come to the Reinwald home; she knew it, but she could not will the feeling away.

"You seemed to be having a nice chat with Sarah," RaeLyn said.

"She's a good kid. She has quite a sense of humor."

"Did you get a big thrill out of having her squeeze you leg like that?"

"She didn't mean anything by that...that's just her way. She's a toucher."

"But you noticed it, then...you knew she was doing it?"

"Well yeah...but just barely. I was hardly aware of it. It was innocent."

"I'll bet," she snapped.

"Come on, Rae, don't get down my neck. I didn't do anything. She was squeezing my leg, I wasn't squeezing hers."

"You would have, if I hadn't been here."

"I would not. Don't be silly. I was just being congenial. And you weren't exactly rude to Sherm, you know."

"Well, he is a good dancer and a perfect gentleman."

"Are you trying to tell me something?"

"Well, he could teach you a thing or two."

She could have bit off her tongue. In all these months,

she had never tried to hurt him like this—and hurt him she had. She could see that in his eyes.

"You didn't say anything about my drinking the beer," she said.

"You want a medal? I don't have any right to tell you what to drink."

"You were trying to earlier."

"If I was, I didn't realize it. You've never done any drinking when we were anyplace else. I just assumed by now that you didn't drink."

She did not know why, but she wanted him to lose his temper—but he was not going for the bait. "I'd like to dance with Sherm again. . .if you don't mind," she said. Before she pulled away from him, she knew she had stung him good. He just stood there in stunned silence as she stepped back.

At that moment, she was ready to fly back into his arms, apologize, ask him to take her away from this place, but he turned and walked away before she could. She looked around the room for Sherm. He was with Sarah on the same studio couch she had deserted minutes earlier. Sarah was sprawled on his lap, wrapped around him like a boa constrictor. His lips were planted on her neck, and his hands kept sliding down her back, over her round rump, gently, steadily, like a baker kneading bread dough. But Sarah's hand—my God! She had slipped it inside the front of his pants, and RaeLyn could see the slow, rhythmic motion beneath the thin trousers as though Sarah's own hand was keeping time with Sherm's.

It excited RaeLyn in a way she had never experienced before. She stood there, staring, shocked by the absurdity of it, hypnotized by the stark, unadulterated sexuality of it.

Then Sherm looked up and saw her. She could feel the scarlet spreading over her cheeks, but Sherm only smiled, flashing white, even teeth. He pushed Sarah away, a little harshly, RaeLyn thought. And then, apparently unperturbed by RaeLyn's observation, he stood, tucked in his shirt, tugged at his trousers in an obvious effort to reposition their contents and walked toward RaeLyn, who was still immobilized by what she had seen.

"How about another beer?" Sherm asked.

"Pardon?"

"Beer. . .the great tranquilizer," he said, still displaying the broad smile.

He did not seem the least embarrassed or disturbed by the certain knowledge that RaeLyn must have witnessed his and Sarah's acrobatics.

"A beer," she said, "yes, I'll have a beer."

He put his arm around RaeLyn's waist and guided her to the refrigerator. She caught Sarah's killing glare as they walked away, but strangely, it only made her feel triumphant.

RaeLyn stood at the bar, toying with the nearly full beer can. She glanced sideways and met Sherm's smoldering, black eyes. She turned away, but she could feel him scrutinizing her—probably mentally stripping her. That idea both angered and titillated her, and she found herself more confused by the crosscurrent of emotions Sherm stirred within her. At least he was being silent for a change. She was not up to making clever conversation right now.

Her eyes followed John, who was dancing with Sarah now. He was holding her comfortably, but not obscenely close, she admitted to herself. Thank God, Sarah was not working on him the way she had on Sherm. Still, the sight of them together did not please her. John should be tendering her, RaeLyn, his apology right now. Or did she owe the apology? What were they quarreling about anyway? Why were they arguing?

Red was sprawled on a giant cushion near the stereo, almost swallowed by the billowy softness that encompassed him. He looked like a red-haired turtle trapped on its back, she thought. His head bobbed up and down, evidently trying to keep up with the music. He was drunk. Vaguely, she recalled her promise to be attentive to him. Perhaps she should ask him to dance again. Red would like that. John would appreciate it, too; maybe he would forgive her for her

Then it occurred to her that Connie and Sambo had absented themselves from the room; they must have gone home early. "Where's Connie and Sambo?" she asked, turning to Sherm, whose eyes were still studying her appraisingly.

"Upstairs in one of the guest rooms," he said matter-of-factly.

"Oh," she said weakly.

"Don't worry, it's all right. Connie's already pregnant, you know. They're going to get married."

"Yes, I knew that." She guessed that made everything all right. They might as well do it in comfort as in the back seat of a car.

"Yeah," Sherm said. "Looks like the old gang's breaking up. This is probably the last hurrah."

"Oh, you'll probably still get together once in a while," she said.

"Nope. . .this is it." He picked up his can of beer and tipped it to his lips, accomplishing the maneuver without averting his gaze.

He was making her uneasy now, but she met his eyes challengingly, determined not to be intimidated by his demeanor.

"We haven't seen Prof much lately," Sherm said, "but I can understand why."

"What do you mean?"

"If I had a girl like you, I wouldn't want to hang around my old pals much either."

"Oh. . .but you have a girl. Sarah. . .she's pretty, and I've seen you with other girls too. Nobody would call them dogs."

"Sarah is a sow compared to you, my dear," Sherm said.

"That's cruel, Sherm, and you know it. She's crazy about you, and she is good looking."

"She's a slut."

The smooth, gracious host had suddenly disappeared. He had turned surly, and there seemed to be something volatile, even dangerous, about him now.

"What do you think of our house?" Sherm asked, his mood changing abruptly.

"It's beautiful. I've never seen anything like it. Uh...does it have bathrooms?"

He smiled. "Dozens." He pointed down the hallway from where they had entered the room. "Second door to your right."

"I'll be back in a minute," she said.

After relieving herself, RaeLyn freshened her makeup. She preened her hair and straightened her dress before she left the bathroom, then returned to Sherm. She was now increasingly disconcerted. She could see John was sitting with Sarah now, but they appeared to be engaged in a totally proper conversation. When she caught his sideways look, she wished again that he would come and take her away and help her escape from what she was feeling now, but he turned his attention quickly back to Sarah.

When she approached Sherm, he said, "You said you liked the house. Would you like to see the rest of it?"

She hesitated. "Yes, I would."

He took her arm like the sophisticated lord of a manor house, and escorted her away from the recreation area and through the maze of rooms that comprised the Reinwald mansion. She was not disappointed—a dining room that was like a great banquet hall; a kitchen that could accommodate a feast; furnishings and decor that she knew instinctively reflected exquisite taste. She appreciated beautiful things, and she could not help adoring the dreamland she found herself in this night.

After they had explored the lower level and the main floor, Sherm led her up the winding staircase. She assumed the bedrooms were there, since she had seen none on the other floors. She had reservations about the propriety of accompanying him upstairs, but she convinced herself that Sherm was too much of a gentleman to make things difficult for her. Besides, there were others in the house.

Reaching the top of the stairs, he gestured to the long

hallway that stretched to both the left and right of the broad landing. "Twelve bedrooms," he said. "Henry VIII would have been right as home here. Most of the smaller ones are the same. I'll show you a few of the nicer ones."

They turned right and moved down the hallway. A deep moan, sounding not quite like agony or pleasure, came from one of the rooms. RaeLyn jumped involuntarily at the sound. "No ghosts in this house," Sherm said, "but you can't visit that room—that's Sambo's. It's my *special* guest room."

Her heart raced at the thought of what was going on behind the door. Her legs weakened and trembled. She glanced at Sherm; he was looking at her, smiling: He knew exactly what she was thinking.

Come here," he said, "let me show you something."

He led her to the room adjacent to Sambo's love nest and she found herself in an ocean of blue. The room had a white ceiling, and one wall was covered with paper of blue and silver geometric patterns. Otherwise, the room, including the bedspread that covered the king-sized bed, was done in varying shades of blue. It seemed cold; still it was an exciting, stimulating coldness, like walking out of a hot, stuffy house into the first snowfall of winter.

"This is my room," Sherm said.

That surprised her, because it did not look like a typical teenager's room. No pinups, trophies or other paraphernalia scattered haphazardly about. The room was more a showcase, immaculate. Neatly framed paintings and wall plaques were positioned tastefully on the walls. Sherm seemed older, frighteningly sophisticated, in the setting.

He moved to the wall that separated the room from the one Sambo and Connie had claimed, and carefully removed an abstract painting. With a smirk on his lips, he said, "Take a look at this."

She moved closer to the wall and saw the neat, round hole, just about the diameter of a lead pencil, that had been drilled through the plaster.

"What's that?" she asked.

"See for yourself."

She looked into the hole and found herself looking through a telescopelike tube that opened into the next room and was angled precisely to provide a perfect view of the bed where Connie and Sambo were carnally entangled. She was unable to pull her eyes away from the wet, naked beings engaged in coitis on the large bed. Sambo was stretched out, flat on his back, his eyes closed as though he were lost in some unimaginable ecstacy. Connie was straddled over his hips, her hands resting on each side. RaeLyn could hear the girl sighing as her body writhed and gyrated on the stiff spear that impaled her. RaeLyn had never imagined anything like it in her wildest fantasies.

Abruptly, Sambo thrust his hips sharply upward, and she could see his slender-muscled buttocks quiver. Connie fell forward and collapsed on top of him. RaeLyn backed away from the peephole. Suddenly, she felt dirty, almost perverted, not because of what she had seen, but because she was a part of the grossest invasion of privacy she could imagine. She was nothing more than a peeping tom.

Sherm put the painting back in place. "Connie and Sambo are regular visitors here. I told Sambo they can make themselves at home whenever my folks are out of town. They put on quite a show, don't they? Of course, I have other guests up once in a while. . .for variety."

"That's a dirty thing to do, Sherm," she said. "It's sick."

"But you liked it. . .I could tell."

"No. . .no! It made me feel dirty."

But he was right—she had liked it. Or at least had been fascinated, excited, by what she saw. Even now, she was tormented by the sensations that raced through her body. She wanted to do what Sambo and Connie were doing. She had to find John and have him take her away from here. They would do it together; he only needed her encouragement. She knew John wanted to as bad as she.

She started for the door and was surprised to find it had been pushed shut since they had entered the room. As she reached for the knob, she was stopped by Sherm's firm grasp on her arm. "Now, wait a minute, RaeLyn," he said. "We didn't come up here just to look at the house. . .you know that as well as I do. I could see what you wanted when you were watching Sarah and me downstairs. You wanted my prick for yourself." He jerked her closer. "I've wanted to screw you ever since you started going with Prof; he doesn't deserve something as delicious as you."

She pulled away. "No, I don't want to. Leave me alone."

But he grabbed her and, with a strength that belied his small stature, yanked her back, swung her onto the huge bed and was on top of her before she could move. She opened her mouth to scream, but could not as his lips covered hers. Reflexively, she clawed at his face and shoulders as she fought to break free, but in the course of their struggle, he maneuvered his hips between her own, working the skirt of her dress above her thighs at the same time. Beneath the sheer panties, she could feel his swelling organ pressing urgently against her pubes. Oh, she wanted him—she could not help it. She had to have him.

Sherm's lips slid down her cheek and to her ear. "No more trouble?"

She sighed. "No. . .no more trouble."

With obvious expertise, he untied the thin straps that anchored the dress to her shoulders, then slid down the zipper that held her dress in place. No clumsiness, no fumbling. He undressed her slowly, deliberately, like a skilled surgeon performing a delicate operation. Then he escaped deftly from his own garments. In a matter of moments, they both lay naked on the bed.

In the course of her disrobing, her passion has subsided slightly. Still she wanted him. This was new to her. She felt like a child in comparison to the knowledgeable young man beside her. But he promptly put her fears to rest as he began to caress her thighs, gently knead her turgid nipples, then dance his fingers lightly down her belly through the silky down of her pubic bush till they came to rest on her throbbing clitoris. Perhaps it was the electrifying atmosphere of the moment. She had never had such a wild, mind-blowing sensation. When his fingers began to stroke her tenderly, it took her breath away, and she was overcome by weakness, as her thighs quivered with pre-orgasmic twitches.

Then he moved his hands between them and spread her legs, moving between them and raising himself above her on his knees. Lightheaded and confused, she looked down and saw his smooth-headed shaft erupting from the black, tangled nest that encompassed its root.

"Are you a virgin?" he asked softly. She was speechless, but she nodded her head affirmatively. He lowered himself onto her and at the same time guided her hand to his pulsating phallus. "You'll have to help," he said.

Following his instructions, she did, and when he entered, she had only a brief instant of burning discomfort before she was filled with the organ of his manhood. She had heard it was supposed to hurt the first time, but it didn't. It felt good; it belonged there.

"I thought you said you were a virgin," he said.

"I am."

"You can't be. It was too easy, and you're too wet."

"I was," she said, suddenly and unexplainably defensive, the transitory beauty of the moment passing and descending into ugliness. She sensed there was something about the notion of her virginity that excited him, perhaps the thrill of conquest, the adventure of the unexplored. He was using her like he used everyone—like he had used John.

John. Oh, God, what was she doing here? Then Sherm's mouth was on her lips again and his hips were thrusting very lightly, provocatively against hers, gradually raising her desire into a crescendo that cried out for climax. She did not care anymore. She responded and moved with him—but he stopped.

"It's okay," she said, "please. . .go on."

"Not yet. Only if you say fuck me."

"Just do it."

"Only if you say it."

"Okay. . .fuck me."

"Say it again. . . .only this time say please."

"Please, fuck me."

He drove deeply. She was glued to him, her body rising and falling with his, matching him thrust for thrust. She felt the pulsating of his organ as he prepared to empty his semen, and suddenly he pulled free from her, lifting himself back to his knees as he discharged in quick, successive spurts upon the bedspread.

She had not come and she felt unsatisfied, cheated—used. "What's wrong?" she asked.

He looked at her comtemptuously. She was no longer the shining princess; she was a dirty beggar girl. She could see that in his eyes.

"Shit," he said, "I wasn't using anything. You don't think I'm going to take a chance on knocking you up. You're a hell of a good fuck, but I don't want anything to do with babies or marriage. Next time I'll have a rubber."

She started to inch out from under him. "There won't be any *next* time, Sherm," she said threateningly. "There shouldn't have been any *this* time."

Then the bedroom door came open, casting a streak of bright light across the dimly-lit room. Gripped by panic, she scooted out from under Sherm, who still towered over her, and raised herself up to look over his sweat-slickened shoulders. It was John. He was staring at them, his face emotionless, but his eyes pained and hurt. She shoved Sherm away, and he rolled over on the other side of the bed, only then becoming aware of John's presence in the room.

"Prof," he said sheepishly but not remorsefully, "join the party."

John looked at him disbelievingly and silently. There was still no anger in his face—only sadness.

Tears welled up in RaeLyn's eyes. "John. . .John. . .I didn't mean for it to happen." She crossed her hands over her breasts, reflexively trying to cover her nakedness.

"I'll see you around, RaeLyn," John said, then he whirled and stormed out of the room.

She called out after him. "John! Wait a minute.. . .I can

explain...please!" She snatched up her undergarments, hurrying to get dressed. She was clumsy now, all thumbs, moving turtlelike, it seemed to her. Sherm watched her silently with traces of a smirk upon his lips. When she was dressed, she ran into the hallway, reaching the landing just in time to see John leave through the mansion's double doors. She walked slowly and numbly back to the bedroom where Sherm still lay naked.

"Prof get away?" Sherm asked.

"Yes," she said, tears beginning to stream down her cheeks.

"Aw, shit," Sherm said, "he'll get over it. It was all in fun. Want to try again?"

"Go to hell, Sherm!" She sat down on the edge of the bed, buried her face in her hands and began to sob, her entire body trembling and heaving as despair overtook her. She did not have to ponder her future with John Armstrong anymore—it had been decided for her this evening.

14

"Hey, Prof," Red said, "did you hear about my latest? Ain't no girl at Borderview High gonna forget old Red was there." Red giggled like a little boy who had just pulled a prank on a playmate. The Dodge swerved on the rough, graveled road momentarily and abruptly jolted John back from his dream world.

"What did you say, Red?" he asked unenthusiastically.

"I wanted to know if you'd heard about my latest caper?"

Red was undaunted by John's indifference. "Well, last Friday, after school was out, I sneaked into the girl's potty room . . . the one on the main floor. I carved a little gem on the wall above the sink. A Red Murphy Original."

"That's nice."

"Do you want to know what it was?"

"Shit, I thought you'd never ask. It goes like this—'As every little girl should know, fucking makes a woman glow; it opens her eyes and spreads her thighs, and gives her ass good exercise.'" John was silent. "Well? What do you think?"

"I think they call that vandalism."

"Shit, Prof, that ain't what I meant, you know that. What

do you think of the poem?"

Beautiful poem, Red," John said scarcastically. "Keats couldn't have done it any better."

"Keats? Does he go to Schonberg High?"

John did not reply.

"Jesus you're a grouch tonight," Red said. "You know something, Prof? You're just no fun to be around anymore."

"You're the one who asked me to come along. I'd just as soon be home anyway."

"Aw, come on, Prof. One last party . . . for old times' sake. Shit, we're high school graduates as of last night. There's a great big world out there just waiting for us to screw it up. Won't be long, and the Beavers will be going their separate ways."

"The Beavers already have, Red . . . in case you hadn't noticed."

"Well, physically, maybe—not in spirit. The spirit's still there, ain't it, Prof? Huh, ain't it?"

"The Beavers are already shot to hell, Red. We had some good times, but things fizzled out a long time ago."

"Now, Prof, just 'cause you and Sherm got into it over something . . ."

"It's more than that. I don't hold any grudges against Sherm. I talked to him this morning, in fact . . . before he left for the trip back East with his folks."

"Yeah, I heard about the trip. What's it all about? Why couldn't old Sherm stay around for a few days? This is senior party time."

"Well, for one thing, he's going to pick up a new Thunderbird in Detroit on the way back. Graduation present from his dad. For another, Sherm's going to be a Harvard man, and they're going to scout out the territory. This is the only time his dad could get away—besides, he's supposed to start learning about the electronics business this summer. From the ground up, he says."

"Old Sherm won't be on the ground very long—not with his old man's dough. Sherm's sharp enough, though. He don't need his old man's money to make a bundle. He'd make a million bucks someday anyhow."

"Yeah, you're right. He'd dream up a racket of some kind; then sell it like hell."

"Guess Sambo's got things decided for him," Red went on. "Connie's gettin' knocked up sort of took care of that. He told me he's going to work at the packing house. Fuck. Ain't it hard to believe . . . in a couple of days, Sambo's gonna be an old married man."

"Yeah," John answered. "I hope things work out for them. Sambo's a good guy, and Connie's all right, too. What about you, Red? Where do you go from here?"

"Shit, I don't know. Who cares? One day at a time. Been thinking about giving the fuckin' Navy a chance."

"Sounds like a good idea."

"Yeash, maybe so. Nothing to keep me around here." Red was trying to be nonchalant, but John thought he detected a twinge of sadness in the tone of his voice.

Red pulled off the dark, winding road and onto a deeply rutted, weed-covered trail that led to Secham's Beach. The term "beach" was a misnomer, since they were actually headed for one of the countless, narrow sandbars that edged the slow-moving, muddy waters of the Skeeter River. The area happened to join farmland owned by a local lawyer, Gabriel Sechman, who good-naturedly overlooked the technical trespasses committted by Schonberg High students.

Most of the shelves of gravel deposited by the river along its fringes were protected by screens of towering cottonwoods and knotted undergrowth that provided perfect hideaways for the wild parties and beer blasts that erupted spontaneously every spring before and after high school graduation exercises. It is an unwritten law that Schonberg High seniors and their guests had first claim to Secham's Beach during graduation week and, as Red's car pulled out of the surrounding woods and onto the pebble-hardened ridge above the beach, John could see that half the senior class was there, already well embarked on a night of partying. Several crackling fires cast their iridescent glow on the shimmering waters of the quiet river, presenting a placid picture that belied the supercharged atmosphere on the beach. Ice chests well-stocked with cans of beer were strung along the sandbar. It was an informal, no-host celebration, and the party-goers congregated in noisy clusters on the sand.

Some had already paired off and moved with blankets to the shadowy privacy provided by the cottonwoods and dense growth of willows that rimmed the sandbar. A few muscular, he-man types, John noted, splashed and yelled in the Skeeter's cool waters. It was evident they had already indulged themselves on too much booze.

Red leaped out and moved to the trunk of the car. "Boy, oh boy, oh boy. Ain't we gonna have a blast tonight! Come on, help me with this cooler."

John joined Red at the rear of the car, then shook his head resignedly as his friend opened it to display his treasure. He not only had the cooler bulging to the brim with booze, but he had three or four cases of beer in reserve, ready to fill the ice-jammed chest when supplies got low. "You going to drink all that yourself?" John asked.

Red snatched out a beer, deftly opened it and proceeded to pour the contents down his throat. He belched and grinned with satisfaction, wiping his mouth with his forearm. "Hell, no Prof," he said, "I got a free beer for everybody. This is old Red's farewell party. It's one for the road from old Red." He yanked out another can, "Here, Prof, for you . . . Let's drink to the Beavers."

John waved it away and said, "No, thanks, I'm not thirsty."

Red's brow wrinkled, and his lower lip slid out in a pout. "Aw, come on, Prof, you ain't gonna screw up everybody's fun tonight."

John shook his head disgustedly and accepted the can. He opened it, then hoisted it ceremoniously in the air. "To the Eager Beavers," he said softly and took a sip of the cold beer. This one would last him the night.

After they had lugged the cooler and extra cases down to

the beach, Red was quickly off to make his presence known. John watched with only half-interest as Red moved from one group to another, rendering his seemingly infinite repertoire of crude greetings as he went, interjecting a dirty story when a lull in the conversation gave him the chance—sometimes even when it did not.

Poor Red. Always working for the laugh. A born clown. But no one ever laughed. Not *with* him anyway. *At* him, maybe, sometimes.

John's eyes moved to the soothing motion of the Skeeter's waters, and he stood pensively gazing at the river, hypnotized by the low murmur of the slow, rolling water. Red was a pathetic soul, he thought. No one liked him very much—too obnoxious, too obscene for most who had any sense of propriety. Even with the Beavers, he had always been something of a tagalong, who had held a status comparable to a nonvoting member of a society who paid his dues but otherwise whose presence was accepted with no more than cool tolerance.

Suddenly, John felt a twinge of guilt. Red always affected him that way. Still, he suspected Red had an instinct for feeding on that guilt, forcing himself into John's company when John preferred otherwise. That was the way it had been tonight. Red had pleaded and cajoled when he dropped by John's home earlier. He called up memories of the good old days and insisted John come along this one last time. Red did not like to be alone and John had the feeling that his presence gave Red something to hang on to, a mooring for security.

Red had been alone ever since the Beavers started breaking up. For a while, John had had RaeLyn and of course, there were other interests and opportunities that presented themselves like so many gratuities from heaven to the class valedictorian. And, he had his books. Hell, he didn't have anything going this summer, though—a summer job to make some money before college started. A lot of reading. He vowed that he would spend some time with Red before he went away to school in the fall.

"A penny for your thoughts," a soft, feminine voice came from behind him.

He turned to see Sarah Remington walking slowly, tentatively, toward him as if she were afraid he might turn upon her like an angry bear. "Hi, Sarah," he said. "How's it going?"

She sipped at the beer in her hand and shrugged. "Not so bad, I guess. Want some company?"

He moved toward her, "Yeah, sure." His eyes moved unavoidably to the firm, round grapefruits that threatened to burst from her bikini top. She was short, but not quite plump. Someday, she would be fat like her mother. But now she was any red-blooded American male's stereotype of well-stacked.

"Let's walk," she said.

"Okay."

They walked lackadaisically along the river's edge, away from the chaos that was beginning to envelop the beach. John kicked at the sand with his tennis-shoe covered feet and Sarah let the saltlike grains work up between her toes. There was an awkward, gnawing silence between them, begging to be broken.

Finally John said, "It's been a long time since I've seen you any place without Sherm."

"You just don't get out much anymore," she answered. "Sherm and I haven't been together since you and RaeLyn were at his house that night."

"I see."

"We never were a regular thing . . . never went steady or anything like that. Sherm's not the kind of guy to stick with one girl. I pity the woman he marries. You know Sherm."

"Yeah, I know Sherm." He was silent a moment. "But you like Sherm, don't you?"

She finished off her beer and flipped the can onto the sand, then reached out and took the can from his hand. "Don't drink much, do you."

No, I don't care for it really."

I don't either, but I drink it anyway. I've only had one;

I'll finish yours." She took another swig of beer. "Yeah, I like Sherm. It's more than like I guess." She turned her head toward John, looking up at him with big, sad eyes. "You're nice Prof. You won't say anything, will you?"

"No."

"Well, the truth is, I'm crazy about him. I love him more than anything. I'd do anything for him . . . and I guess I have done about anything." Her voice cracked, and tears trickled down her cheeks. "But he doesn't care, Prof. He doesn't give a damn about me. I'm just a plaything, another broad to . . . to . . . screw."

He did not know what to say, so he took her hand and squeezed it gently, and they continued walking. A few minutes later, Sarah said, "He did it to RaeLyn that night, didn't he? I saw them come out of his bedroom upstairs after you left. Sherm had that look—like the cat that ate the canary. I could tell. They were screwing up there, weren't they?"

"I don't know," he lied.

"I think you know, but you won't say. And you and RaeLyn broke up after that. Some of the girls said Sherm was bragging about it, too, like he was proud of it."

"Sherm's always had a big mouth."

"You're telling me. John, like I said, I did see RaeLyn when she came out. She was in tears, and she didn't have any use for Sherm then. Sherm was going to take her home, but she wouldn't go with him. She ran out of the house . . . walked home, I guess. John, for what it's worth, RaeLyn's not that kind of girl. Whatever happened, she didn't mean for it to . . . it just did. And I don't think she's been out with anybody since. Maybe you should try to understand."

"It doesn't matter," he said, "it's over."

"You guys are all a bunch of hypocrites . . . every damn one of you. I always thought you might be different, Prof, but you're not. You expect your girl to be a virgin, to save herself, just for you. You've got to be the only guy in her life. But no, the guy, he can tomcat around with every girl he gets his hands on. That's okay . . . that's no excuse for a girl to drop him."

"You're probably right," he said wryly, "but I don't want to talk about it."

They had wandered some distance away from the others now, and when he looked back he could barely make out the flickering campfire flames that looked like tiny birthday candles against the blackness of the night. They paused at the water's edge, John taking a few steps backward as a gentle breeze swept across the river and sent water lapping like a miniature tidal wave onto the beach, saturating his canvas shoes.

"Been swimming yet?" Sarah asked. "The water's warm for this time of the year."

"Didn't bring my swimming suit."

"Go skinny dipping," she teased.

"I'm shy."

"You like to swim?"

"That's my sport."

"Let's both go skinny dipping," she said.

"You're kidding."

"No, I'm not." She started upstream. "I'll just walk up here a ways; it's dark. I won't infringe upon your modesty." She scurried away before he could respond, untying her bikini strings as she went. She did not go so far, however, that kept him from seeing the tantalizing silhouette released from its skimpy bonds.

She was in the water, swimming easily against the current and reached midstream before he even pulled his shirt off. "Come on in," she called.

He kicked off his shoes and slipped out of his jeans and, a few moments later, splashed into the water. He breast-stroked away from the shore, permitting himself to drift downstream a respectable distance from Sarah.

"Come on up this way," she taunted. "Scared of me?"

"No, just enjoying the water."

Except for a few holes that could be treacherous to an unskilled swimmer, the Skeeter was a shallow river, and its waters barely reached Sarah's breasts as she stood in the channel. Suddenly, she squealed and flipped over as though her feet had been pulled out from under her. She came bobbing toward John like a piece of driftwood caught up in the river's current. "Help!" she yelled as she approached, struggling and floundering with her arms as she tried to regain her balance.

Reflexively, John took a few strokes in her direction, then stopped and extended his hand. She reached out and grabbed the hand, drawing herself to him in an effort to pull herself upright and, upon reaching him, flung her arms around his neck for support.

Suddenly, all he could think of was the soft, naked flesh that hugged his own nude body. The river's flow gushed between them, pushing her away momentarily. Then she pulled frantically at his neck. He lost his footing and feared for a moment the river was going to lift them both into its current and sweep them down to the spot where their classmates frolicked. But he pulled back and pressed his feet hard into the sandy river bottom, bracing his legs against the current. He wrapped his arms around her waist, anchoring there as the water swept around them. He laughed, all at once abandoning his melancholy, casting away his self-consciousness. "You're safe now, my dear," he said. "Not even a giant could tear you away from these mighty arms."

She giggled and let her legs float up around his thighs before they locked around him. As her soft mound brushed against his own genitals, a fire swept through his loins. He pulled her tighter against him, pressing his tumescence against her supple body, squeezing her water-slick, full breasts against his chest. She clung to him, willingly, boldly, and when their lips touched he could not say whether it was he or she who had made the first move. He was riding a tide of spontaneity, responding instinctively and without resistance to what his body demanded of him.

"Prof," she whispered, urgency in her tone, "let's go back to the beach."

Clinging to each other, they half-swam, half-crawled to the river bank. She fell down, her back flat against the sand.

John leaned over her and then hesitated. She guessed this was his first time and reached up and pulled him to her, then moved one hand to his engorged organ and guided it home.

He copulated eagerly and excitedly with this demon-girl, who reared and bucked like a rodeo horse, digging her fingernails into his back, gasping out encouragement between their violent thrusts. "Keep it up, keep it up, Prof. Slower . . . slower . . ." Then she squealed and shivered, arching her back and driving her hips upward with full force. It was more than he could stand. He ejaculated before he realized he was ready to come.

"Oh, God," she said as she fell back against her sandy bed, "just hold it a minute, we'll go again."

But he felt himself going limp. The fire was dying just as quickly as it had been ignited. Now he was consumed by a hodgepodge of emotions that ran from guilt to embarrassment. They slipped apart and rolled away. He lay beside her for a spell, not daring to meet her eyes.

"Prof," she said softly, "I could go again. How about you?"

"I don't think so," he mumbled.

"I never guessed it was your first time," she said. "You mean you and RaeLyn never . . .? Oh, I see. Wouldn't Sherm have cats if he knew what we just did?"

John turned his head slowly and looked at her with bewilderment. "You mean you did this just to spite Sherm?"

She turned toward him and threw her arms across his chest. "Of course not . . . I did it because I wanted to. I like you, Prof. I like you a lot . . . And I like doing this . . . if not with Sherm, then with somebody else. And you were good, Prof. And I was ripe for tonight. It's that time of month."

Oh, God, did she mean what he thought she meant? What if? No, it was unthinkable.

As if she had read his mind she said, "Don't worry, Prof, I'm on the pill. Sherm took me to a doctor in Omaha. You know Sherm, he plans ahead. I always thought it would be funny if I didn't take them and he got me pregnant. But I know he wouldn't marry me. I could have an abortion or a bastard . . . he'd give me my choice. He'd probably pay for the abortion, but not the bastard."

Whether she realized it or not, John thought, she was spiting Sherm. God, this whole thing was crazy. His first time should have been passionate and tender with someone he really cared for—RaeLyn. Now that it was over, he could not say that screwing Sarah had given him any more satisfaction than masturbating in the bathroom.

He got up and moved to find his clothes. "What's the matter, Prof?" Sarah asked. "Didn't you like it? You queer or something?" He shot her a killing look, but it was too dark for her to see it.

Then a terrifying scream echoed through the night, sending shivers racing down John's spine. It was followed quickly by a scatttering of other screams from the main body of seniors downstream. The first sounds had been female, but now masculine voices joined in the pandemonium. Several shouted loudly as though trying to be heard above the increasing din. The pitches of the voices, something about their intensity, signaled that something tragic was unfolding.

Hurriedly pulling up his pants and slipping into his tennis shoes, John snatched up his shirt and took off in the direction of the noisy melee. Sarah sat up, still naked, "Where are you going?" she asked, but he did not answer. "Prof," Sarah called, "it's dark here . . . don't leave me alone . . . you good-for-nothing bastard!"

But he was gone, charging frantically along the sandbar that bounded the river. Approaching the scene of the party, he saw his classmates lined along the river's bank, looking out into the dark waters. The noise was dying down, although several girls still screamed hysterically. Most of the observers just stared in stunned silence. A few others called unintelligible instructions to several swimmers who were diving beneath the river's surface. The divers emerged periodically for air, then shook their heads negatively and arched back into the water.

John recognized Sambo's powerful neck and shoulders rising from the river and, kicking off his shoes, dashed into the water toward him.

"Sambo, what happened?" As he neared, he could hear Sambo's labored breathing. When his friend answered, John could tell he was on the verge of tears.

"It's Red! I saw him horsing around on the other side of the river. He looked like he stepped off into a hole—just stepped out of sight. I checked. There's a deep one, all right. I couldn't reach the bottom . . . it's never been there before. It must have washed out with the last flood. There's some driftwood above it a ways; it seems to make sort of a whirlpool near the hole."

"But Red can swim . . . he's a good swimmer."

"Prof, he was so tanked up he could hardly walk, let alone swim. He was getting nasty as hell. You know how he is when he's had too much."

"You're looking in the wrong place," John said, reaching into the water where he stood knee-deep and pulling off his tennis shoes. "The current would have carried him downstream." After tossing the shoes and his heavy, sopping trousers to one of the boys standing closer to shore, he dived in, letting the current do most of the work as it carried him some forty yards downstream. Sambo and another swimmer followed. When John thought they had gone far enough, he called, "Work your way back upstream. If he's gone any further, we don't have a chance of finding him anyway."

Depending upon the water's depth, they swam or trudged their way upstream, John searching the far side, where the treacherous hole had been. He was inching his way toward a grotesquely-twisted island of driftwood when he saw it— the slender white arm with the lifeless, bent hand sticking out from the debris, bouncing in the water like a springy willow branch. His stomach turned and he swallowed hard, fighting to hold back the vomit that tried to spill from his throat. "Over here!" he yelled. He swam with rapid, powerful strokes around the debris so he could come at it from upstream and move into the pocket where the river's victim had been trapped. The body was just dislogding from its precarious location when he got there. He wrapped his arm around Red's slender waist, anchoring him there so that the river could not reclaim the corpse. He had never touched a dead person before, but he knew instantly that Red was beyond help. They were on no rescue mission; it was an act of retrieval.

And still, there had to be hope. He could not wait for the others. With strength he did not know he had, he forced the body from the water, slinging it like a sack of grain over the trunk of one of the trees that had captured it. He pulled himself up on the slippery timber and began pressing forcefully and rhythmically on Red's back, desperately seeking some response, some faint sign of life.

"Christ, he's dead. He knew there were holes in this damn river . . . he shouldn't have been out there in his condition. Oh, Jesus, why didn't I stay with him?" John thought. "He shouldn't have been alone tonight—he needed me and I was up the river, screwing Sarah Remington."

He began pounding on Red's rib cage. "Red! God damn it," he yelled, "wake up! Come on, you can make it . . . you can't die. Red! You scrawny son-of-a-bitch . . . don't die on us. Red, you're not even trying! . . . Oh, God."

"Prof, he's dead," came Sambo's voice. "It's too late; we can't do anything for him."

John looked down to see Sambo and Art Timmerman looking at him, wide-eyed and glum, chest-deep in the Skeeter's muddy waters. "Art," John said, "get across the river. Send somebody for the sheriff; tell them to get hold of an ambulance."

"You going to wait for help?" Art asked.

"No, Sambo and I will bring him across . . . it's our job."

Art glided back into the river and swam toward the body of silent spectators who could barely make out the dark outlines of the swimmers downstream, but could see enough to guess what they had found there.

"Ready, Sambo?" John asked. "I'm going to let him down."

"Go ahead, Prof."

John wedged his hands beneath Red's armpits and lifted the body upward before letting the limp form slide feet-first into the water. Sambo took hold of the body there, holding it steady while John slipped back into the river. Then they flipped the body on its back, each grabbing one side beneath the armpit. Without so much as a word, like an experienced team of horses, they began the exhausting pull upstream and across the river.

By the time they dragged Red's body upon the beach, it was almost deserted, virtually all evidence of the illegal beer party having been erased like chalk marks on a blackboard. The fires had been extinguished, the beer cans gathered up and a mass evacuation accomplished so efficiently it would have made the county civil defense director drool with envy.

Art Timmerman was waiting for them when they got there. "Jess Rafferty went to the farm down the road to call for help," Art said. "You can see everybody else is getting the hell out of here. The sheriff will probably be here pretty quick."

The last remnants of the party-goers were pulling out, and a few minutes later only Art, John, Sambo and Connie remained to keep a silent vigil by Red's body until the authorities arrived.

"John," Connie said, pointing to a spot on the sandbar some twenty feet upstream, "your clothes are up there. So are Sambo's."

Suddenly realizing he was clad only in wet, clingy, now almost-transparent jockey shorts, John nodded and headed up the sandbar to get dressed. Sambo followed.

They heard the mournful wail of the sirens long before they were blinded by the flashing lights of the ambulance that roared out of the timber and onto the sandy beach. It was followed by two cars decorated with the sheriff's five-star emblem.

The ambulance attendants confirmed what John and Sambo already knew. Patrick Murphy was dead. He had been long before he emerged from the water. Quickly and expertly, the attendants put the frail, white corpse on a stretcher. It was a macabre scene, but, for some reason the reality of Red's death did not strike home until the white sheet was pulled over his freckled face and the stretcher-bearers lifted the body and slid it impersonally into the ambulance.

Sheriff Jake Meyer, who had watched silently up to this point, told the ambulance driver, "Take him to Schonberg Memorial. I imagine the County Attorney will want an autopsy just to confirm things."

Then, as the ambulance pulled slowly away, the stocky, white-haired officer turned to the teenagers. "Okay, what happened, kids?"

The others looked at John. "He stepped into a hole," John said.

"Yeah," Sambo interjected. "He just disappeared all at once. We dived for him . . . tried to help him . . . but we didn't find him again until later, when Prof saw him in a pile of driftwood downriver."

"Could he swim?"

"Yes," John said.

"The river's running slow and shallow right now. A good swimmer should have had no trouble."

"Yeah," said John, "I don't know what happened."

"Had he been drinking?" asked the sheriff.

Sambo looked at John, and the latter shrugged.

"Okay, kids, my deputies have been checking out the beach, but I can read what happened here without their help. You aren't going to tell me that you kids made all those tracks here on the beach . . . or that you needed three or four fires to keep warm on a night like this."

"No," John said, "there were others, but they left."

"Well, John," the sheriff said, "I won't ask you for their names now; we'll wait and see what comes of this. You boys pull him in?"

"Yes," John said, "he was our friend."

"It wasn't a very happy experience, was it?" said the sheriff.

"No, sir," answered John.

"Well, kids," said the sheriff, "I'm going to let you go, but I may want to talk to you again. I'd just like you to think about something else. I suppose that boy had nobody to blame but himself for what happened here tonight, but I know his family. Rozella Murphy's a widow, and this young man was her only child. I've got to go break the news to her in a little bit. Think about that."

The sheriff shook his head resignedly and made his way to the car. A few minutes later, with sirens quiet and flashing lights extinguished, the sheriff's vehicles moved in tandem away from the beach.

"Well, I guess I'll be going," Art said.

"Yeah," John said, "thanks a lot, Art. I appreciate your helping us and staying with us."

"Prof," Sambo said, "what about Red's car? You going to take it back?"

"Not now," John said. "We'll wait till tomorrow. I'll check with Red's family or the Sheriff."

"You can ride back with me and Connie."

"Yeah, okay."

"It's not going to be the same without old Red around is it, Prof?" Sambo said as he wrapped his arm around Connie's shoulders and started down the beach toward the car.

"No, Sambo, nothing ever stays the same."

15

He was in front of the store when he saw her. His instinct was to veer sharply toward the street, in pretense of pursuing some pressing errand on the other side, but that would be too obvious. He caught sight of the nervous smile that crossed her lips when she spied him as she leisurely window-shopped her way up the sidewalk toward him. He waved a timid greeting.

It was mid-July. He had not seen her all summer. He had been working at the Klein Feedlots since graduation, from six in the morning till seven or eight at night. This was one of those rare afternoons off, when he escaped from the ever-present odor of sweat, sour grain and fermenting manure.

He had heard RaeLyn was working as a lifeguard at the Schonberg Municipal Pool. She looked it. Her skin was baked to the color of strong tea and her hair sun-bleached like fresh, golden wheat. God, she was something, one of those striking, poised girls, who could not walk down the street unnoticed.

She wore pale yellow shorts, comfortably snug, but not skin-tight. The neckline of her white tank-top revealed just enough of her bare flesh to stimulate the imagination, yet discreetly covered the cleavage of her bosom. The garments were sexy on her long, willowy limbs, and still, by modern standards, they were well within the bounds of discriminating taste.

He had showered and shaved before embarking on his stroll downtown, but suddenly he fretted he had not showered away the lingering cattle smell that had been with him since taking on his summer job.

"Hi, John," RaeLyn said, coming up to him, taking his hand as though there had never been a rift between them. Then, sensing his uneasiness, she quickly released it.

"Hi, RaeLyn," he said. "I hear you're working at the pool this summer."

"Yeah, I like it. It's a nice change from school, and I've always spent my summers cooped up before, working in Dad's office, reading, things like that. This keeps me outdoors . . . gives me exercise . . . all that good stuff. You know." She stepped back, put her hands on her hips and cocked her head to one side, studying him. She smiled.

God, it was heaven to see those big brown eyes again . . . and that mischievous glint was back.

"You've been working hard," she said matter-of-factly. "Lost some weight, muscled up."

"Yeah, a little, I guess," he said, basking in the warmth of her approval. "I've been working at Klein's."

"Oh, that *is* work they tell me. Like it?"

"Like the money, not the work. It'll be a big help with college. Scholarships still don't take care of clothes and all the extras." Then he smiled back and shrugged, "It also makes a guy more determined to get an education; I'll say that."

She nodded but gave him no indication she planned to respond. She also did not appear inclined to move on after their exchange of pleasantries.

"What are you up to?" John asked.

"Just window shopping," she said. "I'm off this afternoon; I've got evening guard duty."

"You must shop like my mother," he said, "never buy, just look."

"Looking's a big part of the fun," she said, "and I buy sometimes. So does your mother. You just don't understand the art."

"I don't think I want to. Uh . . . I'm off this afternoon, too. First weekday afternoon in a month. Would you . . . uh . . . like a Coke? It's a scorcher this afternoon, and I'm thirsty as heck myself."

"I'd like one," she answered without hesitation.

"Let's go over to Doc's."

In his spare time, when Doc Sedgewick was not on scoutmaster duty with Schonberg's reknowned Troop 2, he had to make a living like other people. He was the pharmacist and proprietor of Sedgewick Drug, a modern pharmacy that had a single similarity to its counterpart of an earlier era—a bonafide soda fountain adjoined by a scattering of old-fashioned, circular, wrought-iron tables and matching chairs. The fountain area was not a money-maker, but Doc maintained a little section of his store as a respectable hangout for Schonberg's "good kids," as he called them.

"Hey, Prof!" Doc called from behind the prescription counter as they entered. "How's it going?"

"Pretty good, Doc."

The gray-haired man behind the counter had a healthy tan that belied his indoor occupation. Deep creases lined his cheeks and forehead, and his lean, erect body appeared too young for the weathered face that went with it. His translucent eyes twinkled. He winked at John. "Long time, no see, the two of you. We've got to celebrate. Drinks are on the house today."

"Drinks were on the house the last time we were here."

"Nothing's too good for my Eagles."

Doc's Eagle Scouts had a special place in his heart, and he made no bones about it. He had a special place in John's too. He would have to tell Doc that sometime, let him know how much he appreciated everything he had done for him.

A pert, green-eyed girl brought the Cokes to their table. She hesitated awkwardly, and her face flushed. "Uh, Prof," she said.

He looked up at the girl, "You're Sambo's little sister, aren't you?"

"Judy. I'll be a freshman this fall."

"I'm sorry. You're not a little sister anymore. Any normal American male ought to see that."

"She blushed. "Uh, Doc wanted me to tell you something."

"I should have known; he usually has a price for these 'free' Cokes. What's the message?"

"Well, I don't know what he's talking about, but he says don't forget Alexander Pope."

"Alexander Pope? Oh . . . ." He shook his head in understanding. "Tell him I'll try not to. Thanks, Judy." The girl scurried away.

"What was that all about?" RaeLyn asked, her eyes searching his.

He wished he did not have to look at them; they evoked too many memories, forced him to remember what they had been to each other, made him think of what might have been. "You've heard of Alexander Pope, I presume."

She feigned insult, "No, I never heard of the English poet, the one who wrote 'The Rape of the Lock' and 'An Essay on Criticism.' I've never heard of the man who gave us 'to err is human; to forgive divine.' "

Ouch. He had forgotten that one. He left himself open for that. She knew it, too. She had not spoken sarcastically, but her face had an impish look and she was not unaware of the implications of her words.

"You always were a show-off," he teased.

"You're evading my question," she said.

"Well, Alexander Pope wrote some other thing, too. Doc's kind of an intellectual in his own way—reads a lot. In the scout troop, when some of the guys would get out of line, he would give them a piece of paper with some poetry or some famous lines of prose on it, then send them off to their tents to memorize it. They couldn't join the group again until they were ready to recite the words to the troop. Worked pretty well, too. If you're out hiking and camping, you don't like spending your time memorizing boring phrases."

"What does that have to do with Alexander Pope?"

"Doc always said I had too much pride. I guess I was stubborn. If I had an argument with somebody, even if I was wrong, I couldn't bring myself to apologize or take the initiative to patch things up." He expected her to say something, but she did not, although she was attentive, her face serious now. "Anyway, Sherm and I had a knock-down, drag-out fight one afternoon. We weren't very old . . . it wasn't long after we both got into scouts. I whipped Sherm, but worse yet, I said things that really hurt him. I don't even remember what they were now. Anyway, he ran off to his tent, crying, stayed there most of the afternoon and wouldn't come out for supper. Doc tactfully suggested I go talk to him and tell him I was sorry. I told him I wasn't—that Sherm was the one who should apologize. Doc pointed out that once the fight was over, it didn't make any difference . . . that Sherm was my friend, and when friends are involved you put pride aside once in a while. I still didn't go talk to Sherm, so Doc went back into his tent and dug into his little notebook and brought me one of his sheets of paper. He told me to memorize it before I thought about getting supper. It was the only time Doc ever gave me one of those sheets; for some reason, I never did forget what was on it. I guess it was because he made me repeat it every once in a while as the years went on. Before the evening was up, I apologized to Sherm, and we made peace."

"You haven't told me what the verse was. Do you still know it?"

"Yeah, it went like this . . . 'Of all the causes which conspire to blind man's erring judgement and misguide the mind, what the weak head with strongest bias rules is pride, the never failing vice of fools.' Doc was trying to tell me something just now."

"About us?"

"I think so."

"John, about that night at Sherm's. You know, we never

talked about that. In fact, we never talked at all until today. When you saw me in the hall at school, and I know you did, you always turned your head. I guess maybe I did too. I was so ashamed, I didn't think I could ever look you in the eye again." Their eyes locked now. "But I can."

"There really wasn't anything to talk about . . . and you don't owe me any explanations."

"You're right, I probably don't, but I'd like to explain. John, it was the only time. There was nobody before, nobody since. I'm not blaming Sherm . . . he didn't rape me. And I'm not sure that what happened was wrong in itself. It was my disloyalty to you that made it cheap. I may have had too much beer, and I guess I was in one of those rotten, impulsive spells of mine, like the time with the snowmobile. I always pay the price for it, too," she added. "Anyway, I'm not making excuses, I just wanted you to know. It didn't have anything to do with the way I felt about you . . . or about Sherm, for that matter."

"I said you don't owe me any explanations."

"No, but like I say, I wanted you to have one . . . after what we meant to each other. But you never gave me a chance. You've avoided me like the plague ever since. John, can you ever forgive what happened?"

"I can forgive, all right. I'm not mad or bitter—at least I don't think so—I just can't forget it."

"Nothing stays the same, John. You always said that."

That phrase was beginning to sound like a broken record in his life.

She reached across the table and took his hand. He savored her touch and almost spilled out the words to heal their breach. Instead, he pulled his hand slowly away.

"At least you'll be free to go with other guys. I'll be going away to school this fall; it wouldn't be good for you to be tied down to one guy anyway."

"It depends on the guy," she said. Her eyes were moist with tears that threatened to break loose. "John, remember when we were going together, and you would tell me that you loved me, and I would never really answer . . . not the way you wanted me to? I could never say it the way you could. I'm going to swallow my own pride now. I loved you then—I love you now."

God, she melted him with those words. His resistance was fading fast. "I loved you then," he said.

"What do you feel for me now?" she asked.

"I don't know . . . I just don't know." But he did know. Now he was the one who could not say it.

She sensed his discomfort, for she forced a smile and turned blithely to another subject. "Are you still headed for the University of Missouri?"

"Yeah, still journalism school."

"When do you leave?"

"Another month."

"I see. They're supposed to have a great school."

"Yeah," he said. "that's why I'm going there."

"Still want to write books?"

"Someday. But I'll have to find a way to make a living first. Don't have the money to just hole up somewhere and start writing."

"You will, though. I know you will."

"I think so, but we've got two successful people at this table. You'll go places, too."

"I know."

They sat there silently, toying with their glasses, neither seeking out the other's eyes. Then RaeLyn raised her eyes. "John, I just want to say one more thing about that night, then I'll never mention it again. I don't know why, but for some reason I was trying to spite you. Maybe I was trying to deny what I felt for you. I told you, I still feel those things, John. I know how you feel about trust and loyalty—you just can't overlook what you see as a betrayal. It can't ever be the same between us, John, but just because it can't be the same, doesn't mean it can't be good . . . maybe even better than it was before. But I can see we're not going to wipe it all away today. I just want you to know this, John—if you ever need a friend, I'll be there. You can count on it. And you can trust me. That's all I have to say. Can't we at least be friends?"

"Sure," he muttered, "we can be friends, but . . . but . . . I don't know, I just don't know what to say right now about anything else."

"Let's just give it time," she said, "and see what happens. I'd be glad to see you anytime you want to see me. If you write from school, I'll write back." She glanced at her watch and started to rise. "I've got to go. I have to pick Mom up at the beauty parlor." She brightened and smiled. "I'll see you around, okay? Thanks for the Coke. I'm glad we got to talk."

"Yeah, I'll see you around," he said.

As he watched her walk out the door, a voice called out from behind, "Blew it, didn't you, Prof?"

He turned in his chair and looked up to see Doc with a disgusted expression on his face, looking sternly down at him. "Yeah, I guess I did, Doc."

"Tripping on your own pride again, aren't you?"

"I suppose," he said glumly.

"She's a good one, Prof, and you're right for each other. You know what Pope said?"

"Yeah, I know . . . 'pride is the vice of fools.' "

Walking the eight blocks home, he was oblivious to the scorching sun that cooked his back and forced out the sweat that soaked his shirt. He could think only of his meeting with RaeLyn. Damn, he was just getting used to the idea of life without her. Then she had to screw up everything by meeting him downtown. He could not deny it. The magic was still there. How he had missed their evenings together, their closeness, the love they had shared! Intellectually, he could accept what had happened that night at Sherm's; he understood the frailty of the human race and had always found it relatively easy to overlook the mistakes of others. That night with Sarah—had that been any different? He did not love the girl he had tumbled with—but he had not been going with RaeLyn then. He had not broken any trust.

Hell, who was he kidding? He was holding RaeLyn to a double standard. He would let things cool another week or so, make sure of his feelings, but he was certain he wanted to be with her again. It was that simple.

16

John tried to call RaeLyn several times before he went away to college that summer, but no one answered the telephone at her home. Finally, he drove by the swimming pool where she had worked in an attempt to contact her there. He was told by one of the other lifeguards that RaeLyn had flown to Phoenix with her parents to be with her critically ill grandfather. She had called the pool manager and resigned her job, indicating her family would not return for a month or more.

John abandoned his attempts to reach RaeLyn after that. He would write her after he went away to school. But the young man who proposed to make his living as a writer never wrote to RaeLyn, and when he returned for midterm break that winter, he learned that RaeLyn's father had decided to take charge of his own ailing father's wholesale business in Phoenix. He obtained RaeLyn's address from Connie Hanson, who had corresponded with RaeLyn several times since the move to Arizona, most recently a month previously to inform RaeLyn about hers and Sambo's nine-pound baby boy. He misplaced the slip with the address on it before he returned to school, however. Before he had the chance to get the address from Connie again, he met another girl.

Like himself, she was a freshman at the University of Missouri and, like him, she resided in one of the campus dormitories. She was nearby and tangible; RaeLyn was 1500 miles away. She was a lovely memory from his past. But he could not see her, could not touch her. While he would not forget her, he learned he could live without her.

PART 2

1978–1979

17

"Pea-brained kid," she muttered to herself as she rolled over and squinted at the digital clock on her bedstand. Only 6:30, and Saturday morning, too. She could have slept till noon. What did the kid have against her? Monday through Friday he quietly placed the newspaper beside the door of her townhouse apartment. Saturdays and Sundays he slammed it against the door with a resounding crash. Earthquake McGoon she had dubbed him sardonically. She was spooky about earthquakes ever since she had moved to Los Angeles and ridden out her first tremor. She speculated that this was the reason the loud thunk of the newspaper always jolted her awake.

She cast a sideways glance at Federico Castro, sprawled limply on the other side of her king-size bed. He lay face-up, one arm tossed back against the pillow, his face tilted slightly toward hers. The heavy black mustache that shrouded his upper lip, the smooth olive-tinted skin—he looked like a stereotypical Latin lover, she thought. His performance in bed qualified, too, she admitted. Her eyes traveled down the black, curly mat that blanketed his slender, but muscular chest. The white satin sheet was draped over his lower extremities, but just below his waist, the flimsy cloth arched upward, rising like a circus tent over the rigid pole beneath. If his smug smile had left any doubt, the healthiness of his erection confirmed Federico's dream.

Goosebumps erupted around the nipples of her firm breasts at the sight of the maleness that stirred beneath the sheet. She was suddenly aware of the onset of the soft pulsating between her own thighs. She toyed with the thought of flipping back the sheets, mounting that long slender rod and attacking him like a tigress. Just then, he rolled over on his side and curled up like a baby nestled in its mother's womb. Something about his movement doused the smoldering fire of her passion. She sat up and slipped quietly out of bed.

She tiptoed through the rich, luxuriant carpet and went into the bathroom. She emerged shortly after a soapy, hot shower, feeling relaxed and refreshed. She pulled a pair of skimpy panties over her slender hips and encased her breasts, that were perhaps a bit too large for one so slender, in a white, tricot bra. Without so much as tossing on a robe, she walked to the outer apartment door, opened it and peeked out to see if the coast was clear. She winced when the bright sun already piercing through the smog struck her eyes and blinded her. Then, seeing no one and spotting the newspaper some three feet out on the concrete veranda, she snatched it up and darted back into the apartment.

She perched herself on one of the huge pillows that were scattered helter-skelter about the living area. Pulling her legs under her Indian-style, she slipped the rubber band off the rolled newspaper and shook it open. Then she scanned the large, black headlines that broke the grayness of the front page.

"RaeLyn," came a masculine voice from the bedroom.

"Out here, Freddie. I got the paper."

"Hey, it's Saturday," he protested. "Come back to bed."

"What for?"

"What do you mean, what for? You know what the hell for."

"Take a cold shower, Freddie. I'll be there in fifteen minutes."

Freddie was starting to get too demanding, she thought. For the last six months, he had been spending most weekends and an occasional weeknight at her apartment. Suddenly, she wondered what their relationship was all about. What did they have in common? Where were they going?

They were both lawyers, very junior associates with the gargantuan firm of Howe & Lowenstein. What else? She smiled to herself: they both liked to fuck—especially each other. That was about it. They rarely ate out, seldom went to movies or plays together. She went alone to things like that. They danced only occasionally. It was a shallow relationship at best, but there could be worse things than two young, vibrant people finding pleasure in each other's body.

She was tiring of Freddie, though, and she suspected his own eyes were wandering, looking now for something different. No, a lifetime commitment was the farthest thing from either of their minds.

She flipped the newspaper quickly, running through the financial pages, passing up the sports section, then taking a quick gander at the obscure back pages, which usually featured brief reports from around the country. Ordinarily, she was alert for some news item from Nebraska. She had spent the first seventeen years of her life there and, after graduation from Pepperdine Law School, had returned to her home state and had associated with the Howe & Lowenstein Omaha branch office. A few months after passing the Nebraska bar exams, she was offered a promotion which necessitated her moving to the Los Angeles home office. She was ambitious and jumped at the chance. But she was still Nebraskan to the bone; that's where her roots were sunk.

Of course, she rarely picked up anything about her home state. Nebraska did not give birth to many news-making, national crises. But today there *was* news from home. Her eyes fastened on the tiny, 12 point headline above a one-column story not more than three or four inches long: GOVERNOR UNDER SEIGE; KEY AIDE TO TESTIFY. The story was datelined Lincoln, Nebraska. She read on:

> "Nebraska Governor Clarke Heywood's administrative assistant has been subpoenaed to testify before the state legislature's Special Inquiry Committee on Tuesday. John Armstrong, who served as the Governor's campaign manager during the Heywood election effort, has been a key Heywood advisor, and last summer was tapped as Chief of Staff in the scandal-racked administration. So far, Armstrong has not been implicated in any of the sundry bribery-kickback charges leveled against Heywood and key appointees. According to one unidentified state senator, Armstrong 'knows where the bodies are buried.' The legislative committee's announcement that Armstrong had been subpoenaed was followed immediately by a statement from the Governor's office that a citizens' committee calling itself 'Friends of Heywood' has been formed for the purpose of establishing a legal-defense fund for the besieged Governor and his associates. A source close to the Governor speculated that an announcement would be forthcoming of the retention of the California-based firm of Howe & Lowenstein as legal counsel for the committee."

Slowly, deliberately, she folded the paper and placed it on the floor beside her. It wasn't her John Armstrong. No, it couldn't be.

Who was she kidding? It *was* her John Armstrong. Connie Hanson had dropped her a note with a Christmas card several year ago. John was involved in some political campaign. He was happily married and had a child, Connie had written. She remembered the card well, because it had come on the heels of her divorce from Hal Weston, an aspiring actor. She had been struck at that time by the divergent courses that hers and John's lives had taken.

An unexpected melancholy had come over her after Connie's letter, but she was convinced that that chapter of her life was behind her. She had gone on to other things. Not that she had forgotten John—one probably never entirely shakes off the residue of first love, she guessed. John still entered her thoughts occasionally, but briefly, and she found life interesting and fun—good enough for now anyway.

"Rae," called Federico, "it's been fifteen minutes and twenty seconds. You going to get your ass in here?"

"Go to hell."

Freddie appeared at the bedroom door, his semi-erect phallus swaying in front of his dark, lithe body like a supple tree branch in a wicked gale. "Hey, what's with you?"

"Poor Federico," she chided, "spoiled rotten . . . just like a sultan with his harem—clap, clap, the naked beauties run to his bed."

"What's got into you?" he asked, noticing her serene-looking, cross-legged position on the pillow. "You into yoga now or something?"

"No, just reading."

"Well, I mean, don't you want to?"

"Wow, talk about a command performance."

He looked affectionately at the prized instrument between his legs. "You've demanded more than old Pedro here could give more than once."

She smiled patronizingly at him, like a mother catering to her small child. She sprang up from the floor and walked toward him seductively, swaying her hips just enough to whet his lust. "My dear Federico," she cooed. She teasingly reached out to touch his granite-hard erection. "You men just can't conceal your passion, can you?"

He clasped his hands tightly on her firm buttocks and pulled her close. "Sometimes you're a sadistic bitch," he whispered in her ear.

"But you like me, don't you?" she answered softly.

"Uh, huh. Most of the time." He slipped his hands beneath her panties and worked them slowly down her thighs.

"Let's go back to bed," she said.

In reply, he hoisted her in his sinewy arms and carried her back into the bedroom. It was one of their quickies, but as usual, she came as quickly as he and, sleepily content now after their early morning love-making, they lolled leisurely on the large bed.

She stared dreamily at the ceiling. "Freddie, have you read anything about this political scandal in Nebraska . . . the one some governor's involved in?"

"I hadn't heard anything about it until yesterday. Scuttlebutt is the firm's been retained by some committee supporting the governor. Could be some fat fees."

It was not surprising that RaeLyn had not heard about it at the office. Some five hundred lawyers were associated with Howe & Lowenstein at its offices around the country; several hundred of these were engaged in the firm's Los Angeles home office. "Is Omaha handling everything?" she asked.

"They'll take care of most of the staffing, but Harper's flying out to take charge of the case. He got his start in Omaha, and he's admitted to the Nebraska bar . . . probably take a few from our office along for back up."

Harper was the showhorse of the firm's criminal division. He was a top-notch trial lawyer, with an instinct for the jugular. The productive years for a lawyer were supposed to be the ones from forty-five to sixty. Jarred Harper was forty-three and had been an acknowledged pro in his field since thirty. Good as he was, he was not necessarily the firm's most competent trial attorney, certainly not its most thorough one. But he had a tongue glazed with pure gold, and he had a flair for the flamboyant, a style that attracted reporters like firemen to a fire.

ReaLyn worked in tax and real estate, but she had encountered Harper a time or two. He had propositioned her once in the elevator of the firm's office building. He was handsome and trim, a man she found physically attractive. But he was also arrogant and aloof, and instinctively she had not liked him. She did not sleep with someone she did not like.

"You're in criminal," she said to Federico. "Is there a chance you'll be going to Lincoln?"

"Not much. I'm Harrison's chief errand-boy on the Carilla murder case. I don't speak Spanish; I suppose somebody did in my family five generations ago. But if we have a Spanish defendant, you know who gets in on the act."

"Do you think Harper would let me go?"

"Would he let you go? You're not in criminal."

"No, but I'm a member of the Nebraska bar . . . and I knew the governor's administrative assistant once . . . it might help."

"You slept with him?"

"Is that all you ever think about? No, I didn't sleep with him. We were . . . were close once . . . in high school."

"You never slept with him?"

"No."

"Wish you had?"

"Yes."

"I don't know if you could swing it or not. You might have a crack at it. All Harper needs from the L.A. office is a couple of coolies to run his errands, do some interviews, maybe a little research. On second thought, he likes to be surrounded by class. With your looks, you might pull it off. Do you have any scruples?"

"What do you mean?"

"Would you go to bed with him?"

"No, I don't think so. Not just to get a trip to Lincoln anyway."

"Would you let him think you might?"

"That's a tougher question; I'll have to think about that." She was silent for a few moments. "I've thought about it. I'd let him think I might."

"I'll get word to Harper this afternoon that you know everything there is to know about this administrative assistant. What's his name?"

"Armstrong. John Armstrong."

"Yeah. Well, I may have to stretch the truth a little. Harper's probably in the office today; you may have to go in and talk to him later. He'll probably fly to Omaha tomorrow evening."

"Freddie, you're a doll." She leaned over and kissed him warmly on the lips. "Oh, there's something else."

"What now?"

"I think it's about over for us."

"I thought so." He sighed. "What will I do now?"

"Exactly what you've been doing," she said, "only more of it. You think I don't know you've been screwing that new redhead in criminal on the sly? Federico, shame on you."

"You don't miss much, do you?"

"Not much, Freddie, but it's been fun."

"How about one last fuck for the road?" he asked and rolled toward her. She obliged enthusiastically.

18

"Flight 232 for Omaha now ready for boarding," the voice came over the public address system. RaeLyn was an old hand at flying by now, but there was something about an embarkment at L.A. International that always got her adrenalin pumping. She still felt like she was living out a childhood fantasy. She had read about the international set who flew from one place to another and lived lavishly on their expense accounts, tasting the different cultures of the nation and the world. Deep down, she knew these things never happened to real people—or at least she thought she knew it.

After four years at Howe & Lowenstein, inching her way up, snail-like from the bottom of the legal hierarchy, she quickly learned that some people did indeed live out a substantial portion of their lives in the air space above the nation. But for those who were not free and unattached, they and their families often paid a high price for the unparalleled glamor and financial rewards of such a life-style. She supposed that was why a bachelor like Harper could pursue his ambitions with such all-consuming desire and enthusiasm. As near as she knew, he had no other life to interfere. Neither did she right now, for that matter, but she doubted if she would live out her life that way. There was still too much Nebraska in her.

"Ready, sweetheart?" Harper asked, smiling confidently as he wrapped his arm around her shoulders. Discreetly, she slipped away and moved closer to Dave Stern, the young associate a few years her junior, who was also making the trip.

They entered the waiting area and walked briskly through the accordianlike tunnel that led into the vast belly of the jet, there to be lifted in a matter of a few hours to their destination—halfway across the country.

It had been easier than she anticipated. Federico must have felt he owed her something for the redhead; he had done a great selling job. She had been called to the Howe & Lowenstein office by Harper's private secretary Saturday afternoon. Later, she had met with Harper, who seemed only minimally interested in her legal qualifications, totally unconcerned about her lack of background in criminal law. She suffered slight twinges of guilt now, but none she could not endure.

She was only a nominal feminist. She had always demanded equality in the professional world and generally received it. She had been a brilliant student and would someday be an excellent lawyer. She was confident of that. Her ability and intelligence had always been enough to take her where she wanted. But this time she had compromised herself. She had been exceedingly friendly, probably flirtatious, with a man she didn't like. She had struck no bargains with the suave, smooth-tongued lawyer, but she could sense that he was a hunter, eager like some birddog for the pursuit. She had done nothing to discourage what was likely his notion that she was willing prey. Already she was sick of "sweetheart" this and "honey" that. She had a name and expected it to be used. She would demand it when the plane arrived in Omaha.

She cringed at the familiar, although sometimes amusing, way Harper pressed and probed her unwilling flesh with his hands. That, too, would stop. He doubtless thought he was being accompanied by an easy lay—primed and hot-to-trot as soon as they checked into the hotel. Well, they had reservations for separate rooms, and she intended to sleep in hers tonight. Alone.

This whole trip was silly, she thought. She and John Armstrong had had a severe case of puppy love. He had a family now, and she never played the role of homewrecker. She never would. Still, when she saw his name in the news story, she knew she had to go. There was no logic to it. He probably would not even remember her.

She was something of a mystic, however, and had learned to trust her instincts. It was strange that she had read the newspaper article that morning; stranger still that her own law firm should somehow be connected to John Armstrong. And it had been almost too easy for her to become part of the scenario. Coincidence? Probably. Nonetheless, she was impatient to find out what fate had in store after they made the short drive from Omaha to the capitol tomorrow morning.

19

RaeLyn looked out of the window of her fifth-story room in the new Omaha Hilton. It was nearly 10:00 and it was dark, but the multi-colored flashing neon lights and the well-lit streets unveiled an excellent view into the heart of downtown Omaha. When she talked about her Nebraska roots with her sophisticated Los Angeles friends, they raised their eyebrows and, with a look of incredulity, shifted their voices to a condescending tone. They listened politely enough, all right, but their questions and their responses always left her with the feeling that, despite her fair hair and skin, she was under suspicion of being a refugee from a Sioux Indian village. Certainly no sophisticated person ever rose from the plains of Nebraska. She would inform her friends then that Johnny Carson was a native son of the state, that Henry Fonda was an Omahan and then go on to recite her roster of other famous Nebraskans. Statistically, she would point out, Nebraska and other so-called backward, Midwestern states, dwarfed all of the others, especially those on either coast, in the per capita production of noted political figures, business executives, writers, professional men and others who might be considered movers of the nation.

If only her disbelieving friends could see Omaha tonight. It was decidedly not the manure-rank cow town her disbelieving friends envisioned. It was a city on the move. Signs of new construction and renovating were everywhere. Magnificent new structures, housing financial institutions and offices, were rapidly displacing the old, worn-out buildings that had been constructed before the turn of the century. Some blocks west was an enormous, indoor shopping center claimed by local enthusiasts to be the largest of its kind in the world.

No, Omaha was as twentieth century as anything she had seen. Still, its builders had accomplished this without total obliteration of the genuineness and the rugged individualism that were characteristic of the farmers and ranchers who, in the last analysis, were still the city's lifeblood. And there was no smog.

There were several sharp raps at her door. They had an authoritative sound, and she knew it must be Harper. She turned and walked to her bed to pick up the sheer dressing gown draped across it. Damn, it would barely cover her bikini pajamas, and they were black satin, yet. She had brought nightclothes more appropriate to a weekend orgy than a business trip, and Harper did not need that kind of encouragement. He had all the signs of a stud on the make at dinner this evening—patronizing son-of-a-bitch.

She opened the door without fastening the safety latch. She was aware of her oversight after it was too late. Fortunately, it was Harper, as she had guessed, and she was hardly in a position to keep him out. "Hello, Jarred," she said coolly.

"May I come in, RaeLyn?" he asked.

She hesitated. "Well, I was just getting ready for bed."

"I need to get some background from you before we meet with Governor Heywood and this assistant of his tomorrow. We haven't had a chance to discuss the case much."

"Okay," she said, "come in." She recalled that she had tried to bring up the subject on the flight out, but he had put her off with some abruptness, saying there would be plenty of time to review the details later. He did not have his briefcase or legal pad with him, she noted.

He took one of the stuffed chairs near the coffee table, and she took the other, feeling suddenly naked when she caught his narrow eyes brazenly studying her figure.

"Mind if I smoke?" he asked as he pressed a cigarette to his lips and flicked on the flame of his lighter.

"No, go ahead." She did mind, but she did not care to make an issue of it.

He leaned back and inhaled deeply, then exhaled, sending a cloud of acrid smoke toward RaeLyn's face. She turned her head slightly away, letting her tear ducts soothe the burn. "You said you wanted to talk about the meeting tomorrow, Jarred."

He put his fist to his mouth and coughed. Then he unveiled a broad, disarming smile. "That's right, I did say that, didn't I? Yes, I guess so . . . unless you have a better idea, sweetheart," he said meaningfully.

"My name's RaeLyn; you can call me Rae, if you like. But I would rather you didn't call me sweetheart." She caught a sudden, almost imperceptible angry glint in his eyes, but his smile could have been chiseled in granite.

"Sure . . . uh . . . RaeLyn. Anything you say; I was just being friendly."

"Now, about the Heywood case," she said, "what would you like to know?"

"According to your friend Castro, you know this assistant of the governor's—his chief of staff. Uh . . . what's his name?"

"John Armstrong. Yes, I know him. Perhaps I should say I *knew* him. We were in school together—it's been a long time."

Harper's face turned serious and attentive. She was relieved to see his mind had indeed shifted to business. He had that innate ability of instant concentration, so typical of truly competent lawyers she had known, a knack of moving from one subject to another and back again with little interference with the chain of thought.

"He seems to be the key to Heywood's future," Harper said. "He evidently knows more about running the governor's office than the governor does himself. Heywood delegated a lot of responsibility to this guy; he seemed to be able to handle it. Heywood's a better politician than administrator, so he concentrated on the politics of the job. You know, the speeches, social schedule, contacts with the party, that sort of thing. As near as we can tell, the administration's been run as efficient as hell. Where they got their balls in a ringer was on the political end. Maybe your friend Armstrong should have handled that, too. Anyway, he's close to the governor. Probably knows more than is good for Heywood's health. We'll find that out tomorrow. But I'd like to know more about this boy genius before we get there."

"I'll tell you all I can," she said. "Like I say, it's been a few years."

"Okay, our job's to save Heywood's skin. That's what we're here for. The people we're looking for don't care what happens to his hatchetmen—including this chief of staff. According to our contact here, though, Heywood's very protective of this man Armstrong, trusts him implicitly. He doesn't want him to be a scapegoat although, with his nearness to the governor, he's the logical one to play that role."

Now she remembered why she had gravitated to tax and real estate specialties. Criminal law always had a sickening side, and already she was receiving bad vibrations about this case. "I didn't think we came here to find a scapegoat," she said. "I thought we were here to defend the governor."

"This is politics we're in right now, sweetheart . . . uh, RaeLyn. Law has very little to do with the guilt or innocence of a politician who's involved. Public opinion makes the law. Any crimes directly attributable to the governor are probably trivial, the type of thing a prosecutor would laugh at if commited by an ordinary citizen. You're talking about politicians versus politicians here, not the law versus the governor. The best bet for our side is to make it politically inexpedient for Heywood's political opposition to scream for prosecution. The best way we can do that is to blame somebody else."

"It doesn't sound very honorable."

"I didn't say it was. Now, about this Armstrong. I need to know something. There's a dozen or more payoff and bribery allegations against the governor. Most of them are nickel-and-dime things, irresponsible charges that can easily be put down as politically motivated. There's one that has substance, though. It involves a purchase of a couple million dollars worth of sophisticated computer equipment by the state tax commissioner's office some months back. The department advertised for bids as the law required, but it happened that the specifications approved personally by the tax commissioner could be met by only one company . . . and the president of that company happened to be the top contributor to the governor's campaign. The tax commissioner resigned because of the turmoil, but so far he's stonewalling it. Bets are though, that he'll crack, especially if he's offered immunity from prosecution. But the real rub is that the president of the company is a childhood chum of your Mr. Armstrong. The press just pounced on that tidbit last week, and now the focus has been switched from the governor to Armstrong. Interesting, huh?"

With a sense of foreboding, she asked him, "The president of this company, what's his name?"

"It's Rein . . . something."

"Reinwald. Sherm Reinwald," she said, "of Reinwald Electronics, Inc."

"Yeah, that's it. How did you know?"

"My father use to be executive vice president of the company. I knew Sherm Reinwald, too."

Harper snuffed his cigarette in the ashtray and reached for another. "Say, you might just be a little gold mine of information. What about these birds? Let's take Armstrong; is he honest?"

"Yes."

He squinted, looking at her suspiciously. "You seem awfully certain of yourself. How long has it been since you last saw him?"

"Ten or twelve years."

"People change in that time."

"Some do," she said. "I doubt if he has . . . not in that way."

"I have a feeling this Armstrong is more than just an old friend."

"He was a boyfriend of mine; we were serious once, but things didn't work out. We haven't been in touch all these years."

"Well, I can't give much weight to your opinion about some high school boyfriend. That bastard Juarez, or whatever his name is, sure as hell misled me about your background on this case."

"His name is Castro, and I'm sure he didn't intentionally mislead you. I told him that I knew John Armstrong very well . . . I didn't say how long ago."

"All right, let's say Armstrong hasn't changed all that much. I'll swallow that with a grain of salt. What if the governor is involved in this scandal? If Armstrong's an honest man, I suppose he'll tell the investigating committee everything he knows, even if it incriminates the Governor."

"That depends."

"Depends on what?"

"How he feels about the governor."

"In what way?"

"The John Armstrong I knew was an extremely loyal person. If a friend or someone who trusted him was involved, he'd stick by them through anything . . . even if it meant his own disgrace or serious punishment for himself. I know, I've seen him do it. In fact this whole thing makes me feel like I'm reliving a part of my past."

"This guy sounds like some boy scout."

"As a matter of fact, he was, literally. I'm just saying that, if he's the same John Armstrong, he won't act like most people would under pressure. He'll probably follow his conscience. That doesn't necessarily mean he'll do what's right or moral; he'll do what he *thinks* is right, and he'll be tenacious as a bulldog once he decides what he is going to do." She smiled faintly. "And if he doesn't go the way you want, Jarred, you'll hate his guts."

"I don't want to hear any more about this saint of yours," Harper said. "You're blinded by your teenage romance and, frankly, I don't think I can take anything you've said at face value. What about Reinwald; can you do any better there?"

"He's no good."

"Jesus. You sound like a woman scorned."

"Not quite, but I remember Sherm Reinwald. I don't see him as any more likely to change than John. They were both young men with very predictable patterns of behavior, and those patterns were deeply ingrained—even in high school."

"Okay, so what about Reinwald? I gather you think he's a prick. Why?"

"He'd pimp for his mother, if he thought he could make a buck . . . sell her into white slavery. Not that he's ever needed the money, and I doubt he does now. With him, it's all just a game. See how many guys you can screw and how bad you can screw them." She smiled wistfully as she thought of the irony of her choice of words. "Jarred, this guy stole teachers' copies of exams in high school, then sold them to his classmates. He was willing to let a good friend take the rap for what he did. He's amoral." Yes, she remembered, that's what John had said about Sherm. It had been a matter-of-fact observation made uncritically. John had always been slow to judge—too slow.

"I take it you see this Reinwald as a likely candidate for a scandal like this?"

"Yes."

"But you don't think Armstrong would be involved."

"I'd bet on it."

"Don't bet too much, honey. I've got a hunch your friend Armstrong's going to be everybody's top candidate before long." She glared at him with smoldering eyes, her lips tight. "Pardon me. RaeLyn, I mean." He glanced at his watch. "We'll talk about this more on the way to Lincoln tomorrow; we've had enough business for tonight." He looked at her, smiled lecherously and bent forward to squeeze her knee as he snuffed out his second cigarette.

She stood up and moved away. "I don't like to be pawed," she said coldly.

His smile faded. He looked at her uncomprehendingly, as though it were unthinkable anyone would treat the great Jarred Harper so rudely. "Most women don't find me unattractive," he said.

"I'm not most women."

"Aw, come on now, a doll like you. Don't tell me you don't fuck."

"I don't think that's any of your business. I'm an attorney for Howe & Lowenstein, and I'm here to handle any legal assignment you want. But I'm not a whore for the senior partners."

His face flushed. He rose from his chair. "Look, lady, I didn't say that. I checked you out before I came; you're tagged as one of the promising juniors. They say you're damned good for a woman."

"I'm damned good for anybody," she said evenly. "And now, if you'll excuse me, I want to go to bed . . . alone."

He stalked silently to the door, slamming it harshly as he went out. She snapped the safety latch in place and breathed a sigh of relief. Arrogant son-of-a-bitch. A woman was a piece of ass to him, nothing else. A lousy, fucking machine.

She was here for a visit back home. She'd carry the water bucket for the captain of the team. More than that, Harper would see to it. It suddenly occurred to her that Harper carried a lot of weight with the other senior partners; she might not have a job when she got back to L.A. Oh, well, she'd been having reservations about the slow climb up the corporate ladder anyway. Association with a small firm where her tax know-how would be welcome, or putting out her own shingle—those notions had become more intriguing in recent weeks. Of course, her father would welcome her back to Phoenix as general counsel for his own company.

But why hadn't she gone to bed with Harper? Even now, she found the idea titillating, interesting. He was an attractive man. She suspected he'd be pretty good at sex, like he was at most things he took on. She didn't think of herself as promiscuous, but she did enjoy the sheer physical aspects of sexual relations and did not think herself above a good-time fuck. On the other hand, she had known only three men intimately—four, if she counted Sherm. One was her ex-husband, who bailed out because he was intimidated by her ambition but whom she still looked upon with some fondness. The other two were long-term lovers, who had not been intimidated and whom she was also very fond of. None had been casual, one-night stands. None, except Sherm, had used her. Their contracts had been for the duration of mutual satisfaction. Neither she nor her ex-husband, much as they had used the term, had ever grasped the meaning of the word love. It had not even been used in connection with her other relationships.

A life-long commitment with one man? Right now, she doubted it. Children? Yes, something from deep inside told her this was a fulfillment she desired, but not without at least a reasonable prospect of carrying off that lifetime commitment with the man who fathered them.

No, if Harper had been a different kind of man, she might have welcomed his nearness in her bed tonight, but he was not a different kind of man.

She slipped beneath the sheets and switched off the bedside lamp. Sleep came almost as soon as her head sank into the pillow.

20

RaeLyn had been mildly shocked when they finally met in the conference room of the Howe & Lowenstein Omaha office. Out of the blue, Harper informed her that she would accompany him to Lincoln for a meeting with the governor. Dave would stay behind and organize the support team for the governor's defense and see that the research got into high gear. She had seen the disappointment in Dave's eyes at being passed over and she could imagine what he was thinking, how he would conclude she had earned the trip.

They had departed from the Omaha office in a rental car about 10:30. Harper even trusted her to drive. The trip to Lincoln from Omaha via the interstate was less than an hour's drive, but after fighting downtown traffic in Lincoln, they made it to the capitol only minutes before their 12:30 luncheon engagement with the governor.

Harper had treated her with deference on the trip to Lincoln. She suspected he was switching his tactics, trying another approach. She was doubtless something to be conquered now. Still, she hoped she was not deluding herself that she sensed a grudging respect for her in his manner. During their drive, she was not surprised to learn she had been selected for the trip for reasons other than her superior legal talents.

"I know Dave's disappointed," Harper had said, "but he's got a background in criminal. You're not qualified to set up a criminal trial and research team. Besides, I planned to talk to the governor alone, but he refused to meet with me unless this guy Armstrong's present. In light of your background, I thought your presence might provide a little spice for our encounter."

She felt him studying her face as he talked, and he apparently noted the tautness there at the mention of the prospect of a meeting with the governor and John Armstrong.

"Jesus, you don't still have the hots for that guy, do you? You were a teeny-bopper back then."

"No, but I might be on a nostalgia trip. We were close once. But he's got his life, and I've got mine. I doubt if we have anything in common anymore. I'm curious."

"That's understandable. I hope you're not disappointed."

There had been sincerity in Harper's tone that she found halfway likeable. But was it all an act? Trial lawyers were notoriously good actors, and she was still wary of the man.

They were seated now in the governor's wood-paneled office on the main floor of the state's capitol building. The Tower of the Plains, it had been appropriately dubbed. Governor Heywood leaned back comfortably in his high-backed chair, seeming larger than life with the American flag on one side of his desk, the blue and gold medallioned Nebraska flag on the other side and the Great Nebraska Seal emblazoned on the wall behind him. Slender and erect, she estimated his age in the early fifties, but he had a full, thick head of white hair that made him seem older. He also had an honest face that would surely come off well on television. Doubtless, his campaign staff had pushed the man's charismatic policies in that medium.

"We'll be going to the mansion for lunch," the governor said. "If it's all right with you, Mr. Harper, we'll talk business there."

"That's fine," Harper said. "I assume Mr. Armstrong

will be coming."

"Yes, he's to meet us there. He's tied up at the tax commissioner's office downstairs right now. He's talking to some of the staff people about the Reinwald specs. You know about them, I assume?"

"Yes, from what our Omaha people tell me, that's your big problem, Governor. If we can handle this one, the other charges will probably fade away."

"John and I will tell you everything we know . . . I promise you that," the governor said, "but you're going to find we know very little." He turned to RaeLyn. "Miss Hunter, when I talked to Mr. Harper this morning, he said you were an old friend of John's. He suggested that I not tell John you were coming, so I'm sure we're going to have a very pleasant surprise for my chief of staff shortly."

"I hope it's a pleasant one," she said. "We knew each other in high school, so it's been a long time. He may not even remember me."

"Well, I, for one, am delighted you are here. It's time for John to be with some young ladies again. I hope he has as good taste as I think he does."

The governor was not making any sense, but she thought it unseemly to press for an explanation.

The governor rose. "Now, let's see what Liz has for lunch."

The governor's mansion was across the street, south of the capitol building. It was a warm, mid-May day. The governor peeled off his coat and flung it over his arm as they emerged from the capitol and headed down the steps on the way to the magnificent red-brick mansion that was framed by budding trees and blooming flowers.

Spring in Nebraska. She had forgotten how sweet and how fresh it smelled. For the better part of the past ten years, she had lived in places seemingly without seasons; Nebraska had four of them, each distinct, each unmistakably having a character of its own. She missed that.

"Hello, Clark," said a middle-aged man to the governor as they passed on the sidewalk that fringed the capitol grounds.

"Hi, Jersey," answered Heywood. "How's everything going?"

"Just great."

It was like that all the way to the mansion door, the governor calling greetings, half of the respondents calling him by his first name. He had no body guards, no uniformed officers escorting him to the mansion. He might have been any John Q. Citizen on his way home for lunch. This, too, was Nebraska.

At the door they were met not by a maid, but by the state's first lady. The governor's wife, Elizabeth—Liz, she asked RaeLyn to call her—was gracious and charming, a naturally cheerful lady, it seemed to RaeLyn, who would have been just as happy, probably more so, if she were still hosting barbecues on the couple's Sand Hills ranch.

Mrs. Heywood's face was lined by too many years of exposure to the baking sun, but although significantly shorter than RaeLyn, she had a hard, trim figure that most women twenty years younger would envy, and her long, sable hair had a natural, wholesome sheen to it. RaeLyn liked her instantly. She hoped that Liz's husband would weather the storm unscathed.

"John's waiting in the dining room," Liz said as she led them down the hall. "I haven't told him about our surprise guest. I'm so glad you came, Miss Hunter. We think so much of John, and he's been so lonely these days."

Mrs. Heywood acted like she was playing the role of matchmaker, but John was married and had a family. Still, Mrs. Heywood would be the last person in the world to promote an inappropriate relationship, RaeLyn thought.

When they entered the dining room, John had his back to them, his hands clasped behind him, his eyes fixed on some activity outside the window. "John," Elizabeth Heywood said, "we have a guest today we think you'll be pleased to see."

John turned around to greet his luncheon companions. His eyes settled on RaeLyn, widening in disbelief when he recognized her.

"Hello, John," she said, moving toward him and extending her hand. "It's been a long time."

"Rae," he said, accepting her hand and holding it lingeringly. "I don't believe it."

He responded with that same shy smile, the one she remembered so well. He *was* glad to see her.

Suddenly, it was like their first meeting again, the night of the school mixer. There was the same emotional atmosphere, the unexplainable feeling of anticipation.

"Miss Hunter's one of our attorneys, John," the governor interjected. "She'll be assisting Mr. Harper here."

John turned to the sharp-featured, fashionably dressed man whose intent eyes were studying him appraisingly. "Nice to meet you, Mr. Harper. We're glad to have you on our side. You have a reputation for being one of the best."

Harper took John's hand in a firm grip. Neither man smiled, RaeLyn noticed, and they seemed to eye each other warily. After they released their grip, she sensed there was a reciprocal, instinctive dislike between the two men.

"Won't you all be seated?" Mrs. Heywood said, breaking the chill.

Mrs. Heywood sensed it, too, RaeLyn thought.

In what appeared to be a contrived departure from protocol, RaeLyn was seated at John's right at the long dining room table, with Mrs. Heywood next to RaeLyn at one end, the governor next to John at the other. Harper sat across the table from John, where he could easily converse with the governor and his chief of staff.

As they were being served their luncheon, which featured a tantalizing array of salads, RaeLyn surveyed the gold-hued room that, with its cool formality, had little of the first lady's personality. She was especially fascinated by a small but ornate alcove in which was displayed an elegant, silver punchbowl with candelabras rising from each side.

She cast a furtive glance at John. They had exchanged a few pleasantries, but there was an awkwardness between them, and he seemed relieved to respond to an inquiry the governor had made. He was still trim and his manner much the same as she remembered—intense, deferential, genuine—but there was a tired, almost defeated look in his eyes. His face had the pallid, haggard appearance of a man who worked hard and spent too many hours indoors. Dark circles under his eyes gave further evidence of fatigue; she thought she even detected a few flecks of gray in his wiry, sandy hair.

The governor turned to Harper. "I have to be back in the office for an appointment at 2:00, Mr. Harper, so perhaps we should get down to business. Maybe we can discuss this while we eat; Liz and I have no secrets, and John can hear anything I have to say . . . so fire away."

"All right, Governor," Harper said, "but I would like to point out, especially for Mr. Armstrong's benefit, that I'm retained by the Friends of Heywood Committee, and my instructions are to do anything to help you. Your interests could, at some point, conflict with Mr. Armstrong's. He may want his own legal counsel before this is finished."

"I doubt that John and I will ever have any conflicting interests in this case," Heywood said, "and I may insist that the committee employ your firm to represent John, also. I can't expect him to face financial ruin simply because he took a job in my administration."

Harper was stone-faced but shot a sharp glance at John. "Very well, Governor, that's between you and the Committee. As long as we don't see a conflict of interest, we can represent whoever the Committee authorizes us to. Now, I've been pretty well briefed by our Omaha staff about the charges that have been made against your administration. I understand that the legislative committee meeting tomorrow is limited to the allegations about the revenue department's computer systems. I've already told you that I think that's where your greatest vulnerability lies. Now, so far you haven't been subpoenaed, and our people are checking the legislature's statutory and constitutional authority to do this. If it gets to the courts, there's no question about subpoena power. In any case, there are going to be three witnesses—

your former tax commissioner, Logan Harlowe; Sherman Reinwald of Reinwald Electronics; and, of course, Mr. Armstrong here. The accusations are simple—Reinwald bribed you, your tax commissioner and Armstrong to see that specifications for the computer systems were drafted in a way that only Reinwald Electronics could satisfy. Regardless of how it came about, the facts are indisputable that Reinwald was the only firm whose product could meet the specs. . .and the company ended up with the contracts.

"Now, gentlemen, regardless of the political implications here, we're talking about felonies. You can end up in your state penitentiary or federal prison for this sort of thing."

"I'll take the federal prison, if you don't mind," Heywood said wryly.

Harper was unamused. "I'm serious, Governor. We have a double standard in this country that works out much differently than the average citizen thinks. Joe Blow assumes the politicians get off easy; in fact, our courts bend over backwards to show impartiality. Judges seem to feel an obligation to make examples out of politicians. Private citizens might get six months probation and a fine on a federal bribery charge; a governor and his chief of staff might do a few years jail time on top of the fine. Yes, there's a double standard, but it works just the opposite of what most people think . . . and political figures get the public disgrace and ridicule on top of it."

Governor Heywood was grim now. "You can spare us further details, Mr. Harper."

"All right. All I want is the truth. If you tell me you're guilty, that doesn't change my position at all; it's still my job to defend you, and I'll do everything I can. Now, Governor, suppose you tell me where you fit into this—what you knew, when you knew it—that sort of thing."

Heywood lifted his napkin from his lap, folding it neatly before he placed it on the table. "I was approached by Harlowe six or eight months back when the revenue department was working up the specifications for the new computer system. He and Reinwald were friends; Harlowe had been with the C.P.A. firm that handled the Reinwald Electronics account before he joined the tax commissioner's office. Reinwald was a big contributor to our campaign; I respected his ability and financial know-how. He was the one who suggested Harlowe's name as a prospect for state tax commissioner. John and Harlowe never hit it off very well. For some reason John, here, has never cared much for Reinwald, even though I know they were schoolmates. Anyway, Harlowe told me that Reinwald Electronics had the best computer system, but if our specifications were too general, Reinwald couldn't compete pricewise with other firms . . . not within thousands of dollars. He convinced me that over the next five years the Reinwald computer would save the state millions of dollars. The initial cost would be infinitesimal in comparison to the long-term savings to be achieved by the Reinwald's system. I have since made some inquiries on my own and found that, while Harlowe probably over-stated the virtues of the Reinwald computers, the system was still the best buy for the taxpayers of the state."

"What about the bribery allegations?"

"There was no mention of money. I authorized Harlowe to proceed with the restrictive specifications; I gave final approval when they were returned to me a few weeks later, although I'll admit I don't understand a damn thing about computers. It's all just a bunch of hocus-pocus to me. In retrospect, I can see I handled it stupidly. I should have obtained advice from someone other than Harlowe; I should have talked to John here. But I didn't, and I'll admit quite frankly that my judgment was clouded by the fact that Reinwald was involved. Subconsciously, I'm sure, I was not unaware all he had done for my campaign, but I had never had any prior agreements with the man. Any communication I had with him during this period of time was through Harlowe. Anyway, the revenue department advertised for bids. There were two other bidders besides Reinwald, although Harlowe said they were courtesy bids well above the Reinwald figure. I can see now it was probably something Reinwald worked out to make the bid-letting look respectable. Everybody seemed happy enough until someone, probably another computer company, complained to a reporter at the *World Herald*. Then, if you'll excuse the expression, the shit hit the fan."

"What about Harlowe? Do you think some money crossed palms? What's he going to do?"

"I can answer that," John interrupted. "Harlowe's been on Reinwald's payroll from the beginning. The tax commissioner's job has been a well-paid hobby for him. I've checked in the secretary of states' office; the corporation division there has checked the annual occupation tax filings. Those records show that Harlowe's on the board of directors of at least three corporations controlled by Sherman Reinwald. Of course, he's not on the board of Reinwald Electronics, so there's probably no technical conflict of interest, but it certainly raises ethical questions . . . And what will he do? He'll perjure himself to save his own neck without the bat of an eye."

"Did he resign voluntarily?" Harper asked.

"No," the governor said, "I gave him the choice of resigning or being fired. I should have fired him. He has greater credibility, having resigned. He's already announced that he couldn't, with clear conscience, stay with our corrupt administration."

"When he testifies before the legislature tomorrow, what's he going to say?"

"My guess," John said, "is that he'll say the specifications were dictated by the governor's office; that he will admit he was guilty of gross oversight in not studying them more closely, but that he had nothing to do with the development of the plans."

"Can you find someone in the revenue department who was close enough to the situation to refute that?"

"I'm working on that," said John, "but Harlowe hired his top two or three assistants personally. They'll probably be resigning soon, and they, no doubt, know where their bread is buttered."

"Okay," said Harper, "let's assume you're right about Harlowe, and he tries to cast all the blame on the governor. That still doesn't get Reinwald off the hook. If Harlowe was on his payroll like you say, it doesn't fit. Reinwald's subpoenaed. I assume he'll have something to say about this. What's his position?"

"He hasn't said a word so far," John said. "I tried to talk to him; he's in town. . .but he's not available. But I've known Sherm Reinwald a long time. He's got things figured out, you can count on that. And when the dust is settled, the odds are Sherm won't be hurting too bad. I can't figure out what he's going to do. . .what he's going to say. The truth won't get in his way, though."

"You and RaeLyn seem to have the same opinion of this guy. I'll bet there's an interesting story behind that," Harper said meaningfully. "I'd sure like to get next to this bird, get some inkling as to what he's up to. If I take what you gentlemen tell me at face value, there may have been a political crime or two on the governor's part, but nothing criminal in the legal sense."

RaeLyn had remained silent, absorbing the meaning of what the conversation's participants had been saying, sorting out the possibilities in light of what she knew. "Jarred," she said, "I think Sherm Reinwald would talk to me."

Harper looked at her, his eyebrows lifting in mild surprise. "You really think so?"

"Yes, there's a good chance. . .no, I'd say an excellent chance, if he's still the same Sherm Reinwald I knew." She cast a quick glance at John, whose face was impassive.

"Well," Harper said, "there's no ethical problem with you talking to him. We're not adverse parties at this point; he's just another witness who has been subpoenaed by the legislature. It might be worth a try. I should be back at the Omaha office by 4:00; maybe I'd better stake you out in Lincoln. I should have had you bring your things."

"She'll stay here at the mansion with us. I'm sure we can find some things to see her through to tomorrow," said Mrs. Heywood.

"Thank you, Mrs. Heywood, I'd love to stay."

"Liz," Mrs. Heywood reminded her. "You'll be very welcome here."

"Why don't you call the Omaha Hilton and let them know someone will be picking up your things?" Harper said. "Then you can call our office and have them send someone out to get your clothes together. I'll bring them back here tomorrow. I guess you're elected to be our capitol contact."

Why had Harper changed his attitude toward her so quickly, she wondered? Then it occurred to her, why not? She was in a unique position to gather information usable to the defense. Besides, she sensed that the governor and Mrs. Heywood liked her. She and John were old acquaintances; she could be helpful to Jarred Harper here, and he was too smart not to see that. This man was no paper tiger; he had an astute, keen mind and an enviable ability to make objective, dispassionate decisions in behalf of his clients. She felt now that his judgment was that she was a competent lawyer who could make a worthwhile contribution to his client's cause. . .not just a potential bed partner who came along for the circus.

Harper turned to the governor again. "Governor, what's the political climate over at the legislature? Does your party have a majority on the investigating committee?"

"I presume you're aware of Nebraska's legislative set-up, Mr. Harper. We have a unicameral legislature, you know."

"Yes, I'm aware of that. The only one-house legislature in the country, as near as I know."

"And we have the added distinction of being a non-partisan body. Of course, I use the words 'non-partisan' advisedly."

"Yes," John said cynically, "I call it the Nebraska Non-Partisan Partisan Legislature. The senators are elected without political designation on the ballot, but I assure you that all but a few belong to a political party. And, on the five-man investigating committee, we have only two of our party members. To make things worse, two of the opposition party members covet Governor Heywood's job—Senator Grayson and Senator Stolski—they're both headline grabbers."

"Will the Senators vote the party line on a motion to censure or impeach?" Harper asked.

"It's hard to say. In addition to an unofficial political division in our so-called non-partisan legislature, we have a geographical division segmented into roughly three voting blocks—Omaha, Lincoln and outstate. Governor Heywood's from our ranching country, of course—outstate. Two of the committee senators are from Omaha, two from Lincoln, one from Broken Bow—outstate."

"You don't paint a very optimistic picture."

"No, I guess not, but this business has turned me into a pessimist. The governor calls me his doomsayer." John took a drink of his iced tea, then leaned forward on the dining room table, casting his eyes downward as though he were studying the still half-full plate. There was an uncomfortable silence.

"Well, Governor," Harper said, "I'll be meeting with our Omaha people this afternoon. I'll probably be in touch by telephone later today. I'll need to meet with you and Mr. Armstrong at length tomorrow morning, so I would appreciate it if you would clear your calendar. I think Mr. Armstong's testimony is scheduled last. My guess is he won't be on for several days, maybe a week, so we should have some time to firm up our position. At least we'll have a chance to find out what your former friends are going to say before Armstrong takes the stand." He looked at John. "Frankly, Mr. Armstrong, you're something of an enigma to me. Your only involvement seems to be after the fact, but I have a gut feeling you're going to be more important in this case than we can even conceive right now. I can see you've got a special relationship with the governor, and you have these past ties to Reinwald. I'm not giving you a clean bill of health and, in any case, I think the press and the committee's going to make it hot for you. What if the tide starts to go against the governor, starts to take him down, maybe starts to take you with him . . . are you going to be joining up with Harlowe and Reinwald?"

John glared at the lawyer. "I resent your question, Mr. Harper, but if you have to have an answer, the answer is no. I'll go down with the governor."

"We'll see," said Harper dubiously. "We'll see." Harper rose from the table. "It was a fine lunch, Mrs. Heywood. You're a gracious hostess."

"Thank you, Mr. Harper," said Mrs. Heywood. "I'm certain we'll enjoy your company again before you leave Nebraska."

"Governor Heywood," Harper said, extending his hand as the governor stood, "I'll be in touch."

21

RaeLyn sat on a claw-footed divan in the living room of the governor's mansion, waiting for Mrs. Heywood to return with the coffee pot. Earlier, the governor's wife had shown RaeLyn to her luxurious room on the second floor of the mansion, pointed out the telephone and left her to pursue the arrangements for a meeting with Sherm Reinwald. Mrs. Heywood had left with the parting admonition, however, that RaeLyn was expected downstairs for coffee at three. Liz obviously had some things of her own to say.

John's departure after lunch had been as perfunctory as his greeting. "It was nice to see you again, RaeLyn," he said, and she responded, "Nice to see you, John." Such an original dialogue. There had been no hint of their one-time closeness, no warmth. Still she knew he was not displeased to see her. There was something she could not quite put her finger on. It was as if he were covered by a camouflage and she would have to tear it aside to find out what lay hidden beneath. Whoops, cut your curiosity short, she reprimanded herself. John Armstrong has his own life; you have yours. Keep it that way; do your job.

Her telephone conversation with Sherm went well. She might have been talking to the Sherman Reinwald of ten years ago. "RaeLyn Hunter! Jesus, great to hear from you . . . you'd like to see me? Sure . . . privately? How about dinner at my apartment, say sevenish? We'll talk over old times."

She felt a bit devious for not having informed Sherm of her mission. On the other hand, she was dealing with Sherman Reinwald. When in Rome . . .

Mrs. Heywood entered the room, placing an ornate sterling silver tea service on the coffee table. She took a place beside RaeLyn and offered her some of the hors d'oeuvres from the half-filled tray.

"Thank you, Mrs. Heywood," RaeLyn said. "You're going to think I'm terrible; I have an enormous appetite."

"Liz," Mrs. Heywood smiled. "We're going to be friends, I think. And eat all you want. You're probably one of those persons that the Good Lord unfairly blessed with the capacity to eat without converting calories into pounds. Unfortunately, I'm not. I have to work like sin to hold my weight. But so much for small talk. RaeLyn, I want to help you any way I can, and I have a feeling we can talk."

"I think so, too, Mrs. Hey . . . Liz . . . and I think my main job right now is to learn about the people involved in this thing, get a feel for them, so we can gauge how they might react if certain developments take place. A law professor I had at Pepperdine said a good lawyer is half psychiatrist. I think that's true. We have to always remember we're dealing with people. And if we don't understand them, we're going to make poor judgments. I intend to learn more about Mr. Reinwald this evening."

"You've contacted him, then?"

"Yes."

"I'm surprised he would see you."

She shrugged; her lips parted in a sheepish smile. "I guess I was less than honest with Sherm . . . he doesn't know I'm with Howe & Lowenstein. I'm afraid he thinks our little rendezvous has other possibilities."

Mrs. Heywood smiled knowingly. "I gather you and Sherm Reinwald were more than just speaking acquaintances in your high school days."

"Yes and no," RaeLyn said. "No one was ever close to Sherman Reinwald in the real sense. But I knew him, knew what kind of person he was. He was John's worst enemy, although John never recognized it—or maybe I should say, never admitted it. He always put up with Sherm's little games, and he always got burned in the process. It's ironic that ten years later Sherm's playing the same role."

"Speaking of John," the governor's wife said, "I think he's the one we both really want to talk about."

"Why do you say that?"

"I saw your eyes when you met John this noon; you looked like a teenage girl seeing her first love."

Had she been that transparent? RaeLyn eyed Mrs. Heywood warily. No, the petite lady meant her no harm.

"You're probably not far from wrong," RaeLyn admitted. "John was my first love, and I was his."

Softly, understandingly, Mrs. Heywood said, "I thought as much. Don't worry, John didn't see what was in your eyes any more than you saw what was in his. Mr. Harper probably saw it; that man doesn't miss much. But I have a feeling you don't care what Mr. Harper thinks—professionally, maybe, but not personally."

"You don't miss much either," RaeLyn said. "But what did you see in John's eyes?"

"Beneath the sadness, I saw a young man who suddenly caught a glimpse of life again."

"But why the sadness? I saw that, too. I know that the present crisis must put terrible pressure on your husband and John, but John has the look of a man who has been torn to shreds by something. He doesn't look well, physically or emotionally."

"He's probably not. Oh I don't mean he's a candidate for an insane asylum, or anything like that, but after all he's been through, he's just . . . just . . . drained. I can't think of a better way to put it."

"What do you mean 'after all he's been through?'"

Mrs. Heywood's voice softened to a whisper. "RaeLyn,

I'm sorry. I've been talking in riddles. You didn't know about John's tragedy; my God, I feel like a fool."

"I don't know anything about John. I haven't talked to him or heard much about him for years. I know he's married and has a child. It was only a few days ago that I read in the newspaper he was working with the governor . . . What tragedy?"

"He lost his wife less than six months ago in an automobile accident. John was to speak at a party fund-raising dinner in Buffalo County, but the press had broken the story about the Reinwald contracts the same day, and he had to stay in Lincoln to meet with Clarke and other advisors about the situation. Becky was a good speaker, very personable, and popular with our rank and file party members, so she made the trip as John's surrogate, so to speak. It was nearly midnight when she left Kearny after the speaking engagement. It was a one-car accident; they think she probably dozed off, because a driver who was following her said the car just swerved off the road before it rolled over the embankment. She was killed instantly."

"How terrible. Now I understand why John seemed so distant and sad."

"Yes, it's been a difficult time. He has a three-year-old daughter, Karin. They moved their home into a town house apartment last week. He has an elderly housekeeper who comes in days and watches Karin. She adores the little girl." Tears glistened in Mrs. Heywood's amber eyes. "But it's impossible to explain to a little girl Karin's age why her mommy won't be coming home any more. And, John—I don't think he's shed a tear. He's done all his crying on the inside."

"He must have loved her very much."

"Yes, they were a very close couple. They complemented each other well. Becky was more an extrovert than John—bubbly, an easy person to know, one hell of a politician, Clarke always said. Clarke had political ambitions for John, but even my chauvinistic husband admitted that Becky might have been happier and better-suited as the candidate. Very pretty, petite, sharp as a tack."

"John is more than just your husband's chief of staff, isn't he?"

"Yes, much more. He and Becky were our dear friends. Clarke and I have three lovely daughters who are grown now and have lives of their own. John's the son we never had. We would trust him with our very lives. Clarke hired him as a speechwriter when he was fresh out of college. Clarke was running for Congress that year, and he was defeated—quite soundly, I might add—but he and John became very close. They shared a common philosophy that less government is better government. But it was more a personal rapport than a philosophical one. John took a reporting job after that campaign, but when Clarke announced his run for governor two years ago, John took on the job as campaign manager and directed a beautiful campaign."

"It's strange," RaeLyn said. "When we were in high school, I never had any doubts about John's abilities, or his character for that matter, but he always seemed too shy and reserved to get into politics. It's the last place I would have expected to see him."

"He's not happy here. He doesn't belong here. He could be governor himself, but he doesn't have the stomach for it. John was meant to be a mover in other ways—the backslapping, the wheeling and dealing, the hypocrisy you have to tolerate in this game—John's not comfortable with that, and it's starting to make him miserable. And now, with the scandal allegations, the hearings, the threats of criminal prosecution, John's unhappiness is on the verge of turning to bitterness. He can't stay with us much longer; Clarke and I know that. He needs to move on to something else . . . a new life . . . then he'll be all right again. But I know he won't leave until we've weathered the present storm . . . and it may be a long one. I'm glad you're here to be with us, RaeLyn."

"Why? I don't understand."

"Selfishly, I'm glad to have someone to talk to in confidence. Two of our daughters live back on our Sand Hills ranch with their husbands; our other is attending college in Arizona. I've been very guarded, bordering on paranoia, ever since these terrible accusations started. But, I'm pleased more for John's sake. He needs someone to talk to, a younger person . . . more specifically, a woman. Now, don't misunderstand me, I'm not a devious old matchmaker. But maybe I am a little old-fashioned. I may be too much a romantic, but I believe in the man-woman relationship—that a man needs a woman to turn to when things are rough, just as much as a woman needs a man. The Good Lord just meant it to be that way. I know He did. John needs a friend, RaeLyn, a friend who is also a woman."

"He has one—you. And I'll try to be as good a friend, if he needs me. I owe him that much." Mrs. Heywood looked at RaeLyn quizzically. "I betrayed John once, and when I did, I betrayed myself. I want the chance to make it right."

22

"RaeLyn! Come in," Sherm said as he opened the door. "My God, you're stunning." He smiled that perfect smile of his. She could feel his eyes surveying every feminine curve of her body, pausing longer than good taste would ordinarily permit at the cleavage revealed by her new evening dress. Yes, same old Sherm—he had to undress her mentally before he was ready for conversation.

"It's been a few years, Sherm," she said.

"What? Oh, yeah, too many, Rae. But they've treated you great."

"Thank you. You're looking very well yourself."

Well, sit down," he said. "We've got a lot to talk about. Care for a drink? You name it; I've got my own supply here."

She took a seat on the circular sofa that formed a conversation area at one end of his living room. "A white wine would be nice, if you have it."

"Certainly. Make yourself at home; I'll be right with you."

She studied the apartment with casual interest, finding that it evoked memories of that night years before when she and John had gone to the party at Sherm's house. This room was rich, lavishly furnished and decorated, like the Reinwald mansion had been. She had lived in comfortable surroundings since, had visited elegant, plush homes. No doubt she had seen places that represented significantly greater financial investments on the part of the owners, but the Reinwalds had a knack for making things look expensive, in this instance at the sacrifice of taste.

The walls of this room were covered with a gold foil streaked with veins of silver. Dazzling, yes. And it created a kingly atmosphere, projecting wealth and power throughout the room. But he might as well have papered the room with thousand dollar bills.

Sherm was evidently undaunted by the festering political storm. He exuded robust health. Trim, obviously fit, his dark eyes were bright and alert. His black hair was styled meticulously and showed no sign of thinning. It seemed that, unlike John, Sherm had been unscathed by the passing years.

"Here, Rae," he said, handing her a crystal goblet. "Asti Spumante. It's a good white wine. Take my word for it."

"I will, Sherm. I suspect that as a connoisseur of fine wine and women, I can trust you implicitly."

Sherm sat down beside her. "I'd say that's a fair statement. As for women, on a scale of ten, at this point of the evening, I'd rate you as a ninē."

"Not a ten? And what do you mean by 'this point of the evening?'"

A smug, tight smile crossed his face. "Let's just say I have a complex rating system, and that my evaluation is incomplete at this point."

"You may never complete it. Anyway, why is it men think they're the only ones entitled to a rating system? It so happens, I have one of my own."

He wrinkled his brow and looked at her suspiciously. "Oh? Have I been rated yet?"

"No."

"Oh . . . uh . . . well, tell me about yourself, RaeLyn. Your call this afternoon came out of the blue. Haven't heard a word about you since you left Schonberg. Where have you been? What have you been doing? Have you seen your old . . . uh . . . friend, John?"

"I'll answer your last question first. Yes, I've seen John. I dined with him at the governor's mansion this noon." Sherm's smile evaporated, and she detected a rarely perceptible tenseness in his face.

"Moving in pretty high-class company, aren't you?" he asked.

"Yes. I've enjoyed the company of some very high class people today. The governor seems to be a very personable, genuine person. His wife is a gracious, compassionate lady."

"You said John was there. What about John?"

"John is still John. Battered, deeply hurt, perhaps. A little discouraged." She paused. "Sherm. . .I didn't call you for old times' sake; I'm a lawyer now. . .with the Howe & Lowenstein firm."

"Oh-h, I see. The hotshot California shysters who were hired by the governor's committee."

She ignored the verbal slap at her law firm and took a sip of wine before she fixed her eyes on his and said, coolly, "Yes, I'm assisting Jarred Harper with the case. You've heard of him, I presume."

"I've heard of him. He sent you here on sort of an espionage mission, I take it."

"No, it was my idea. You haven't been very accessible. I used our past acquaintanceship to get a foot in the door. I admit it." She placed her wine glass on the marble-topped coffee table. "I'll leave right now if you like."

He pulled a cigar from his coat pocket and made a little ceremony of nipping off the tip and plucking it delicately from his lips before lighting the slender brown cylinder and inhaling deeply. He exhaled a stream of smoke which she found surprisingly sweet-smelling. "No, stay," he said, "this might be interesting."

"You'll talk about the case?" she asked.

"Sure, hell, why not? I've got nothing to hide."

"All right, you're going to testify before the Special Committee tomorrow, aren't you?"

"Hell, yes, I've been subpoenaed. My lawyers say it's either that or go to the pokey. I don't think I'd like jail much. As you can see, I'm accustomed to better accommodation. Besides that, I've got a wife and kids to support."

"Oh." Her eyes darted reflexively to his hand for the wedding band, which was not there. "I didn't know you had a family, Sherm."

"Yeah, a fat little wife and two kids. Great bunch. My folks live in Florida now; we headquarter in their old home in Schonberg. You remember our house, don't you?" His eyes twinkled suggestively at his last remark.

"I remember," she said unflinchingly.

"Of course, I spend more than half my time here now. We moved the company's main office to Lincoln a few years back; that's where the action is in the electronics business. But Schonberg's better for Rachel and the kids. Small town atmosphere and all that stuff. Rachel bitches like hell about my being gone all the time, but she eats good, and this gives me a little room to move around. . .if you know what I mean. I'll always be a bachelor at heart, but in my business you need the respectability that goes with a wife and kids. The way I live is kind of like having your cake and eating it, too."

"You always had a knack for that, Sherm. Now, back to tomorrow. What's your testimony going to be?"

"Damn, you get right to the point, don't you?" He blew out another thick cloud of smoke. "All right. My testimony. I was planning to save it for a surprise, but for you, RaeLyn, I'll give a sneak preview. But I'm going to tell the truth, and you may not like it."

"Let me decide. What's your story? Did the tax commissioner, Harlowe, take a bribe?"

"Bribe?" he said, exaggerated surprise in his voice. "My God, RaeLyn, what do you take me for? Even if you doubt my honesty, don't question my intelligence. And Harlowe . . . he's a victim, a scapegoat. I've known him for years. A man of absolute integrity."

"Then you're saying the governor's a crook?"

"The man I supported? No, I couldn't be that wrong about anybody. The governor's as much a victim as poor Harlowe. Clarke's a decent man, but naive. . .a little too innocent for the political game. But the governor's a wealthy man—ranching and banking interests. Who would believe he was bought off for a lousy fifty grand? When the lynch mob cools down, that story won't sound plausible."

"Then who?"

"Well, first, RaeLyn, there wasn't any bribe. If there was anything, there was a loan . . . a personal loan to a friend . . . or at least an intended one. And who? Your friend and mine . . . Prof. That's who."

Her eyes flashed. "You're a liar!"

"More wine, RaeLyn?" Sherm asked, smiling confidently.

"No, thank you. What's your story, Sherm?"

"I don't like your tone, RaeLyn. It's not a story; it's fact. It looks like old Prof isn't quite as pure as we were always led to believe. Now, don't look at me like that. Jesus, just because you still have the hots for that guy. . .just hear me out."

"I don't have the 'hots' for anybody, but I'll listen to what you have to say."

"Here's how it happened," Sherm said. "Some months back, Prof came to me. He admitted he had been living above his income. He had a sixty thousand dollar mortgage on his house and other personal debts he had accumulated when he had served as the governor's unpaid campaign manager. Of course, his job with the governor carries a big title, but not much salary—not for the standard of living he's almost forced to maintain. Prof approached me as one old friend to another; he wanted to know if I could refinance him—or at least come up with enough money to get him through his financial crisis. Hell, you know me. I couldn't turn down an old buddy like Prof. I loaned him fifty thousand, interest free, no strings attached. I swear it. It was just a loan to a good friend."

"Well, when the computer contracts came up, Prof interceded on his own with Harlowe—at least that's what Harlowe says. Demanded that the specifications be drafted to fit the Reinwald machines. Harlowe protested, because he worried about how things would appear to the public, but he agreed it would be the best investment for the state, so he saw nothing morally wrong with going along with it. Besides, Prof was the one man in the state who had total direct access to the governor. Harlowe felt the word from Prof was as good as word from the governor, and when he discussed it with the governor at later dates, the governor seemed to be in complete agreement. I'm afraid Prof read more into my loan than he should have; he probably thought he was doing me a favor. As you can see, he didn't. Our company's reputation is worth many times any profit we made on the computer sale."

"I doubt that," RaeLyn said. "So you made John a loan. Do you have the note?"

"No, we didn't need one between friends."

"Do you have the cancelled check for the money you loaned him?"

"No, we made it a cash transaction, so it would be just between us."

"That's not going to wash very well, Sherm. If you testify to that, the committee will scream bribe. So will the press."

"But it's certainly a plausible explanation. And there will be no proof that it was otherwise. Harlowe will back me up on the pressure he got from Prof."

"And, of course," RaeLyn said, "Harlowe's not about to admit he took a bribe while he was on your payroll. John's convenient. Why lay the blame on John, Sherm? First, I think what you're telling me is a blatant lie, but even if it weren't there's no point to it. If there's no bribery involved, just deny it; why implicate someone else?"

"Hell, I can't avoid it. They subpoenaed my bank records. They show a fifty-thousand dollar cash withdrawal several weeks before the final draft of the specifications was approved. Those jackasses on the legislative committee aren't too bright, but somebody's going to jump on that one. I've got to have an answer, one that can't be confirmed."

"I see. And of course, anyone who might have taken money for illegal purposes wouldn't be in a position to confirm he had received it without admitting his own guilt. But if John had accepted a loan from you as you claim, his conduct might be considered unethical, but not necessarily illegal. In the absence of documentation, the committee would have to draw its own conclusion."

"Oh, I'm certain Prof will deny everything. He was especially insistent that we have nothing to document the transaction."

"Sherm, it just doesn't add up. A shrewd, hard-nosed businessman makes a loan, disburses cash, nothing to document it. That sounds like so much crap to me."

"Friendship, RaeLyn. . .friendship. I was prepared to write it off, if I had to. Just a favor to a friend."

"That's your story then?" RaeLyn asked.

"Those are the facts," he replied. He started to rise, depositing his smoldering cigar in an ashtray. "Are you sure you won't have another glass of wine?"

"No thanks. I'll be leaving now." She stood, facing him, her blazing, dark eyes belying her otherwise composed manner.

"But we were going to have dinner. Hell, don't take any of this personally, RaeLyn. I'm not. The evening's young; we'll talk about old times." He cleared his throat. "Maybe relive some."

"I'll pass it up. I think I can find better company."

His lips twisted into a sneer, and he met her glare with ice-cold, unfeeling eyes. "You've become a disagreeable bitch, Rae. You used to have a friendly way about you. Remember your first fuck?"

Her hand whipped out and delivered a stinging blow to his cheek. "It wasn't worth remembering, Sherm. You just weren't that good. I'll gladly forego the encore."

She whirled and headed for the door. Sherm stared after her, rubbing the tender, red imprints on his cheek with a trembling hand.

"Cunt!" he yelled. "Lousy, stinking cunt. You two-bit whore! You're on the wrong side...you hear me? You're on the wrong side."

She could still hear Sherm venting his rage in senseless invective as she closed the door and walked down the hall that led from his apartment. This was a side of Sherm she had not seen in her youth, a hysterical, irrational man who surrendered to childish tantrums when he failed to get his way. She had also seen another of those frightened, lonely men who could never procure enough money to purchase happiness or peace.

She had figuratively emasculated him with her cutting remarks before her dramatic exit. She knew this; she had intended to. Most men, she believed, were insecure, although in varying degrees, about their adequacies in sexual performance. A man like Sherm, deep-down, would be more vulnerable than others on this count. Could he ever be certain that it was not his money, rather than the enigmatic instrument between his legs, that women found attractive?

This much was certain—Sherm was powerful, cold-blooded, and vicious in the use of the money that was the source of his power. But he was not invincible, and he could be stopped. He *had* to be stopped.

23

After RaeLyn's departure, Sherm stormed around the living room of his apartment. He picked up his whiskey glass and slammed it angrily against the wall, then followed it with the wine goblet. He kicked at the coffee table, wincing in pain as the edge clipped his shin bone. "Bitch. . .fucking bitch!" he hissed. He tore off his suede sportcoat and threw it on the couch, then marched to the bar and filled a glass to the brim with Jack Daniels. He honked down the drink and quickly poured himself another. He whirled and walked deliberately to the wall phone. He picked up the receiver and dialed, sipping at his whisky while he waited for an answer.

"Hello," came a high-pitched voice on the other end of the line.

"Shirley," he said, "get your ass in here—now!" He banged down the receiver. RaeLyn Hunter would pay. She and her holier-than-thou attitude. And she hadn't been such a great piece of ass either. A scared kid who didn't even know where her pussy hole was—practically begged to be screwed. Then she had been Miss Innocent after he obliged her.

But he had killed things between her and John. Another

pious son-of-a-bitch. Even when they were kids, he acted like he was everybody's goddamn conscience. He always had an excuse for not having any fun. Mr. Goodie-Two-Shoes. So superior with that over-rated brain of his.

Their friendship—if that was what you called it—had always been shaky. But it was the time they found the exams in Sambo's locker that finally did it. The noble bastard martyred himself over Sambo, and Connie, and, of course, RaeLyn, and whoever else knew about it. And who came up looking like a shit-ass? Good old Sherm. Well, this time it would be John Armstrong's turn to play bad guy, even if he took it in the shorts himself a little in the process.

Sherm downed his drink and moved again toward the bar, when he heard the timid rapping on the apartment door. "Come in," he growled.

The door opened, and the face of a young woman peered in, her green eyes darting uneasily about the room, as though she were expecting a wild animal to attack from some hidden place. She stepped in lightly and closed the door behind her. Her shoulder-length hair was flame-red, and she had a full, voluptuous figure set on long, slender legs. Her milk-white flesh was generously exposed by a backless, emerald-colored evening gown that matched the color of her eyes. She was nineteen, perhaps twenty years old, and her childlike face had a look of innocence that made her seem younger.

"Sherm," she said uncertainly, "is everything okay?"

God, if she didn't have that damn, shrill voice. It made him think of chalk squeaking on a blackboard. But she was ravishing; she would have been a fantastic model, he thought, if her tits weren't so big. She wore her lavish wardrobe well, although she did not need it to turn him on. And she was submissive. In bed, she was game for anything—a gourmet fucker. She was bought and paid for. He furnished her with the luxurious apartment next to his, kept her in the latest styles and paid her a generous allowance—and she had a proper fear of him. She was not about to run out on him, not until he was ready for someone else. And that might be soon.

"Jesus Christ, what are you dressed like that for? We're not going out to dinner; you're going to fix something here."

A disappointed pout formed on her lips. "But you said you were taking this old friend of yours out for dinner, and I heard her leave, Sherm. . .so I figured you would want to take me out. And, Sherm, I peeked out the door and saw her going down the hall; she looked like more than an old friend. Jesus, she was a knockout. Did you try to make it with her, Sherm?"

"You stupid slut! It's none of your goddamn business!"

Her eyes widened in fright. "I didn't mean anything, Sherm. I'm sorry. I guess I'm a little jealous. Sherm, you understand, don't you?" He stared at her silently. Tears welled up in her eyes. "Sherm, I said I didn't mean anything. . .honest."

"Get the hell in the kitchen and fix me something to eat. A sirloin, maybe, and a salad."

"Sure, honey, whatever you want." She walked to him with open arms and started to plant a kiss on his cheek.

He stepped aside, evading her embrace. "Just fix dinner," he said.

She moved away, her cheeks flushed by hurt. "Sure, right away, honey. Why don't you have another drink? I'll get things started."

As she moved toward the kitchen, his eyes were drawn to the sleek lines of her naked back, then they came to rest on the graceful, erotic movement of her firm tight ass. He had always found her walk provocative. "Wait a minute," he called after her. She turned and smiled, looking like a small puppy eager for its master's approval. "Come here," he said softly. She approached him hesitantly. "Take your clothes off."

A look of puzzlement shadowed her face, as she came to a stop not more than five feet from him. "Shall we go into the bedroom?"

"Take off your things. . .here. . .now! Don't make me

tell you again!"

"Sure, honey...whatever you want." Apprehensively, she wriggled out of her gown, freeing her braless breasts. She stepped out of her heels and slipped out of the bikini panties that barely covered her thick, rust-colored pubic thatch. "There. How's that, honey?"

"Do you like me in bed?" he asked. "Do you like my prick?"

She looked at him questioningly. "Sure. Sure, honey. You're the greatest in bed."

Was the cunt lying? How could he tell? "How many men have you had? he asked.

"I don't know," she said, searching for the right answer. "Not many."

"More than five?"

"Yes, I suppose so."

"Who was the best?"

"You, Sherm. You, of course."

He studied her with burning eyes. "You swear I'm the best?"

Tears streamed down her cheeks. "Sherm, I swear, you're the best. Don't be angry. I haven't done anything. I love you, Sherm. Believe me. You're the best." She buried her face in her hands, whimpering softly. "Sherm, I'm afraid of you when you're like this. Please don't hurt me; it can be so good for us." She looked up at him with pitiful eyes. "We'll go to bed. I'll give you anything you want."

He walked over to her, grabbed her arm and jerked her toward him. She shrieked in pain. "Sherm! Please!"

He slapped her face sharply. She tried to pull away. He struck her again on the mouth, drawing droplets of blood to her lower lip. "Don't try to get away from me," he said menacingly.

"I'm sorry, Sherm."

He moved toward the couch, yanking her roughly behind him. "Put your hands on the couch and bend over," he commanded.

"Sherm, no please! I don't like it that way. It

hurts. . .terribly. I'll do anything else, Sherm."

"You'll do what I say." She obeyed and stood there, tense and motionless, bent over the couch; Sherm stood behind her, gazing at the smooth round buttocks raised and ready. The thought occurred to him that her ass looked like it was split in a huge, vertical smile. Yes, it was a smile inviting him—no begging him—to enter, lusting, crying, for the world's greatest cock. He unzipped his trousers and his tumescent penis sprang out. He moved closer until he felt flesh against flesh. "Spread your ass, RaeLyn!"

"Sherm!" the choked. "It's Shirley. I'm Shirley. Please don't, Sherm."

He slid one hand along her ribcage until it came to rest on a full, suspended breast. He grabbed it and twisted mercilessly until she screamed in pain. "Scream all you want, RaeLyn," he said, "it won't help."

With his other hand, he guided his organ between the soft cheeks of her buttocks, located his target, then rammed it home with full force. The girl screamed and sobbed hysterically as he hammered at her again and again, pounded on her back with his clenched fist, wrenched and raked at her torso with the other hand. He was like a man berserk, oblivious to her forlorn pleas and, in whispered tones oozing out between labored gasps, he said, "Like it, RaeLyn? Like it, RaeLyn?"

24

John ran his fingers tenderly through the silky, golden curls of the fragile-looking little girl who lay sleeping in his arms. Karin was so like her mother—petite, translucent blue eyes, fair skin, sensitive and shy in some ways, assertive and extroverted in others. The similarities were pleasant reminders of Becky and what she had been to him, and yet they evoked memories he was certain would pain him the rest of his life.

He glanced at his watch. It was nearly 9:00; he should take her to her bed, but he had promised RaeLyn when she called earlier, that she could see his little girl. Besides, it was not as if Karin were being kept from her sleep. She slumbered secure and content in his arms now, and he suspected that even lost in sleep, her subconscious derived some assurance from his protective holding. Poor, sweet kid. She and Becky had been so close.

Becky. He vaguely remembered their having a few rough spots in their marriage, a skirmish or two precipitated, at least in part, by the political life they had opted for. Tension, long hours, job insecurity. But in his grief he focused on their good times, and there had been many of them.

John had met Rebecca James when he was a coed at the

University of Missouri, majoring in speech and drama. He met her when they were both freshmen. In their junior years they married. They could not afford it, of course, but they were in love. John had a full scholarship; Becky had a partial. Like John, Becky's family was of modest means, so there was no help from home. But they both worked parttime and made ends meet until graduation.

After graduation, John took a reporting job with the *Lincoln Journal* and he and his Missouri wife returned to Nebraska. Becky enrolled as a graduate student at Nebraska Wesleyan, with an eye toward a master's degree and an eventual college teaching career. John was to get his masters, perhaps teaching part time, until he made it as a freelance.

They both shared a casual interest in politics and took an excursion to North Platte one weekend to hear a nationally-known Senator on the hustings for an obscure, rancher Congressional candidate. The rancher, Clarke Heywood, stole the show with his down-to-earth manner and simple, forthright political philosophy. Later, they met Clarke Heywood and his wife, Elizabeth, on the receiving line. Becky struck up a conversation with Mrs. Heywood, who quickly elicited the Armstrongs' backgrounds. Knowing that her husband needed a speechwriter and advance man for the campaign, she told Heywood about the young couple. Would John be interested in the job? In the heavy atmosphere of the circuslike political gathering, John agreed to give it a try. As a bonus, Heywood acquired a "firecracker of a stump-speaker" as Heywood called Becky. Neither of them got around to completing their masters' degrees.

After Heywood's defeat, they responded to reality and the need to earn a living. John took a job as an interim editor for the *Schonberg Journal-News* while the publisher-editor was incapacitated with a stroke. Becky, in the meantime, put her education to dubious application as a salesclerk in a women's clothing shop.

When Clarke Heywood called one evening and informed them he was planning to announce for the governor's race, they realized they were hooked. Like two old warhorses, they made arrangements to sever their Schonberg ties and join the Heywood campaign as full-time staff members—John acting as general manager and Becky handling advance work when she was not performing as a surrogate speaker at some small, county fund-raiser. Becky on the speaker's dais—he smiled to himself as he thought of it. "Sweet little thing," the old ladies would chortle as she approched the speaker's podium. "Wow, with legs like that, we've got the wrong candidate for governor," he heard one man say. "She can have my vote anytime."

Then, like a little David, she would tear into the opposition party candidate, lambasting the hapless man and his policies with the fervor of an evangelist and the simple logic of a skilled teacher. At the end, when she walked away from the rostrum, Becky James Armstrong also walked away with the hearts of the party faithful. Clarke Heywood tromped three opponents in the primary. The summer faded into autumn, and John, too, hit the campaign trail. After some coaching from Becky, he blossomed into an accomplished speaker in his own low-key style. But when the election was over, John knew that Becky had been the key to the victorious campaign. Or perhaps Karin, indirectly, could be given credit.

As the campaign moved into the October stretch, it was obvious to the inquisitive press and curious public that the growing bulge in Becky's abdomen was not the result of over-eating on the mashed potato circuit. She was undeniably *enciente*. The child was neither planned nor unplanned. They had wanted a child for several years, but Becky had been unable to conceive. No physiological reason, the doctors said, but John and Becky had nearly given up. Her timing, politically, could not have been better, because the news of Becky's pregnancy captured the woman's pages and made her a continuing focal point of public interest—Does campaigning tire you? When is the baby due? What do you hope for your child? There was nothing phony about Becky, and the people saw that—even those who opposed Clarke Heywood's policies and would never vote for him liked Becky. "Too bad she's not the candidate," they said.

But Heywood's opponent failed to recognize Becky's personal popularity, and in the closing days of the campaign, he turned on her like a tiger, responding acridly and viciously to Becky's own barbed attacks. He committed his political suicide in an interview on statewide television the week before election. "What do you think about Becky Armstrong's role in the campaign?" the interviewer had asked.

"Frankly," the candidate had said, "I find her appearance these days more than a little obscene. If I was her husband, I'd lock her up at home. Keep them barefoot and pregnant, I always say."

John and Clarke Heywood were watching the interview in the lobby of a Lincoln hotel. "It's all over," Heywood remarked after his adversary's comment. John agreed, but he had a twinge of remorse that the election turned on such irrelevant incidents and slips of the tongue. He had always seen Clarke Heywood's opponent as an essentially decent man, and there was no real rancor in the tenor of his remarks. It probably slipped out as a bad joke, but the poor guy would have hell to pay in the newspapers the next day. And, indeed, the press ripped him apart. One group called him a chauvinist pig. Mothers, present, past and future, were offended. Men did not like the coarse treatment given little Becky. Clarke Heywood won by a landslide. The right man won, John thought, but probably for the wrong reasons.

But how short the memory of the press and public. Here, a few short years later, they had turned with a similar vengeance on Clarke Heywood, and now, he had only a tenuous hold on the governor's chair and could all but abandon any ambitions for re-election.

The public loved Becky, but it did not ever really know her. In their private lives, she was soft-spoken, gentle, nothing like Clarke Heywood's "little firecracker." Like John, she savored their privacy and neither foresaw a long-term future in the public eye. He could see her now. Tiny, almost birdlike, she barely cleared five feet. In spite of her delicate features, she had a full figure; it was a miniature of larger women he had known. "I've got oranges where others have cantaloupes," Becky often joked. It was true. She was small-breasted but well-formed and shapely, slim but with the requisite womanly curves.

He missed her most at night, especially those hours he lay awake in bed, trying in vain to capture that elusive sleep. Becky would not have tolerated his insomnia. She would have reached over and touched his cheeks gingerly. "Need a tranquilizer?" she would have said, and then have pulled him to her, and they would have made slow and tender love.

John sat, the little girl cradled in his arms, staring pensively at the apartment wall. The doorbell rang, and he was abruptly jolted back to the present. "Come in," he said, "it's not locked."

RaeLyn opened the door and stepped in. "Hi," she said, her eyes moving to the little girl. "Don't get up, John, let her sleep."

"I'll do that. Sit down, Rae."

She took an armchair across from John's cushioned rocker. She studied the little girl's face. "She's precious, John. Karin, that's her name, isn't it?"

"Yes, how'd you know?"

"Liz told me."

"Oh, then you probably got the low-down on what I've been doing these past years. Why don't you tell me about yourself?"

"I'd like to sometime, but not tonight. I've got to talk to you about some other things."

Karin's eyes blinked open, and she looked confusedly at RaeLyn before she looked up at her father. "Who's the pretty lady, Daddy?" she asked.

"Her name's Miss Hunter," John said. "She's an old friend of mine."

"My name's Raelyn. You can call me Rae."

"Did you know my Mommy?"

RaeLyn cast an uncomfortable glance at John. "No, Karin, I'm afraid I didn't."

"My Mommy went to heaven. Me and my Daddy are sad."

"I know, Karin, but someday you will be happy again. Your Mommy would want that."

Karin smiled. "You're a nice lady."

RaeLyn smiled back. "Thank you, Karin."

"And I think you'd better get to bed now, toots," John said.

"Oh, Daddy, please."

"No arguments," he said sternly. "Grandma Armstrong's going to be here early in the morning. You're going to go visit her, remember?"

"I know, Daddy, but can't you go too?"

"I wish I could, honey, but I'll come to Schonberg soon. I promise. Now, to bed."

"Can Rae come with us?" Karin asked.

John looked at RaeLyn questioningly. "I'd love to," she said, taking Karin's hand as she stood. "You lead the way."

In Karin's bedroom, John and Raelyn tucked the little girl in bed. John turned on the nightlight beside the bed and bent over to kiss his daughter on the forehead. "Good night, honey. Sweet dreams."

Karin looked up at RaeLyn with wide, blue eyes. "My Mommy used to kiss me good night, too. You can kiss me, if you want to."

John caught a glimpse of moistness in RaeLyn's eyes. She smiled tenderly and bent over to kiss Karin. "I'd love to, Karin."

When they were seated again in the living room, Raelyn said, "Wow, that's quite a little girl you have there. She's a heartbreaker."

"She's special . . . I don't know what I'd do without her. She liked you."

"I'm glad."

"I'm going to miss her after she leaves tomorrow."

"I take it she's going to stay with your mother for a while?"

"Yes, I've got a housekeeper who's been staying days and fixing most of our meals, but her daughter in New York had a baby, and she's flying east to be with her for a month or so . . . and my hours aren't going to be very reliable for a while, I'm afraid."

"Karin needs to be with you, John. It's too bad you can't work something out."

"Well, I'll try to drive out to Schonberg on weekends. Believe me, I'm going to be thinking of a way to get her back as soon as possible."

"I'm sorry, John, for what you've been through."

"It's been tough, and I know I've been feeling sorry for myself. Others have endured the same thing; a lot of people have suffered worse. But that's someone else's tragedy. We have to have our own, I guess, to really know what it's like. It just seems so unfair. Becky was so young and had everything going for her. And Karin left without a mother. You know, we didn't even have a kiss good-bye, just a quick call home that morning to see if she could handle the speech for me—then, good-bye. See you later, I said . . I didn't even tell her I love her. I knew I had been cool with her that morning—all the pressures on the governor, the Reinwald scandal—I'd been preoccupied. I tend to clam up and brood when things aren't going right. If only I could have told her how I felt about her . . . how much I loved her . . . how much I cared."

"She knew that, John. She understood. Words are nice, but love is more than words."

For the first time he was struck by the femininity of his visitor. It was nice to hear the sound of a woman's voice in the room, and he was suddenly acutely aware that he was in the presence of no ordinary woman. RaeLyn was class. Yes, that was what he thought years ago that night at the mixer—class. It was an intangible something that few people had, but you recognized it instantly when it was there. Becky had it; RaeLyn had it.

"Sorry," he said, "I didn't mean to cry on your shoulder. You came to talk to me about the hearing tomorrow, I presume."

"I didn't consider it crying on my shoulder, John. I think maybe you need to talk, and I try to be a good listener."

"You always were," he said, "and I might take you up on that one of these days, but it's getting late, so we'd better talk business."

"All right, John. I visited Sherm earlier this evening. After I left his place, I called Jarred Harper and told him what Sherm's testimony is going to be. He suggested I contact you and see what you had to say about it. Before I go ahead, though, I should warn you—Harper wants to drop you like a hot potato. He thinks we should confine our defense to the governor, and it's only because of Governor Heywood's insistence that our firm's representing you."

"I understand that," John said, " but you sound ominous . . . like there's some reason Clarke should disassociate himself from me. What is it?"

She related the gist of her conversation with Sherman Reinwald, omitting the details of their parting exchange. "And that's it," she said finally. "Sherm's going to testify he gave you fifty thousand dollars cash as a loan and that you misinterpreted it as something else and acted accordingly."

John felt a gnawing deep in his gut and leaned back in his chair, overwhelmed by a sense of despair. "I don't believe it," he said. "Why?"

"Because he hates you. That was obvious when I talked to him. God knows why . . . some kind of deep-seated resentment, I guess, that probably goes back years. But, John, as a lawyer, I have to ask you some blunt questions. It embarrasses me to do this because, as impersonal as I'd like to be, we're not strangers."

"Fire away."

"Did you ever receive money from Sherm? A loan or anything else?"

"No."

"Did you ever ask him for a loan?"

"No."

"Is there any truth in what he said? Anything that might give credence to his testimony?"

"I don't know what it would be. At this point, Clarke isn't going to testify, but he can say I never discussed the specifications with him prior to their approval. In fact, I was completely unaware of the whole bid-letting process until the *World-Herald* story. Sherm was right about one thing, though, and I suppose he didn't have much trouble finding that out. I was in a pretty bad financial bind about that time. Becky and I spent too much time the last five years in no-pay or low-pay political jobs. We had more house than we could afford, and I was having one heck of a time generating enough cash flow to meet the mortgage payments and keep us eating too. But we probably weren't any different than half the people in our country. That seems to be the way of life for a lot of people in our age group. Anyway, it wasn't a problem that couldn't be resolved by sale of the house. After I lost Becky, I sold the house and paid off the mortgage. Now, I've probably got ten thousand in the bank . . . and every dollar of that can be traced to the house sale.

"There's another thing, Rae. Sherm would be the last guy I would go to for help. A matter of pride, I guess. I can't think of anything more humiliating than having to beg Sherm for money. He was a heavy contributor to Clarke's campaign, but I wasn't the contact. I couldn't even bring myself to ask him for a political contribution. If I had been as desperate as Sherm claims, I would have gone to Clarke first. He's offered to loan me money in the past—even pay me a private salary on top of what I get from the state. I've always turned it down, because I was afraid I'd lose my independence. I knew it was just Clarke's way of expressing his confidence in me. That's all I can say, Rae. Sherm's story is pure fabrication and unadulterated lies. You'll just have to decide whom you're going to believe."

"I didn't believe Sherm even before I heard your side, John, but what I think doesn't count. It's a matter of convincing the legislative committee and the public. Jarred Harper told me he doesn't think a single indictment's going to come out of all of this turmoil; he's reviewed everything with our Omaha staff, and he's convinced it's just a question of who's going to walk away disgraced. He insists it's a political trial, not a legal one. There may be some charges filed by the federal district attorney to placate the public and the press, but when things have cooled off, Jarred thinks any charges will be quietly dismissed. If they aren't, he's extremely confident he can win an acquittal. Of course, his appraisal of the situation can change, if some new evidence pops up."

"Well, I don't know what it would be," John said. "I believe in Clarke Heywood's integrity; I'd stake my life on it—I guess I already have in some ways. But he's made some mistakes, some bad appointments. He's human like the rest of us and perhaps too trusting to be a successful politician. But I don't think anything can save him—not in this climate. The public wants scalp . . . I'm sorry. I imagine my bitterness is pretty obvious. I've become cynical about this whole damn business. People seem to think they're electing gods to public office, and when the officials perform like the mere mortals they are, the drums start beating for a lynch mob. No one receives less compassion and understanding than our country's political figures. Damn. If every voter could spend just one day in the shoes of a governor or senator or congressman, not to mention the President, they'd see things differently. Oh, sure, there's some crooks, but by and large I've got a hell of a lot of respect for most of the elected public officials I've met at all levels of government. Most of them are honest, sincere people—regardless of their philosophies—trying to make their particular component of government better. But they're held in such low esteem . . . and it's getting worse. I'm starting to wonder where we're going to find people to take these jobs. *I've* had it; I know that. I don't want any part of it anymore. And it always comes back to this, RaeLyn—the people. Most of them get better government than they deserve. I always think of that quote of Kennedy's—'Ask not what your country can do for you, ask what you can do for your country.' Hell, seventy-five percent of the people out there could not care less about doing something for their country. The government's in business to do something for them; that's the way they see it. The congressmen, the governors, all the public officials are supposed to play Robin Hood—take something from somebody else and give it to them. Tax one group to pay another. Cut one group's public services to give them to another that screams louder."

He looked at RaeLyn with tired eyes. She did not appear to be judging him too harshly, and he thought he saw a glint of understanding in her eyes. Or was he just seeing what he wanted to see? God, he just needed somebody to talk to—like Becky.

"I'm sorry, Rae, I'm rambling again."

"I'm not complaining."

He wanted to tell her just what he had been through, strip his soul naked and have her listen in her non-judgmental way. He did not need advice or counsel; he needed a listener. But he fought off the urge to talk.

"I think you've had enough of my pontificating for tonight. It's getting late. Is there anything else you need to know?"

"There is one thing. Assuming our firm represents you and Governor Heywood jointly, Harper still sees the governor as our primary responsibility, and he wants that understood. He also feels that our firm's profile with you should be low-key. Harper, of course, is the main lawyer on this case; he prefers to be personally identified only with the governor. He wants me to appear with you at the legislative hearing tomorrow and to handle at least the public aspects of your involvement. John, I'm not a criminal lawyer, and Harper will still be calling the shots, but I want to know how you'd feel about my handling this in light of . . . of our past relationship."

He smiled faintly. "I want the best damn lawyer I can get;

I think you'll do fine. And there won't be any conflict with your firm representing the governor; I'll go down the line with Clarke."

"But what if we find out later he hasn't been completely honest with you? That he's not clean?"

"Then I would resign from his administration at the first opportune moment . . . but I wouldn't turn on him. Most people wouldn't understand this, but a governor, president, or any other policy-making official needs a few people around he can trust implicitly. If he can't, he'll never get any feedback. He'll operate within the narrow confines of his own mind, won't be free to test his ideas. Governing can't be a one-man job, but it seems like we're trying to make it that way. I have nothing but contempt for people who work close to a public official, then resign in a huff and make a bundle, telling all. I'll never be a Judas. I may have to leave the administration, but when I do, I'll go without a whimper. I think Clarke knows that."

"Yes, I think he does," RaeLyn agreed, "and it's obvious he and Liz care a great deal about you. I just hope we can hold off the hordes so that none of you get hurt."

25

The hearing room in the east wing of the marble-floored capitol building was cold and austere. The room had probably changed little since the construction of the statehouse more than fifty years before. It was simply furnished—a long oak table and complementing chairs were the focal point in the room's center; spectator chairs lined the panel-sheeted walls that reached to the high ceilings mandated by another era. In spite of all the publicity, the hearing room was not packed with observers and could easily have accommodated another dozen persons.

Casting his eyes along the row of observers' chairs, John found he could match most of the familiar faces to one branch of the news media or another—the *Omaha World-Herald*, the *Lincoln Journal-Star*, KOLN-TV from Lincoln, WOW-TV out of Omaha. Evidently, his fellow Nebraskans were content to let the working press spoonfeed their version of the testimony to the readers and listeners of the state. Not even the chairman or other officials of the governor's minority party were present to offer moral support. They were hedging their bets, John guessed. While they doubtless hoped that John and Clarke Heywood weathered this storm, the party leaders wanted no part of the rough and tumble right now. They wanted to be in a position to pick up the pieces if the Heywood adminstration went down the tube.

In politics, John had long since concluded, one generally moved in a shaky conglomeration of fair-weather friends. Lately, John had felt like a leper. With the exception of Clarke and Liz Heywood, his old political friends were keeping a discreet distance.

John glanced at his watch. Ten o'clock. The hearing was to have convened at 9:30. His own performance had been delayed two days. Sherm's testimony had taken the better part of Tuesday, and Harlowe, the governor's former tax commissioner, had corroborated what he could of Sherm's story yesterday. Sherm's testimony had not deviated in the slightest from what he told RaeLyn it would be. Even at the risk of implicating himself in what could be interpreted as a bribe, Sherm insisted he had made the fifty thousand dollar loan to John.

Why? Revenge for some deeply-harbored resentment he had carried all these years? It was total fabrication, and still John was convinced that the representatives of the press believed it and had, in turn, unconsciously and inadvertently, sold the public on John's guilt. RaeLyn had assured John prior to this morning's hearing there was no evidence sufficient to support a criminal indictment. But that was small consolation. His good reputation seemed irretrievable at this point.

His eyes turned to RaeLyn, seated beside him at one end of the long hearing table. She looked pensively at the table, then, as though suddenly struck by inspiration, her hand moved to the yellow legal pad in front of her and jotted down some quick notes. As she had been for the past several days, she was all business this morning. They had conferred frequently, but with the exception of a few casual inquiries about Karin's adjustment with his mother, RaeLyn had confined their conversations to his legal-political problems. She was not acting as a long-lost love or even an old friend; she was a lawyer, and he was beginning to feel very secure under her guidance. Surprisingly, as the crisis intensified, he felt some easing of his personal pressures. Having someone else call the shots was a relief.

When she had come to his apartment several nights ago after her meeting with Sherm, he was not unaware of the tastefully suggestive dress she had on. The pretty, nubile RaeLyn had grown into a striking woman. Even now, dressed in a conservative, rust-brown pantsuit, he knew that the eyes of most of the men were covertly perusing the unmistakeably female figure.

She looked up at him and met his eyes, holding his gaze for a moment. "Ready?"

"As I'll ever be," he replied wryly.

"Questions?"

"No, I'll just tell the truth."

"All right, I'm going to make a brief opening statement in your behalf. After that, it's up to you. Remember . . . don't amplify on any of your answers. Respond only to the question that's asked, and make your answer brief. If you're uncertain about something, ask to confer with your counsel."

"I will," he said.

The thick, heavy door of the hearing room creaked open, and the committee members walked in single-file, taking their places at the opposite end of the table from John and RaeLyn. Officially, the committee was non-partisan, but it did not take an especially astute politician to single out the two members of John's own minority party. They were easily identifiable by their downcast eyes and glum faces. Dwight Ranson, a farmer-rancher from Clarke Heywood's own Sand Hills country, rubbed his white sideburns and fidgeted nervously in his chair, betraying that he would rather be back home, branding calves. Charlie Schuman, a sixtyish country lawyer, dabbed with a handkerchief at his shiny, hairless scalp, then looked at John and shrugged, signaling that things had not gone well for the minority party at the pre-hearing session of the committee. John knew Schuman and Ranson as capable, honest men, but neither was a professional politician. He was certain they had no ambitions for higher office. They were citizen-legislators, uncomfortable with the political infighting their jobs sometimes called for. He imagined that each would have forfeited his $4800-a-year salary in order to escape this hapless role in the inquiry.

Unfortunately, two of the three majority party members of the committee were drawn from the young, ambitious faction of the Nebraska unicameral—Adam Grayson and Peter Stolski—each in his late thirties, each actively interested in his party's gubernatorial nomination. John surmised that Grayson, the chairman, would be the next governor. Tall and trim, with Kennedyish good looks, he would win the beauty contest hands down. He was extremely articulate and had a sincere, affidavit face. Clarke Heywood always said that Grayson could feed the voters cowshit, tell them it was hamburger and make them believe it. Too bad. The son-of-a-bitch was a liar, and a stupid one, to boot. That was the worst kind.

Stolski was equally ruthless and partisan, but John had found him to be quick and intelligent and a man of his word, although they rarely agreed on political issues. In a primary, Stolski would lose to Grayson. He was overweight and dumpy, with a receding hairline. Baggy eyes and sagging jowls made him look much older than Grayson, who was actually several years Stolski's senior. No, Stolski was not charismatic—only competent.

The other majority party member, Sy Lonberg, like Grayson a member of the Omaha delegation, was an elderly, retired machinist with a white beard and mustache that reminded John of Colonel Sanders. He would sleep through the hearing and vote with Grayson and Stolski.

Grayson picked up the gavel and rapped sharply on the oak table top. "The Special Committee is now in session," he declared. "We are convened this morning to take the testimony of the governor's chief of staff, Mr. John Armstrong." He nodded at John. "Do you have an opening statement, Mr. Armstrong, before we have you sworn and proceed with our business?"

RaeLyn rose. "Senator Grayson. My name is RaeLyn Hunter. I'm acting as Mr. Armstrong's legal counsel, and I would like to make an opening statement in his behalf, if I may."

Grayson eyed her suspiciously. "You're with the Howe & Lowenstein firm that is representing Governor Heywood, is that correct?"

"Yes, that's right, Senator."

"Since your firm represents the governor, I assume you are representing Mr. Armstrong with the governor's consent."

"That's correct."

"Then are we to take it that the governor approves of everything Mr. Armstrong has done? That he condones Mr. Armstrong's questionable conduct or was perhaps a participant?" Grayson smiled smugly and looked around the room as though he were expecting a round of applause from the spectators.

"With all due respect, Mr. Chairman," RaeLyn said, "may I point out that this committee is conducting an inquiry, that no judgments of guilt have been made at this point. I would hope that everyone on your committee is approaching Mr. Armstrong's testimony with an open mind. I have been told that the people of Nebraska are proud of their legislature's non-partisanship, and I trust that Mr. Armstrong will not be exploited for anyone's personal political benefit."

Grayson glared. "Exploited! I think that word is uncalled for, counselor."

"You're absolutely right," RaeLyn said. "I apologize to the committee. I did not mean to insinuate that Mr. Armstrong would not be treated fairly. Now, if I may proceed with my opening statement . . ."

The committee members' eyes were fastened on RaeLyn, and John could see she had effectively captured their attention. Grayson was not going to intimidate her, and he would have to be on his guard, for she had nearly raised the question of partisan politics, and the press was alerted now to the implications of any overkill on the parts of Grayson and Stolski.

"Mr. Chairman," RaeLyn said, "members of the Special Committee. I need not remind you that John Armstrong is not on trial here today. The Special Committee is charged with the responsibility of determining whether there has been any improper or unethical conduct on the part of Governor Heywood or his subordinates in administering the affairs of this state. This is the proper function of your legislative body, and Mr. Armstrong has been instructed to cooperate fully with your committee.

"Mr. Armstrong is aware of the testimony that has been given to this committee by Sherman Reinwald and Mr. Harlowe, and he is prepared to respond to your inquiries pertaining to their testimony."

The door of the hearing room opened. John glanced to one side, distracted momentarily from RaeLyn's remarks. The ruddy-faced man who quietly entered the room shot a nervous look at the hearing table before he let himself down into one of the empty chairs along the wall. He was clearly out of place in the setting. He was a tall, heavy-framed man who, although not obese, packed too much weight on his chest and belly. He was tieless and wore a drab, gray sportcoat that probably had not fit him for five years. He was a tired-looking man, with that look of defeat that so often seems to settle on the laboring man who has long since surrendered to the dream of an easier life. The late arrival's bloodshot eyes met his own for a moment, and he gave John a barely perceptible nod before turning his attention to RaeLyn who was concluding her remarks.

My God, he knew the man. But it couldn't be. Sambo! After all these years. What was he doing here?

"Mr. Armstrong!" came the grating voice. "We assume you still plan to give us your testimony."

He felt RaeLyn's hand on his arm. "John," she whispered, "what's the matter? They're ready to swear you in."

"What? Oh, I'm sorry. Pardon me, Senator Grayson.

Yes, I'm ready now."

"I hope we're not boring you," Grayson said sarcastically.

"No, Senator, not at all. I apologize."

He was sworn in, and the first hour of testimony went very routinely. Of course they were setting him up, trying to lull him into a false sense of security. Grayson and Stolski would not be able to restrain themselves much longer. They had rehashed his close relationship with Clarke Heywood until they were beginning to sound like a broken record. And, of course, Grayson and Stolski had carefully cemented John's connection to the minority party. So, now the spectators were properly confused as to what crimes or misdeeds were at issue here, and whether it was John or Governor Heywood or the minority party itself, as a collective entity, that had done whatever had been done.

It was Grayson's turn to interrogate again; he cleared his throat and a hushed silence suddenly descended on the roomful of people, who sensed that something significant was about to take place. He made something of a ritual of pouring a glass of water from the pitcher at the committee end of the table, then sipped it slowly, staring at John as he did so. Placing his glass on the table and tilting his head upward in grand Rooseveltian style, he stated, "Mr. Armstrong, we don't seem to be making much progress here. I'm hard-pressed to think of a single bit of useful information this committee has elicited from your testimony."

"I'm sorry, Senator, but perhaps it's because I don't have much to say. I doubt that I have any information that will shed much light on any of the matters before your committee."

Grayson leaned forward on the hearing table, his eyes boring in on John. "We'll see," said the senator. "You're familiar with Sherman Reinwald's testimony before this committee, I assume?"

"I didn't hear the testimony, Senator, but I read the press accounts of it, of course. And I was briefed on the gist of its content by my attorney. She was present the day Mr.

Reinwald testified."

"I understand you and Mr. Reinwald go back quite a few years."

"You might say so. We were high school classmates; we've seen very little of each other since those days, however."

"Would you classify your early relationship as casual or close?"

"It's difficult to classify, Senator. I wouldn't call it close, but it was certainly more than casual."

"I think you're being evasive, Mr. Armstrong."

"I'm trying not to be, Senator. Perhaps I can put it this way—Sherm Reinwald and I knew each other very well. We were part of a group of boys who spent a lot of time together, but we were never what I would call close friends."

"I see. And you say you've had little contact with Mr. Reinwald since high school?"

"That's correct, Senator."

"But your testimony has shown your closeness to the governor and your political party. You certainly aren't saying you're unaware of the large sums Mr. Reinwald contributed to the Heywood campaign . . . nearly $20,000, I believe. An enormous sum for a state this size."

"I'm aware of it, Senator."

"And you claim you had nothing to do with those contributions?"

"That's right. I never solicited them, and I never discussed them with Mr. Reinwald or the governor's fundraisers."

"But money is the lifeblood of politics, and you were the governor's campaign manager. You're testing our gullibility, Mr. Armstrong."

"We had a separate finance committee that handled the money end of the campaign. I always had a distaste for soliciting campaign funds. I was responsible for campaign strategy and coordination, but my involvement in fundraising was confined to arrangements for small fund-raisers and events in conjunction with the campaign activities. Direct solicitation of larger contributions was left entirely to the finance committee."

"Mr. Armstrong, did you approach Sherman Reinwald for a loan?"

"No, Senator, I did not."

Grayson lifted his eyebrows in mock disbelief, then turned to the gallery with a condescending smile that said "we all know he's not telling the truth." Then he resumed his offensive against John. "You are aware of Mr. Reinwald's testimony on that point."

"Yes, I am."

"Than what was the nature of the $50,000 you acquired from Mr. Reinwald?"

"What $50,00?"

"The $50,000 Mr. Reinwald testified he gave you."

"Mr. Reinwald did not give me $50,000. He did not give me $50. I wouldn't have asked him for it; I wouldn't have accepted it, if he had offered it."

"Mr. Armstrong, our committee has evidence that mortgage indebtedness against your residence in almost that precise amount was paid off slightly over a month ago. This is documented. Where did this money come from?"

"From sale of my house. For some reason, the deed to the property hasn't been recorded by the purchaser yet."

"Mr. Chairman," RaeLyn said, "might I interject something at this point?"

"Yes, Miss Hunter, what is it?" Grayson snapped.

"Mr. Armstrong's testimony on this point is easily verified. I have a sworn affidavit signed by the broker who handled the sale of his residence and a closing statement that will confirm that sale proceeds were used to pay off the outstanding mortgage. We're also making available to the Committee audited bank statements reflecting all transactions in the bank accounts of Mr. Armstrong and his late wife for the past year. We think these will show Mr. Armstrong is not a wealthy man and faced something of a financial struggle . . . as do most of us, I might add. However, they show no indication of sources of money outside his salary as the governor's aide."

Grayson cut RaeLyn short. "Thank you, counselor. We'll receive those documents as evidence and have them reviewed by our own legal counsel and auditors for their evaluation. But none of this precludes the possibility that Mr. Armstrong obtained cash from Mr. Reinwald under some pretense and again disbursed that cash without running it through any bank accounts. Or for that matter, he could still have the cash in his possession."

He turned on John, again. "Mr. Armstrong, Sherman Reinwald was very precise in his testimony. By saying what he did, he even implicated himself to some small extent in an impropriety of sorts."

Impropriety, John thought. It looked like Grayson had found a political benefactor of his own. Sherm was being treated with kid gloves.

"Now, once again," Grayson said, "I acknowledge that you may have received money from Sherman Reinwald for any number of perfectly legitimate purposes. We are merely seeking the truth here. Did you receive $50,000 or any sum of money from Sherman Reinwald?"

"No," John said flatly.

"Then how do you explain Mr. Reinwald's testimony?"

"He's lying," John said matter-of-factly.

The hearing room broke out in a clamor as the press and other spectators talked excitedly at the chance to jump upon the first headline-grabbing utterance of an otherwise monotonous, barely newsworthy session.

Grayson's face flushed, and his gavel struck against the table again and again until the din subsided. When all was quiet, he said, "Calling a man a liar . . . that's a rather harsh statement, Mr. Armstrong."

"I agree," said John.

"Why would Mr. Reinwald lie?"

"I don't know."

"Just a few more questions, Mr. Armstrong. Do you have any personal knowledge concerning the governor's intervention with respect to the specifications for the computer contracts?"

"I do not." He was bordering on perjury, but he had not quite crossed the line, he rationalized. His information was hearsay and after-the-fact, and he was not going to volunteer anything that might embarrass Clarke Heywood. Would he lie for the governor? He could not say.

But Grayson did not press that question, even though Clarke Heywood's involvement was the administration's most vulnerable point. Evidently, Grayson was so convinced of John's guilt that he was bent on bringing down the administration by hanging the chief of staff. At least Sherm's testimony had moved the focus of the investigation away from the governor.

Senator Grayson said, "I must conclude that if anyone would have been aware of the governor's role in this, you would have, Mr. Armstrong. It appears to me that you are nearly admitting your own active participation. As near as I can determine, you are the only member of the administration outside of the governor who would have had the authority to give final approval of the specifications."

"I have to disagree," John replied. "The Governor permits his department heads to be relatively autonomous in their respective areas. He concerns himself with broad questions of policy and doesn't intervene in the day-to-day operation of the agencies, unless some problem has been called to his attention."

"What are you suggesting, Mr. Armstrong?"

"That the decision involving the computer specifications was one that could have been made by the department head himself . . . the tax commissioner, Mr. Harlowe."

"Are you accusing Mr. Harlowe?"

"No, Senator, I'm just pointing out there are other possibilities."

Grayson glanced at his watch. "It's nearly noon, gentlemen," he said, addressing the members of the Special Committee. "I'm going to declare the hearing in recess until 1:30. We should be able to wrap this up easily this afternoon." He rapped his gavel once on the table, signaling the meeting was adjourned.

RaeLyn leaned over to John, smiling reassuringly. "You did a great job. You should have been a lawyer."

"No, thanks, not me. I shouldn't have been a politician either. We really didn't prove anything this morning, did we? It's still Sherm's word against mine."

"That's true, but there's nothing that should provide a basis for filing criminal charges against either you or the governor."

"But there's enough to convict us in the press."

"You don't go to jail for what they write about you in the newspapers. Don't worry about the press."

"In politics there's nothing more serious than the press. That reminds me, I saw Sambo sitting in the press area this morning."

"Sambo?"

"Yes." He turned to where Sambo had been sitting; the chair was empty. He pushed back his own chair and stood. "He's gone. I think we'd better find him."

"Why?"

"I don't know. Somehow, his being here doesn't make sense. I just think we should talk to him." John shoved his way through the crowded room, oblivious to the unrelenting questions of the reporters who swarmed around him. As he broke into the hallway, he caught sight of Sambo, who was nearing the far end and about to turn the corner that led to the capitol rotunda and its main exit. "Sambo!" he called.

The bulky figure stopped and turned, looking around nervously before he caught sight of John, who was rushing down the hall toward him.

"Sambo! It's been a long time," John said as he approached Samuel Hanson, Jr. and extended his hand.

"Hello, Prof. It's good to see you."

Sambo was noticeably ill at ease, twisting his neck back and forth as though trying to escape the strangling shirt collar that encompassed his thick neck.

"Sambo, I saw you in the hearing room. Would you like

to join RaeLyn and me for lunch? Oh, God, I forgot about RaeLyn . . . I left her back in the hearing room. She's probably looking for me now . . . how about it, Sambo? Will you join us?"

"Well . . . I . . . I don't know. I was going to head back to Schonberg." Then he sighed deeply and straightened up, setting his jaw as though he had just made a momentous decision. "Yeah. Damn it, Prof, I'll have lunch with you. I sure as hell didn't drive all the way up here just to watch that circus in there."

26

They had lunch at Abbie's, an old-fashioned restaurant that featured irresistible homemade pies. The atmosphere was casual and informal. As they finished, John thought Sambo seemed significantly more at ease. RaeLyn deserved most of the credit, though. With little difficulty, she had taken up where they had left off ten years earlier. She was adept at small talk, and John was not. He was relieved to have RaeLyn carry the burden of the conversation about the Hansons' expanding family. "How soon is Connie expecting?" RaeLyn asked.

"August," he replied. "Five kids." He shook his head from side to side as though he did not understand it. "That's a lot of shoes."

"But it's worth it, isn't it?"

"Yeah, they're great kids. Connie's nuts about them. I'd say she's a better mother than I am a father."

RaeLyn smiled warmly and touched his arm tenderly. "I'll bet you're a great father, Sambo."

John could see that Sambo was touched by RaeLyn's words. She had a way of saying the right things to melt a man's heart. How well he remembered.

"I get along with the kids," Sambo said, "but I don't

spend enough time with them. I'm in charge of the kill floor at the plant; that means long hours. The kids are in bed a lot of times when I get home, and I have to take on odd jobs most weekends to make ends meet." He looked at RaeLyn, then at John. "That's how I ended up here."

"What do you mean?" John asked.

"Did you think I drove two hundred miles to watch that side show down at the statehouse? There's lots better stuff on television, and that ain't saying much, Prof."

"No," John agreed. "I had a hunch you had something else on your mind . . . that's why I went after you."

"Yeah, you figured right. I just lost my guts. I was going to beat the hell out of there and just forget about it."

"Forget about what?"

"Well, you know I said I took weekend odd jobs . . . they're all for Sherm."

"You work for Sherm?"

"Off and on. He pays good when he can use me."

"What do you do?" RaeLyn asked.

"Like I said, odd jobs. Sometimes I act as chauffeur for his van, like when he takes a bunch of drinking buddies to a football game or some important customers on a hunting trip. Things like that. Then, sometimes, I handle special jobs."

"Such as?" RaeLyn asked.

"Well, I saw a guy do what I do in a movie once. They called him a bagman."

"A bagman?"

"Yeah, kind of like a delivery man. I take envelopes and packages to people Sherm wants to get to them."

RaeLyn asked, "Are you free to say what's in them?"

"I'm not supposed to. Sherm swore me to secrecy, and he pays me big money. He paid me as much as five thousand bucks at a crack. That's why Connie and me live in a new house. Yeah, I know I don't look it, but we live high off the hog. Last year, I made more off Sherm's jobs than on the kill floor at the plant. Sherm's tried to get me to quit and work for him fulltime. I don't think there's much job security there, though. Like, here today, gone tomorrow." He looked at John. "What do you think, Prof?"

"You're probably right."

"Anyway, I've kept my mouth shut. Sherm's warned me, and I know enough that what he's been doing ain't quite legal, but I need his money, and I'm in too deep. Sherm says if he ever gets in trouble, I'll go to jail. It would kill Connie and the kids."

"You're an accessory," RaeLyn said matter-of-factly.

"Yeah, I think he said something like that. Anyway, after what Sherm's done to you, Prof, I don't owe him anything."

"I take it you know something," John said. "Something that might help me."

"Yeah, sort of. I figure that what I've been carrying mostly is money. I don't know how much, and it's almost always in sealed envelopes. But I can make a pretty good guess as to what's in there just by feeling the package. I gave Logan Harlowe—the guy that used to be tax commissioner—one of those envelopes at his house here in Lincoln one Sunday afternoon. It was about the same time they say Sherm took the fifty thousand dollars out of his bank account."

"What about the other times?" RaeLyn asked.

"Same kind of envelopes . . . usually to vice presidents or other people with fancy titles, who work for big companies in Nebraska or Iowa. Sometimes in Kansas. I always guessed it was somebody who had some say about their own company buying something from Sherm's. I remember one time it was a mayor in Kansas. Later I read a newspaper story about the town buying a computer from Reinwald Electronics. I never got to go to college, but it didn't take a genius to figure that one out."

"But you never actually saw the money?" RaeLyn asked.

"No, but I knew what was in the envelope."

"You know," she said. "If you testify to that, the implications would be pretty clear. It would give credibility to what John has been saying."

"Yeah, I figured as much . . . and it would ruin me, too, even if I didn't end up in jail."

"He's right, RaeLyn," John said. "I couldn't let Sambo do that . . . I wouldn't let him. It really wouldn't be conclusive proof anyway, would it?"

"No," she admitted, "but you've been concerned about your reputation with the press; I think you would be cleared there."

They sat there silently for a moment. Finally, John said, "Sambo, I would never force you to testify to anything, but tell me this . . . if I asked you to, would you do it?"

Sambo fidgeted in his chair and pulled a rumpled handkerchief from his coat pocket, then swiped at the perspiration that was forming on his brow. "Yeah, Prof, I'd do it. I wouldn't want to, but I'd do it. I want out anyway. This work I've been doing for Sherm can't lead to anything but trouble. Someday I'll get caught and, knowing how things have always worked out, Sherm won't be the one to go to jail. No, I can't risk it anymore."

"Can I tell Sherm you've told me all of this?"

Sambo hesitated. "Yeah . . . yeah, I guess so. He'll be madder than hell, though, Prof. You ain't seen him much these last years. He can be like a crazy man; he has regular fits."

"Would he harm you or your family?"

"I don't know, but I don't think he'd go that far. I think he'd be scared to. For one thing, I know too much; he can't put on too much heat, like getting me fired at the plant or anything like that."

"I'm not talking about getting fired, I'm talking about physical harm."

Sambo looked at John with a startled expression on his face. "Jesus, I don't know. I can't believe he'd do anything like that."

"John," RaeLyn interjected, "as long as Sherm knew you and I were aware of this and that we had more than a casual interest in Sambo's well being, I don't think he'd do anything drastic. He's an evil man, but not a stupid one."

"I think it's time someone had a talk with Sherm," John said.

"You want me to confront him?" RaeLyn asked.

John thought a moment, meeting her eyes evenly as he weighed his options. "Rae, I don't think so. You might face some ethical problems in doing what has to be done. You're a heck of a good lawyer, but I think this takes a street fighter, and I've learned a little bit about that these past few years." There was a new spark of life in his eyes. "Besides," he said, "I've been guilty of letting you carry the fight for me, and I haven't given Clarke much help either. Let's face it. I've been sitting on my butt, feeling sorry for myself ever since this whole thing broke. I've held my own in a pretty rough game the last three or four years, and I've hit below the belt a few times. I think it's time I started hitting back now." He turned to Sambo. "I'm going to have a little talk with Sherm, Sambo. I'll have to tell him about our conversation, but I want to be sure . . . do I have your permission?"

"Yeah, go ahead."

"And you'll back me if you have to?"

"I'll do it."

"I don't think you'll have to, but I don't like to operate on bluff. All I want to do is keep you out of trouble and get the heat off me and, indirectly, Governor Heywood."

"May I ask how you plan to do this?" RaeLyn asked.

"I don't know, Rae, but I will by the time I talk to Sherm, and that, hopefully, will be tonight." He glanced at his watch. "It's after 1:00. Should we be getting back to the hearing room?"

"Yes, we'd better," she said, "but I think we're through the worst. It shouldn't take long."

"Good." John turned to Sambo, "I can't thank you enough, Sambo. I haven't had a morale booster like this since . . ." he turned back to RaeLyn and gave her a barely-perceptible smile, "since I saw RaeLyn at the governor's mansion."

27

"Sherm," John said when the apartment door opened and he was met by the dark little man inside.

Sherm's face was impassive. "Hello, Prof," Sherm answered, holding his ground in front of the partially-opened door.

"May I come in?" John asked. "I think we need to talk."

"I'm afraid I'm busy right now. It'll have to be some other time."

"I don't think you're that busy. I think you'd rather have me say what I have to say here than before the Special Committee."

Sherm eyed his visitor warily. "All right. Come in." He held out his hands in an empty gesture. "But you can see I wasn't expecting company."

Sherm was not his usual immaculate self, John noted. His cheeks were covered with sandpaperlike stubble, indicating he had not shaved that day. He was barefoot, and the flowered sportshirt he wore was open, revealing the firm, smooth skin of his chest and belly. Affluence had always agreed with Sherm, and it appeared that the years had not changed that.

"Sit down," Sherm said curtly, pointing to a hard-looking armchair with ornately-carved arms and legs. I'll be with you in a minute."

Sherm went into the rear of the apartment and entered what John surmised was a bedroom. John sat down on the proffered chair; it was as hard as it looked. Sherm had not exactly thrown out the welcome mat.

As he sat there, surveying the luxurious surroundings, he could hear muffled voices coming from the room Sherm had entered. One was obviously feminine and unhappy, evidently the target of some hostility on Sherm's part. He thought he heard the sharp crack of flesh against flesh, preceding a short, shrill scream. He started to rise from his chair to investigate, then thought better of it.

From Sherm's standpoint, it was obvious that John's visit was inopportune. Sherm emerged from the room, his shirt buttoned and tucked in. A pair of buckskin-colored shoes added several inches to his height. He was grim-faced, and his eyes were glazed with anger. John could not be certain whether Sherm's wrath was directed at him or at the unfortunate soul in the other room. He did not much care.

Sherm moved to the bar and poured himself a bourbon. "Want a drink?"

"No, thanks."

"Suit yourself." Drink in hand, Sherm walked to an overstuffed chair across the room from John, leaving a good ten feet between them. He let himself down in the chair, sipped his drink, then glowered at John in silence for a few moments. John met his gaze evenly.

"Well," Sherm said, "I'm listening." He glanced at his watch. "I don't have all night, so make it quick."

"First, Sherm, just to satisfy my curiosity, why did you dream up that bullshit about making me a loan?"

Sherm smiled wolfishly. "Oh, that's why you've got a hair up your ass. What did you do with the money, Prof? Have a good time? Hey, you ought to spend some of it on RaeLyn. Jesus, I'll bet she's a great piece of ass."

Sherm rambled on, although it seemed to John the little man was half talking to himself. "She came to see me, you know, Prof . . . first day she was in town. Remember who busted her cherry? Said she never had anything like it since. Begged me for a fuck, but I wouldn't give it to her . . . yeah, begged me for it. I'll give her a chance before she leaves, though." He took another drink. "She let you have any yet, John? Her cunt was just itching for a screw the night she was here. Hell, I bet she'd even let *you* do it now."

John seethed, feeling the warmth spreading on his cheeks as they flushed in anger, but he did not reply.

"Don't be embarrassed, Prof. I see I hit a raw nerve. You never did crawl into that little cubbyhole of hers, did you? Isn't that a hell of a note? And she's probably had a lot of experience now . . . screwed guys till hell wouldn't have it . . . but still a regular prima donna to the only guy she ever loved. Yeah, she's still got the hots for you, Prof; I could see that the night she was here, but she still saves her pussy for guys like me. The real men. Believe me, I know. Some things I'm not so smart about, but broads and money—those I know."

"I came here to talk about money, Sherm, and you still haven't answered my question. Why?"

Sherm got up and walked to the bar to pour himself another drink. "Why . . ." he said, as though pondering. "Why . . . why?" He returned to his chair. "I think it's because I hate your guts, Prof. I've always hated your guts. Well, not always maybe. Those few early years back in Doc Sedgewick's scout troop we might have been friends. Not after we hit high school though. You always looked down your nose at me. I know you did. Your head was full of that crap you picked up in those books. The Brain. Hell, yes, you always had an answer for everything. Then you had to be Mr. Boy Scout too. You had to be sure we felt guilty if we had a little good, clean fun. And you were always after my butt, trying to make me feel like a criminal or something. That time Sambo got caught with the exams in his locker. Pious Prof, he wouldn't cheat. Shit, you didn't have to cheat. What about us poor slobs who didn't have computers in our skulls?"

"You're hardly a poor slob, Sherm. And don't play that dumb act with me,. You're looking to the wrong guy for sympathy."

Sherm had lifted his whisky glass to his lips as John spoke. Suddenly his hand trembled, and he spilled part of the contents down his shirt front. "Sympathy! You high-and-mighty son-of-a-bitch! That isn't what I want from you. It's respect! That's all I ever wanted . . . and I never got it."

"That's something you can't buy, Sherm. I never thought about it, but you're right—I never did respect you. I still don't. I never will. My feeling for you? What would I call it? Yeah, I know—contempt, Sherm. That's what I feel for you . . . contempt."

John could see barely-controlled rage in Sherm's eyes, and he knew he had stabbed his foe deeply. Watching Sherm was like observing a stick of dynamite as the spark burned its way down the fuse, creeping ever closer to the moment of explosion. This was a man perched precariously on the brink of insanity.

"Okay, Sherm, I guess I vaguely understand why you did it. You see it as kind of revenge and, of course, it's a good way to keep your crony Harlowe off the hook. But now I'll have my say. I assume your lawyers filled you in on my testimony at the hearing today."

"Yeah, you bet. They say you weren't very impressive, Prof. Nobody believed you . . . especially not Grayson. The majority party is going to keep on your ass . . . Heywood's too." Regaining his composure somewhat, he slumped down in his chair, stretching out his legs and tossing one over the other.

"Too bad about Heywood. He was always my candidate. Too much country bumpkin in him for the statehouse, though. I feel kind of bad about you, too, Prof, since you're something of an embarrassment to me."

"You've embarrassed yourself, Sherm, and the hearing didn't go all that bad. The committee had cooled by afternoon, and they were finished by three. I think the majority of the committee members thought they were beginning to learn too much. But I didn't really come to talk about the hearing. I want to tell you about the nice lunch I had this noon. RaeLyn and I joined a mutual friend of ours at Abbie's."

John noticed Sherm's hand shaking again, as the latter fumbled reflexively in his shirt pocket for a cigarette that was not there. "What friend?"

"Samuel Hanson, Jr. We used to call him Sambo back in the good old days . . . remember?"

Sherm pulled himself up in the chair and fixed his eyes on the framed painting above John's head. "The last I heard, Sambo still lives in Schonberg and works at the packing plant. He's a hell of long a way from home."

"He had some things to tell me . . . things important enough to justify the drive, he thought. After hearing what he had to say, I agreed, and I'm grateful to him."

"What do you mean?"

"Sambo told me about his part-time job . . . the payoff envelopes he's been carrying for you the past several years. I was interested in one particular envelope. The one that went to the tax commissioner, Harlowe . . . just about the time you withdrew fifty thousand dollars from your account, about the time you said you made a certain loan to me."

Sherm's lips formed in a snarl, and his eyes smoldered. "That dumb son-of-a-bitch!"

"A little slow, maybe, but not dumb, Sherm. We had a long talk. Sambo knows he could be in trouble, too, but he wants out. If necessary, he's agreed to tell everything he knows with names and places. I think the Special Committee could draw some reasonable inferences. My guess is some of the companies and cities involved would be interested in what Sambo has to say. With a little time, they could probably add a little fuel to the fire that is going to cook you, Sherm."

Sherm sat there zombielike, digging his fingernails into the padded chair, his eyes revealing the turmoil boiling within him.

"You're not very talkative right now, Sherm, so let me continue. I've thought about this. What do I do with this information? Morally, I guess if I'm the good boy scout you say I've always been, I should insist that Sambo testify before the committee. I'd get the satisfaction of seeing justice done. As a fringe benefit, I'd get some revenge and maybe see you end up in the pokey. On the other hand, RaeLyn tells me that what Sambo has told us is still pretty flimsy evidence. Sambo cannot testify for a fact that bribery was involved. It's a fine line, but RaeLyn and I could keep quiet, I think, without committing any legal or moral transgression."

"What are you getting at?"

"This. I don't want Sambo to get in any trouble, and I don't want him or his family hurt in any way. Remember, RaeLyn and I know about this, and you can be certain everybody will know about it if anything unfortunate should happen to any of us."

Sherm's face turned ashen, and he remained frozen in his chair. "Go on."

"Sambo has promised to testify, if I ask him to, and RaeLyn's taking his deposition tonight just in case someone tries to persuade him otherwise. But we'd rather not go that route, Sherm, so we're going to give you a chance to redeem yourself."

"Redeem myself?"

"Yes. All you have to do is go before the committee and admit that your testimony about me was false, or file a sworn affidavit to that effect. I just want to get this out of the news as quick as I can . . . for Governor Heywood's sake as well as my own."

"How noble," Sherm said sarcastically.

"Think about it, Sherm. At least you'll only have one bribery charge to deal with. For that matter, maybe you won't have that. Knowing you, you'll find a way to weasel out of it."

"And what do you suggest I tell the committee?"

"You might try the truth for a change. But I don't care what your story is, as long as I'm not in it."

"This is blackmail," Sherm said indignantly.

John smiled and shook his head in disbelief. "I think this is what they mean by the pot calling the kettle black. I'm pleased to see your sudden interest in law and order, Sherm, but call it what you want . . . I want proof by six o'clock tomorrow evening that you have taken steps to correct your testimony. If I don't get it, I intend to go public with Sambo's information."

Suddenly Sherm rocketed out of the chair and charged at John like an enraged badger. His hands locked around John's throat before he realized what was happening. As he tried to struggle free of Sherm's viselike grip, the chair toppled over and sent them both sprawling on the floor. John drove his elbow into Sherm's ribs, and the latter released his hold, enabling John to roll free and get to his feet. Like a tenacious bulldog, Sherm was after him, tears of anger streaming down his face.

"You cocksucker!" he screeched. "You'll pay! You'll pay!" He lunged at John again and drove him into the wall with battering-ram force. John was the bigger man, but he quickly realized that his sedentary life of recent months had taken its toll, and that Sherm was quicker and stronger. But Sherm was also mindless now, obsessed with the idea of getting at John. As a result, he left himself exposed to John's defensive strikes. As Sherm eased back momentarily to muster strength for another assault, John went on the attack. He drove his fist into Sherm's face, sending him reeling backward as John's knuckles crushed into his nose. John held back, hoping that would end the fight and bring Sherm to his senses.

But Sherm recovered quickly and charged again, arms flailing. This time Sherm scored a blow to John's right eye, tearing the flesh above it and unleashing a torrent of blinding crimson. John backed away, trying to wipe away the blood and clear his vision with one hand, while keeping Sherm at bay with the other. But the wild man banged his head into John's chest, almost knocking him to the floor before John locked his hands and hammered them down against the back of Sherm's neck. Sherm grunted in pain and pulled away, but this time John gave no quarter, taking the fight to Sherm with several sharp punches to the stomach and finally, taking no chances, driving his knee into Sherm's groin. That finished it. Sherm collapsed to the floor; John moved back, breathing heavily as he tried to catch his wind. He looked down at the battered man on the floor. Christ, had he done that? He had not remembered inflicting that kind of punishment. Sherm's face was red and swollen, and his twisted nose spewed blood like a leaky garden hose. His lips, too, were puffy and bleeding. For a moment, the pathetic sight evoked John's sympathy, but then he saw the hatred in Sherm's eyes.

"Mother-fucker," Sherm croaked. "You'll pay!"

Suddenly, John as acutely aware of his own injuries—the soreness in his ribs, the tender spot on his bruised breastbone, the painful throbbing above his eye. He pulled a handkerchief from his coat pocket and pressed it firmly against his brow in an attempt to stop the bleeding. Only then was he aware of the red-haired young woman who stood in the kitchen entryway looking upon the scene with wide, frightened eyes. She had a sheet pulled around her body and, as far as John could see, that was all that covered her nakedness. She was a pretty thing, but young, and one side of her face was marred by a large red welt. He nodded at her.

"I'm Shirley," she said. "Is . . . is Sherm all right?"

Sherm was unhearing. He had drafted his shirt into service as a compress. His head was bent over and his broken nose was cradled in silk-cushioned hands.

"He'll be all right, Shirley," John said, "but he'll need a doctor to set his nose."

"He tore off my gown," she said apologetically. "I . . . I live next door; I don't have anything else with me. If I stay here, he'll hurt me. I want to leave him, mister. Can you help me?"

"I don't think he'll bother you tonight," John said. "Go back to your apartment and lock the door."

"But you don't understand . . . that's Sherm's apartment, too. I can't stay there."

"I see," said John, suddenly seeing the young woman's plight. "Just keep your door locked and get your clothes packed. I'll arrange for someone to come and help you move out first thing in the morning. Do you have a place to go?"

"Yes . . . yes, I think so. I have a friend I can stay with for a while, if I can be certain Sherm won't come after me."

"He won't." He turned to Sherm. "Sherm, do you hear that?"

Sherm looked up. He had the look of a sick man but he was comprehending now.

"This young lady's leaving now. She doesn't want to see you again. I'm going to give her my name and phone number in case she ever has any trouble. Do you understand that?" Sherm nodded his head slowly. "And, Sherm, you never did say . . . are you going to take care of that business about the testimony?"

Without answering, Sherm pushed his cumpled, bloody shirt against his nose again.

"We'd better go, Shirley," John said, "it's getting late."

28

The beautiful woman across the table was distracting. John found himself picking at his steak and salad, as his eyes returned again and again to feast on her lovely face. Her silky turquoise dress was high-necked and might have been considered conservative, were it not for the sheer fabric that revealed a suggestive outline of what lay beneath. Intermittently, she would look at him as though feeling his gaze, smile demurely, then return her focus to the meal.

They had spoken little since taking their table, and she seemed as uncomfortable with the silence as he. It was nice to have dinner with a woman again—especially nice when that woman was RaeLyn.

The Cattle Company was an appropriate name for the restaurant in the Beef State's largest city, and although its name had registered images of promising fare, John had not anticipated the exotic setting. But the western atmosphere, stimulated by the rustic decor and oak-beamed ceilings, was romantic in its own way. He was no connoisseur, but the pre-dinner wine had seemed excellent. RaeLyn commented that she had not tasted its equal in Los Angeles, and, of course, Nebraska steaks—Omaha steaks in particular—simply had no competition in the culinary world.

This was RaeLyn's last night in Nebraska. The next morning she would board a flight for L.A. Harper and the other Howe & Lowenstein attorneys had departed several days ago. John was with them in the conference room in the firm's Omaha office when Harper instructed RaeLyn to remain a few days to tie up any "loose ends," as he had put it. Harper winked meaningfully at RaeLyn when he said it, and she had blushed noticeably and turned her attention to the stack of papers in front of her. John was not so naive that he did not catch the implications in Harper's wink, but still he was convinced that Harper misunderstood his closeness to RaeLyn in the several weeks that had transpired since the Special Committee hearing.

Yes, they had spent a great deal of time together, had dinner frequently, shared long hours of conversation. But their discussions had centered on the immediate legal problems John was facing and the political implications of any decisions he might make. Oh, they had reminisced occasionally, and they had shared some personal thoughts, but it was as though they were playing chess—each speaking cautiously and timidly, for fear that he or she might be the first to make the wrong move that would bring about some catastrophe. There was a distance and uneasiness between them that had not been bridged. Certainly, he saw no prospect of romance in their future. Too many years had passed between them, and they were each different persons now.

Or were they? He could not deny that she was an interesting, desirable woman, and he was acutely aware of the warmth he felt when he was with her.

But she had a career halfway across the country, and another woman he had loved deeply had died only six months before, and he had a daughter who needed his attention. He would soon have a new career to start and, financially, he was busted. Something told him that he and RaeLyn were just not meant to be.

But being with her now, and the emotions she evoked for the first time since Becky's death, made him realize there *could* be another woman in his life. Not another like Becky.

There was only one Becky, and he wanted to keep it that way. Someday, there would be another woman, perhaps just as special, but in her own, unique, individual way.

At least the scandal charges had about burned themselves out. Public attention now had shifted to Sherm and Harlowe. The press was directing barbs at Governor Heywood that suggested his incompetence and political naiveté, but reporters and commentators were beginning to concede the governor's integrity. Clarke Heywood was deeply hurt, however, and John wondered if the governor might not have preferred the continued attack on his honesty to the speculation about his administrative ability. But you did not go to jail for incompetence.

Sherm had never made a commitment to retract his testimony, but he had performed as John was certain he would. His attorneys filed a sworn affidavit with the chairman of the Special Committee, totally retracting the testimony that had been given about John. Harlowe was now the scapegoat. The loan request had been made by Harlowe; the loan had been made to Harlowe. The former tax commissioner's public statements now indicated that he would back up the revised loan story. Sherm and Harlowe would maintain that John had been implicated solely because of the apparent impropriety of the tax commissioner taking money, even though, of course, no bribe was intended or involved. Sherm and Harlowe were properly saddened and contrite for what they had done, and they had apologized publicly—although not privately—to John.

Harper had made a prognosis for the scenario that would unfold, one that John, cynically, agreed with. The Special Committee would make a lot of noise for another month or two, then, when it became obvious that they would not hang Governor Heywood with any of the evidence, the committee would quietly terminate the hearing process and promise to study the evidence carefully. The charges would then die a natural death. Sherm would not be charged with contempt or bribery, since he had come forth and rectified the record on his own. He was vulnerable to the filing of criminal charges, but as long as Harlowe backed him up, the evidence was flimsy against each, and probably neither would ever suffer more damage than the public embarrassment they incurred.

However, Sherm would be the kiss of death for any politician in the future, and governmental agencies which provided the greatest market for Reinwald equipment would be extremely wary about doing business with the firm. Sherm would survive, though, and John had no doubt his old nemesis would thrive again.

John had been in Omaha the past three days at the request of Jarred Harper, who had wanted to take depositions at the Omaha office for purposes of preserving a permanent record, just in case the conflict should flare up again and a key witness should not be available.

RaeLyn had remained in Lincoln as the guest of Governor and Mrs. Heywood until she returned to Omaha for the depositions. In the days immediately preceding, she had reviewed pertinent testimony with John and had confidentally elicited any information he might have that could someday be embarrassing to the governor. He had washed all of the Heywood administration's dirty linen, but when they were finally ready to proceed with the depositions, RaeLyn concluded that Clarke Heywood was, in fact, an exemplary man, deserving of John's loyalty. Somehow, receiving her reassurance on that point had given him some relief.

They had completed the depositions yesterday and most of this day had been spent at the Howe & Lowenstein office, with RaeLyn reviewing the transcripts of his testimony. When they had started to shuffle through the mass of typed sheets this morning, RaeLyn shrugged and admitted apologetically that it was busywork. But they nonetheless went through the motions and had some enjoyable coffee breaks. All in all, it had been a relaxing day, and he was glad for the additional time with her.

"Aren't you hungry, John?" RaeLyn asked. "You're making me look like a lumberjack."

"You do stow it away pretty good," he teased.

She smiled. "I'm ravenous tonight . . . but then, I always am. I eat like a horse for a month, but then have to do penance and starve for the next month. That's the story of my life."

"I doubt that," John said. "It seems to me the women I know who are always talking about diets are the ones who don't need them. Anyway, you look great tonight, Rae."

"Thank you. Flattery will get you everywhere. John?"

"Yes."

"Is something bothering you this evening? You seemed so relaxed earlier today . . . more so than I've seen you since I've been in Nebraska. You seem a little up-tight tonight. Want to talk about it? Or am I wrong?"

"You always could see through me. I'm not really upset about anything, though. In fact, I was just counting my blessings, so to speak. Thinking about how well things have turned out. It looked pretty bleak a month ago. But I don't know . . . I feel a little silly saying this . . . but I hate to see you go."

She reached across the table and placed her hand on his. It was the first time since their reunion that she had touched him like this, and he was very conscious of it. "Why should you feel silly saying that, John?"

"I don't know. Maybe it's because I don't have any right to feel that way. God, I feel childish and clumsy tonight. I can't think of the right things to say; I'm like a high school kid on his first date."

"That's a coincidence; I've been the same way. It's been a long time since I felt like this. John, I think we need to talk. Ten years ago we left a lot of things unsaid, and I've always been sorry about that."

"Me too."

"Then let's not let it happen again. I think we've both been fencing. There's an awkwardness between us, and we've been afraid to say what's on our minds. Maybe it's because of what we meant to each other once. Or maybe we're just a couple of shy kids again. Let's grow up and get rid of some of our inhibitions."

"You're right. I'll never forgive myself if I let you get away without my saying what I want to say . . . even if I make a fool of myself."

She squeezed his hand. "You won't make a fool of yourself, John. Just say it."

"It's not that easy."

"Why not?"

"There are some things you can't say without baring your soul—and I'm not sure I can do that. There are just so many things . . ."

"John, let's make a pact. I have some things I want to say, too. It's not going to be easy for either of us, but let's be honest with each other . . . say whatever comes to mind, express what we really feel. No embarrassment. When we walk away, we'll do it without being sorry or feeling foolish about anything we've said. Okay?"

"Yes, I think I'd like that. I think we have to."

"Then, let's do. Let's go someplace where we can talk privately."

"We can go to my room . . . if you don't mind. I have a little wine in the refrigerator, and we won't be interrupted there."

"Terrific. But I'm still hungry; let me finish my steak first."

"Fine. I'll finish mine, too. Suddenly I'm famished."

They smiled at each other as their eyes met.

29

"The wine's good," RaeLyn said as John sat down beside her on the couch in his room at the Granada Royale.

"It's nothing special, but I wouldn't know the difference. I'm not much of a drinker. A little wine now and then, that's about it."

"That much hasn't changed. You never were." She looked around the room. "This is an interesting place. It makes me think of California with the Spanish decor and atmosphere."

"They call it a hometel. I guess because it's almost like an apartment. The living room area here, the kitchen area with the little refrigerator and stove. There's a bedroom and bathroom through that door. It's a very popular place for families. Becky and I used to bring Karin here sometimes for a quick weekend escape."

"I had to close my eyes coming up," she said. "I can't stand heights. Those glass elevators don't do much for me."

"We're only four stories high, and the atrium the rooms are built around—it's beautiful . . . fountain, tropical plants."

"It's beautiful, all right. I noticed it when we were on the main floor, but I couldn't look down at it. You noticed I stayed clear away from the railing when we walked to your room."

He smiled. "I wondered what was wrong with you. I was disappointed that you weren't more interested in the view. Anyway, I'm relieved to find you're afraid of something. I was beginning to think you weren't human."

"I'm afraid of a lot of things."

"I'd never guess it. Sometimes you seem so secure and confident, you scare the hell out of me. What are you afraid of?"

"Well, like everybody, I guess I have a lot of little fears. They're not fears, really, but things that worry me. First, it's my job at Howe & Lowenstein."

"Don't you like it?"

"I like the work well enough, but I have this fear of getting lost in the shuffle. It's such a huge firm, and you're just a number there. I can't complain about the money, and it will be better in another year or two when I get senior associate status . . . big money when I become a partner . . . but that's a long way off. And you never have an identity of your own. The firm will still be Howe & Lowenstein thirty years after the founders are dead and gone. Now," she said, with a twinkle in her eye, "if it could be Hunter & Lowenstein, I might be satisfied. But seriously, you don't even get to know your clients. Most of them are corporate entities or wealthy individuals who deal with five or six members of the firm. I handle a lot of tax and real estate matters without ever even meeting my clients. It's such an impersonal thing, and I've never been satisfied that you can do your best work on an impersonal basis."

"I can understand that," he said. "What are you going to do about it?"

"I don't know, but I'm going to decide soon. I may leave Howe & Lowenstein, start my own office, or go with a small firm that needs somebody with my tax experience. I think businesses are starting to take a look at small firms again; there's a new interest in the personal touch. I'm a good lawyer, John. I'm not worried about handling matters on my own, but I like the financial security I have with Howe."

"But you've already made up your mind."

"I have?"

"Yes. I think you're going to establish your own office."

"Yes, I guess I am. Maybe I just needed somebody to tell me that."

"In L.A.?"

"I think so . . . or at least Orange County. Maybe in a more rural area."

"What else worries you?"

"That's a little tougher to talk about."

"We're going to say what we feel. No embarrassment, remember? Go ahead, then I'll take a turn."

"I'm twenty-nine years old. I was married once . . . I don't think I told you . . . and it didn't work out. I think it was more my fault than his. It wasn't a bitter parting, but I've always chalked it up as one of the failures in my life. I know I'm not an old woman, and there's time for me, but I worry a little about going through life and never truly loving a man again, never having him love me in return. I'm not very religious, John, but I do have a reverence for what there can be between a man and a woman. I never had it in my marriage, but I've seen it in others—that special bond that has to make every day of a lifetime so much more fulfilling. And then there's children. A woman especially can't help but be aware of the limitations of her child-bearing years. I'm in the middle of those prime years, and in a half dozen years or so, for genetic and other reasons, I'd have to think twice about having children. And I do want children. I can't explain why, but it is something that has suddenly become very important to me. Perhaps it has to do with searching for a little bit of immortality. Maybe seeing your little Karin had something to do with it. Sounds silly, doesn't it?"

"We made a pact that nothing we said was going to be silly . . . and it's not. I'm sure you're feeling what a lot of women do. A lot of men, too."

"It's not that the world will end if I don't have those things. I'll have a rewarding life, an exciting one, and I'll try not to look back too much. But I think I'd always wonder what might have been. I've been dwelling on that more than usual the last few weeks."

"Dwelling on what?"

"What might have been."

"For instance?"

"What might have been if we hadn't gone to Sherm Reinwald's to be with the Eager Beavers one spring evening . . . I'm sorry, John. I shouldn't have mentioned that."

"Anything's fair game. It doesn't bother me anymore."

"You're sure?"

"Yes. I reacted childishly, and I never gave you any understanding after that night . . . even when I learned more about the circumstances. It's not important anymore. Maybe we're living in more enlightened times—more than likely I've just grown up—but I'm sure I wouldn't react the same way today. In any case, let's just put Sherm behind us."

"Gladly. Now, it's your turn. I'll be the listener."

He sipped at the red wine he had almost forgotten and placed the glass on the table. "My concerns aren't that much unlike yours. My career, for instance. As you know, I'm planning to resign in another month after things have cooled down a little. Clarke's against it, but I know my leaving the administration would give him his only chance for a fresh start. Besides, I've had it. I'm ready for something else. But what? I'm a journalist by profession. I'd like to write a book . . . perhaps a novel."

"How about an inside story on your work in politics and state government?"

"Never. I could write some pretty hot stuff with what I know, but like I told you before, I've always held those kiss-and-tell guys in contempt. I don't want any part of that kind of book. But I'm a realist. I've got a daughter to support, bills to be paid. I'll have to find something that will generate some steady income. I wouldn't mind a teaching job somewhere if I could find one in my field."

"The governor should have some contacts that would help you."

"Yes, but I don't want to impose on him further."

"Don't be ridiculous. He and Liz would feel better about everything if they could help you. You're like a son to them. Talk to Governor Heywood about it. Please, John, do it for him if not for yourself."

"I'll see. You're probably right."

"I am right. I know it."

"Then there's the other," he said. "The love and family thing . . . like you were talking about. Of course, my position's a little different from yours. I had that special kind of relationship you were talking about, and it's worth it, Rae, I can tell you that. Whatever sacrifices or compromises you have to make to have it, it's worth it. And I'm greedy. I want it again . . . even though it makes me feel disloyal to Becky to be thinking about it so soon."

"You shouldn't feel that way. From everything you and Liz have told me about Becky, she would have wanted it for you. I think she would take it as a tribute that you would want to find that kind of love again. And you will find it, John. I envy you. You're the kind of man who will."

"Now comes the hard part, Rae." He took a deep breath and looked into her eyes. "I'm starting to wonder if I could find it with you."

She did not seem surprised at his remark, but he thought he saw the faintest trace of tears in her eyes, and there was a sadness in her face. She moved her head toward his and brushed her lips lightly against his own.

"Don't you think I've wondered that, too? I think I've sensed what you're feeling, and, believe me, I've been feeling the same thing. But we're both afraid to describe the feeling with words. We're not sure enough to call it love, are we?"

"No. I guess I've wondered if I'm just trying to relive a time in my youth, or maybe because of what I've been through the last six months I'm reaching out for anyone who's warm and feminine and understanding. Someone who will help wash away the loneliness. It would be easy for me to say I love you, Rae, because right now I feel that way. I know I care deeply, and I'm scared to death at the idea of your leaving tomorrow."

"John, I think I'm in love with you, but I've got the same reservations. Besides, there are other considerations. I've got a profession, plans of my own, and I have trouble now seeing how they can jibe with yours. It just seems like we're destined to go our separate ways."

He could see she was on the verge of tears. For the first time, he saw her as a person like himself—vulnerable, confused, torn by conflicting emotions. He reached out and she came into his arms. He held her close, her head resting on his shoulder before their lips met again, this time in a tender, lingering kiss. At that moment, he was struck with an urgency he had not known for months. He wanted her desperately, and he pulled her closer. He slid his hand down the full length of her back, and his mind was suddenly overwhelmed by the image of the two of them together, loving, taking pleasure in each other.

"Rae," he choked.

"Yes . . . yes," she whispered, "I want it, too."

Then, as though on cue, they rose together, and he took her hand in his and led her into the bedroom. As they lay naked on the bed, the image became reality. The fantasy became truth. Her fragrant woman-smell was an anesthesia that eased his hurt. The touch of her body against his was the surgery that exorcised deep scars; the climax was the balm that commenced the healing of his wounded spirits.

30

John sat with RaeLyn in the waiting area at Omaha's Epply Airfield. He glanced at his watch. RaeLyn's flight would be leaving in half an hour. He found himself increasingly depressed as the time for her departure grew nearer.

After last night's love-making, they had slept a drugged sleep. It was nearly ten when they awakened in each other's arms, and they had had to rush frantically to pick up RaeLyn's things at the Hilton and get to the airport in time for her 12:30 flight. There had not been enough time to talk, and there were still so many things he wanted to say.

He put his arm around her shoulder and leaned toward her in an effort to be heard above the terminal racket. "Rae, I don't want you to go."

She looked at him with sad, bewildered eyes and shrugged. "What do you have in mind? What would I do here?"

"I don't know. Couldn't you get assigned to the Omaha office? Or start a practice here? Then we'd have a chance to see each other, give things time."

"You're asking me to throw away all the groundwork I've laid for my career on a mere possibility. John, be honest with me. You aren't prepared to say you're truly in love with me, are you?"

"I can say it . . . but I won't, because I don't know if it's true. I'm mixed up about things right now."

"Let's not read too much into last night, John. It was good. We were two lonely people who needed each other and wanted each other. It was right for last night. But for today, tomorrow, a lifetime? That's doubtful."

"Don't say that. You're probably right, but, God, I don't want to think about it. Things are going to seem so . . . so empty here when you leave. We will see each other again, won't we?"

"I hope so. But I'm a realist, John. In a few days, we'll be back in our old routines, our own environments. When we were kids, we thought we couldn't live without each other . . . but we did. We both made satisfactory lives for ourselves. We'll do it again."

He was mildly irritated at her dispassionate evaluation. "Damn it! Do you always have to be so objective about everything? How can such a warm woman be so cool?" He caught a glint of hurt in her eyes and instantly regretted his remark. "I'm sorry."

"John, I just don't want us to build our dreams on quicksand. I'll always treasure our reunion here. I think we helped each other. That's a good thing for both of us to remember." She paused. "John, why don't you go to Schonberg this weekend? Visit Karin. She needs her father, and you need her."

He nodded in agreement. "That's a good idea. I think I will. After I'm finished with the administration, I'm going to give her a few weeks' time. Maybe take a vacation with her before we settle down to something new."

"She'd love Disneyland," RaeLyn said.

"Isn't she too young to appreciate it?"

"You're never too young for Disneyland . . . never too old, either."

The public address speaker announced RaeLyn's flight. "They're boarding," she said, "I guess this is it."

"I guess so."

They rose and faced each other, their eyes saying what their lips could not, unaware of the stampede of passengers that filed past them. John took her gently in his arms and kissed her lightly on the lips.

"Good bye, Rae . . . for now."

"Good bye, John. Take care." She pulled away abruptly and hurried to take her place in the boarding line, then she disappeared through the doors that would lead her through the embarking tunnel to the 747 that in a short time would carry her back to Los Angeles. So few hours between them, but so many miles.

Hot tears burned RaeLyn's eyes. She could feel them streaming down her cheeks as she went through the doors. She did not look back. She did not want John to see.

She did not remember entering the jet, but somehow she had numbly found her way to the non-smoking section of the plane, secured a window seat and fastened her seatbelt. She stared out the window, unhearing of the friendly chatter of the little old lady who sat beside her.

John's pride had separated them once. Now, was it her own? She could have stayed a few more days, offered him more encouragement. She had been too negative about their prospects. Was their relationship truly as superficial as she had suggested? From John's standpoint, perhaps. But from hers, no. She loved him dearly and wondered now whether she had ever stopped loving him. Her hands moved to unhook the seatbelt. There was still time to tell him how she felt. She started to rise, but then fell back in her seat as the jet's engines roared and the mammoth plane lurched forward.

"Your seatbelt's supposed to be fastened, dear," said the little old lady.

The airplane was racing down the runway now. RaeLyn looked blankly at her traveling companion, then finally comprehending, said, "Oh, thank you. I guess I've been daydreaming." She refastened the belt and leaned back in her seat as the jet rose gradually from the runway, shot into the sky and angled westward.

Postscript

I had gained an hour crossing from the central to the mountain time zones, and my clunker of a Ford was making good time as I headed northward on Interstate 25 toward Buffalo. The remainder of the journey would go slow, however, since the highway that led from Buffalo to our lodge above Ten Sleep Canyon twisted and turned through the rugged mountains and would reduce my car's speed to a snail's pace. With luck, I figured, I would be home a good half hour before nightfall.

As my car rolled smoothly up the interstate through the naked, barren rock that covered most of this part of Wyoming, my thoughts turned back to the sequence of events that had so rapidly brought richness to my life again. All of this in less than two years' time.

Clarke Heywood had helped as RaeLyn said he would. He contacted an old friend of his and, before I knew it, I was on the staff of the University of Wyoming journalism school. I said my good-byes to Clarke and Liz, and I returned to Schonberg for a visit with Mom before Karin and I moved to our new home, a small, off-campus apartment in Laramie.

The second afternoon of my stay in Schonberg, I took Karin for a nostalgic stroll through downtown Schonberg. Of course, a nostalgic trip through Schonberg would not have been complete without a stop at Sedgewick Drug. Doc made a terrible fuss over Karin, stuffed her with ice cream and, with that instinctive rapport he always seemed to have with kids, wasted no time in joining her in meaningless chatter. Finally I convinced Doc that we really had to go, and he said, "Wait a minute. I have something for Karin." The white-haired old gent, still bursting with energy, scurried back to what he called his knickknack department, where he always carried a stock of merchandise that defied drugstore categorization. He returned momentarily with his hands behind his back. Doc's broad smile and the Santa Claus twinkle in his eye told me he had found exactly the right thing for Karin. He stood above her, trying to make his face stern. Karin looked up at him with those big, blue eyes that could melt steel. "Do you like surprises?"

"You betcha," she replied, using her favorite expression.

"Do you like Mickey Mouse?"

"You betcha."

He moved his hand from behind his back and produced a stuffed, felt-covered Mickey Mouse doll. "Would you take care of this for me, Karin?"

"You betcha," she said, taking the doll and pulling it tightly to her bosom. "Oh, thanks, Doc. I'll take good care of Mickey."

"You do that, honey." Doc knelt and squeezed her gently, planting a kiss on one of the downy, golden locks that curled over her ear.

"Mickey Mouse," I said. "That makes me think of Disneyland. RaeLyn lives in Los Angeles, now, did you know that, Doc?"

Doc stood and lifted his wiry, white eyebrows questioningly. "Oh?"

"Yeah. She told me I should take Karin to Disneyland."

"That sounds like a good idea."

"Yeah, but the trip would take about everything I could

scratch up."

"I think you should go. Call RaeLyn . . . tell her what you're thinking about . . . see what she says."

"Maybe I will. Thanks, Doc . . . for everything."

"You betcha, " he replied, winking at Karin.

The trip to Los Angeles seemed to tie together all those loose ends that had been playing havoc with my life. At RaeLyn's insistence, Karin and I stayed at her apartment. She had an extra bedroom which Karin and I shared. My Midwestern, puritan conscience questioned the propriety of our staying with RaeLyn, but Rae had laughed and finally chided me into accepting her invitation. We had a ball. RaeLyn took some vacation time, and we saw Disneyland—twice. We tried Knottsberry Farm and Marineland, and RaeLyn even drove us down to San Diego to see the zoo.

The nights in her apartment were unsettling, though, for when I thought of the woman sleeping alone in the room next to me my mind returned unavoidably to that night at the Granada Royale. I wanted to drink of this woman again . . . and again . . . and again. But Karin's presence was an inhibiting factor. Somehow, it seemed vulgar and irreverant for me to steal away to RaeLyn's room when Karin slept so innocently and soundly on the bed beside me.

By the beginning of the second week, however, I was sleeping in RaeLyn's room. It seemed the most natural thing in the world that we should be there together like that, basking in the warmth and comfort we received from each other. It was as though things had always been that way, that we had never been apart all those years. By the end of the week, neither RaeLyn nor I was willing to chance another separation for however brief a time. We were married in a brief ceremony in a little roadside chapel. We remained in RaeLyn's apartment while she wound up her business with Howe & Lowenstein. Karin and I saw more of Los Angeles and made arrangements for the move to Laramie. But the nights were for RaeLyn and me.

Shortly after Labor Day, the three of us moved temporarily into the cramped Laramie apartment. I commenced my classes at the university, while RaeLyn made the rounds of the real estate brokers. We agreed a family should have a real house, and she looked for a small bungalow-type home, while trying to ferret out some office space for the law practice she planned to establish there. It would work beautifully, she insisted. She could concentrate on her income tax specialty, which would make her workload somewhat seasonal, freeing most of her summers during the time when I would be on my own hiatus.

At one of the brokerage offices, her eyes picked up an interesting listing as she scanned the firm's bulletin board—"Modest two-story lodge in Big Horn Mountains near Ten Sleep. Perfect for summer home."

She off-handedly asked one of the salesmen about the listing. It was a steal, the man insisted. The seller lived in Kansas and had financial troubles. He wanted a quick sale. When she suggested we drive north over the weekend, I protested. "I'm broke. I can barely make payments on one house let alone two."

I've got enough cash saved up, if we like it," she said. "It would take about everything I've got, but it sounds like it would be a good investment, besides a wonderful place to spend our summers."

"I didn't marry you to have you support me," I said.

"Look, you've got a good salary. It will take me four or five years to establish any kind of practice here after I've taken the Wyoming bar. You're going to be carrying the financial load for the next several years, but at least I've got a stake that can help us get something extra. The isolation would be tremendous for your writing, wouldn't it?"

"Yeah, but . . ."

"And a great place for kids."

"Kids?"

"Yes, for Karin and the other children we'll have."

"Oh." Her lips formed in a pout. I couldn't tell if it was real or faked.

"You said we were going to be a family, didn't you?"

"Yeah, but . . ."

"Then what's with this 'his' and 'hers' crap? If we're a family, it's the family's money. That's the way I see it."

I capitulated. "Okay. We'll drive up to Ten Sleep this weekend."

I drove into Buffalo. I was hungry and was tempted to stop for a bite to eat. But I did not even slow down at any of the restaurants. Leaving the interstate, I turned up the narrow highway that led into the stark splendor of the Big Horn Mountains. I would be home in less than two hours, and I was anxious to see my family.